# TO LOVE A WITCH
## A WICKED WITCHES OF THE MIDWEST MYSTERY
## BOOK SIXTEEN

## AMANDA M. LEE

WINCHESTERSHAW PUBLICATIONS

Copyright © 2020 by Amanda M. Lee

All rights reserved.

No part of this book may be reproduced in any form or by any electronic or mechanical means, including information storage and retrieval systems, without written permission from the author, except for the use of brief quotations in a book review.

❀ Created with Vellum

# PROLOGUE

## FIFTEEN YEARS AGO

"I want a man who will pay all the bills so I can stay home and have kids."

I leaned back on my bean bag and fixed Clove with the most dubious look I could muster. "You do not."

My cousin, who had dark hair and a ski-slope nose, managed to convey annoyance with a single hop of her shoulder. "I do. I've given it a lot of thought. I want to be a mommy when I'm old."

I exchanged an incredulous look with my other cousin, Thistle, who was resting on her bed, a magazine open so she could stare at whatever celebrity she was in love with this day.

"You want to be a mommy?" Thistle challenged. "You're saying, like, you want to sit on the couch and hang around with kids all day?"

The dreamy expression Clove sported only moments before fled from her face. "You don't sit around if you're a stay-at-home mother. You do things."

"Like what?"

"Like ... clean the house, take care of the kids, homeschool and stuff." She averted her gaze and stared at the wall. "It's a hard job."

I would never say otherwise, but that didn't mean Clove was designed to accomplish that job. "You hate kids," I pointed out.

"And housework," Thistle added. "You gave me your entire allowance last week because you didn't want to take out the garbage."

Clove made a protesting sound. "The garbage was gross. It was hot ... and the flies had been in it. That means other things were in it. You know I hate those other things."

I didn't even have to ask what "things" she was referring to. I was well aware of her distaste for all things buggy or insect-y. What ended up in the garbage can at the end of a sweltering summer week was even worse than mosquitoes and June bugs. "I don't understand this from a feminist perspective," I argued. "You've been raised by a bunch of women who believe it's important to take care of yourself. Now you're saying you essentially want a man to take care of you. They won't like that."

"I don't like that," Thistle said darkly. She might've been small and wiry, but she was tough. Nobody wanted to fight with her unless there was no way out of it. She had a look about her that said it might become necessary today.

"I'm not saying I want a man to take care of me," Clove countered. "I mean I want to help. I want to contribute to the household."

"Just not with a job," Thistle muttered.

Clove ignored her. "There are different ways to contribute to a household, Bay."

"And you want to be a mommy," I noted.

"Yes." She beamed.

"Have you met our mommies?" Thistle refused to let it go. I was of the mind that the conversation was too deep to delve into on a day when the window air conditioner was churning in an attempt to keep up, emitting sounds suggesting it might soon give up the ghost. Thistle apparently had other ideas. I was hardly surprised. That was her way.

"I've met them," Clove shot back. "I don't want to be like our mothers."

"I'm sure that will make them feel better about your life choices," I said dryly. "Just out of curiosity, though, why don't you want to be like our mothers? I mean ... they're pains in the behind, but they're strong."

"That's why I don't want to be like them." Clove was earnest. "I've seen how hard they work. I'm surprised they're still standing. Things would've been easier for them if they hadn't divorced our fathers."

"I don't think they believe that," Thistle said. "Besides, they seem to like the work. All that stuff they do in the kitchen, yeah, that's more like a hobby they love. Ordering us around, that's also something they enjoy."

"You're missing the point. They did everything on their own because they had to. I don't want that to be necessary when I'm their age."

"Then marry someone who sticks around," Thistle suggested, earning a quelling look from me. She was more practical when it came to adjusting to our fathers being absent from our lives. Clove still held out hope that things would return to how they had been. I tended to lean toward Thistle's way of thinking.

I, Bay Winchester, was something of a Debbie Downer when it came to the big questions in life. I'd been warned about it by every female in the family, that I had to buck up and look toward the good rather than accepting the bad. It had yet to happen.

"You're ridiculous," Thistle said, directing the conversation back to the topic at hand. "Our mothers work because they like it. Sure, some of it is difficult, but they're big fans of being able to say, 'Hey, I did that.' If you marry a guy with the express purpose of him taking care of you, you'll never be able to say that."

Clove folded her arms over her chest, jutting her lip out stubbornly. "Don't make fun of my choices."

"Then don't make it so easy for me to make fun of your choices," Thistle said. "You're setting feminism back fifty years saying stuff like this."

"It's how I feel," Clove persisted.

"Well, it's stupid."

Clove's eyes fired. "You're stupid!"

Thistle clearly wasn't in the mood to be messed with. She narrowed her eyes. "You know who could best settle this argument?"

I knew the name before she even invoked it. "Don't," I warned.

It was too late to rein in Thistle. "Aunt Tillie."

Clove's shoulders jolted, glancing around as if she expected simply saying the name would cause our great-aunt to materialize. As if she was the Candyman or something. "You wouldn't dare." Her voice was a breathy whisper.

"I would." Thistle's eyes flashed with malevolence. "I think she'd want to know how twisted that mind of yours is."

"I'll make you eat dirt," Clove warned. "If you tell her ... ."

It was too late. The bedroom door flew open to allow Aunt Tillie entrance. The look in her eyes as she stood there, nostrils flaring, told me exactly what sort of diatribe we were in for. She was barely five feet tall, yet loomed so much larger in our eyes.

"Oh, crap," Thistle muttered under her breath. No matter how much bravado she'd flashed when threatening Clove, she would never rat out our softer cousin. It was simply a taunt with which we all teased each other. This time, though, the witch in question had obviously been close enough to hear Thistle utter her name.

"You rang," Aunt Tillie said dramatically, her new combat helmet in place.

Before this week, she'd been wearing an old football helmet she'd pilfered from the high school on one of her daily missions, which normally included three bouts of torturing her archnemesis Margaret Little and three stops for doughnuts at the Walkerville Bakery. She'd upgraded thanks to an estate sale down the road. For some reason, the combat helmet seemed to fit her personality, even if it was too big for her head.

"We weren't doing anything," Clove immediately volunteered. "We were just ... talking." She ended the statement with a lame shrug. "You know, talking about nothing important."

Aunt Tillie arched an eyebrow and turned her eyes to me. "What were you talking about?"

It took everything I had to maintain an even expression. She knew darned well that I was likeliest to tell her the truth. I crumbled like a two-week-old cake whenever she started questioning me. In some ways, Clove was the weakest. She could lie with the best of them when the opportunity arose, though.

"We're not doing anything," I said in what I hoped was a believable voice. "We're just hanging around, talking about boys."

"Uh-huh." Aunt Tillie swished her lips as she glanced between us. "I thought perhaps you were talking about future plans, like marriage and kids." Her gaze was dark when it landed on Clove. "Like maybe someone wanted to sit back and let someone else do all the heavy lifting in a marriage or something."

Clove gave a small yelp as Thistle glared.

"If you already knew what we were doing, why go through the charade of pretending you weren't eavesdropping?" Thistle snapped. She and Aunt Tillie were constantly doing battle. Today looked as if it would be no different.

"I don't eavesdrop." Aunt Tillie scowled. "I divine information." She tapped the side of her head for emphasis. "I'm an all-knowing witch. I see everything you do. There's not a single thought you have that I can't pull from your head."

"Oh, yeah?" Thistle narrowed her eyes to slits. "What am I thinking right now?"

I bit my lip to keep from stepping into the middle of their skirmish. I always tried to play peacemaker, but it never worked out for me. There were days Thistle and Aunt Tillie clearly wanted to do battle and this was obviously one of those days.

"You're thinking that you want to be just like me when you grow up," Aunt

Tillie replied, not missing a beat as she patted Thistle's head in a condescending manner. "You're so ... cute."

Thistle's mouth dropped open. "I am not cute. I am the eater of souls."

The response was enough to earn a genuine chuckle from Aunt Tillie. "You really do take your cues from me sometimes. It's frightening. But we don't have time for that today." Her expression was hard to read as she turned back to Clove. "I heard what you said."

Clove swallowed hard. "I ... am not sorry I said it." She found her spine at the oddest of times. This seemed like the absolute worst hill on which to die. She was about to turn thirteen, for crying out loud. She had plenty of time to change her mind. Obviously, she thought differently. "I know what I want out of life."

"Yes, a man to take care of you," Aunt Tillie drawled. "That's just ... lovely." She said the word "lovely" with the same nose wrinkle Clove pulled out when she had to touch the garbage cans after the flies started dropping their larvae on the trash.

"There's nothing wrong with wanting to be married," Clove shot back shrilly. "You were married. Although how you ever found anyone to put up with you is beyond me — unless he was dumb or something."

I sucked in a breath. Things were about to get nasty. I'd never met Uncle Calvin, but family lore painted him as the nicest and most patient man who ever walked the Earth. To cast aspersions on him in front of Aunt Tillie was like waving a red scarf in front of a bull while your shoes were nailed to the ground — except she was far more dangerous than a bull.

Instead of firing back — with magic or dark words — Aunt Tillie shook her head. "No one says you can't get married, but why you'd want to is beyond me. That's not what's annoying."

"Oh, yeah?" Still defiant, Clove had apparently decided she wasn't going to back down. I wondered if her funeral would be well-attended. "How is having a dream annoying?"

"We didn't teach you to want that dream," Aunt Tillie replied, much more reasonably than I expected. "I understand. You miss your father, even more than these other two. You think there's a way to make sure your kids never have that problem.

"You can't guarantee that things will work out forever," she continued. "I hope you find a man who can put up with all your quirks, who will love you for who you really are, and accept you, kvetching and all. But knowing you, you'll probably settle for some idiot without a backbone. The trick is to find a man who wants to do what's right for you while not sacrificing too much of himself. It's a delicate balancing act, but it can be achieved."

Clove's expression remained cloudy. "I just want to have kids and be happy."

"No, you want some mystical husband who will wait on you, take care of you, and somehow arrange things so that you don't have to work. You're lazy when you want to be. You all are. That's a product of your age. You'll grow out of it."

Thistle made a derisive sound deep in her throat, causing Aunt Tillie's gaze to laser in on her.

"Yes, Mouth?" Aunt Tillie prodded. "Do you have something you want to share?"

"Not really." Thistle was blasé. "I was just thinking that I don't ever want to get married. Why would I need anyone other than me?"

She was sucking up. She understood Aunt Tillie would like that reaction best. I knew her better than most and it was obvious she was playing a game.

Apparently Aunt Tillie was aware of that fact, too, because her response was anything but expected. "That's bold talk, but I don't believe it. Besides, you might surprise yourself. The man you end up with will be either a saint or a sinner. I don't think there will be a middle ground with you."

Thistle arched a challenging eyebrow. "Meaning?"

"Meaning you and Clove are talking about different things. She's talking about making herself small to fit into some life she's dreamed up. That will never work. She's just too young to understand that. Give it time.

"As for you, you're cutting off an avenue of happiness that you might need," she continued. "You're a strong girl with a mouth like a sailor and the disposition of a constipated snake. You might be surprised at the sort of man willing to take that on."

Thistle's frown only deepened. "What if I don't want to take on that man?"

"Then you don't have to. But you'll find that your wants and desires will change as you grow older. I'm curious to see what poor sap ends up with you. I'm hoping for sinner so you have your hands full, but I have a sneaking suspicion you'll end up with a saint."

Thistle didn't look convinced. "What about Bay?" She jabbed her finger in my direction. "What do you see in her future?"

The smile Aunt Tillie graced me with was shudder-inducing.

"I don't want to know," I said hurriedly. "I'm fine wondering ... and imagining ... and dreaming for as long as it takes."

Aunt Tillie snickered. "Bay is more difficult to read. She's a mixture of you two, with a little of her mother thrown in, and a lot of outside elements working against her."

"Wait ... are you saying I'm going to end up alone?" That was not what I wanted to hear.

"No, but would you have a problem with that?"

I thought about it and then nodded. "I want to marry Colin Farrell."

She laughed. "Is that one of your movie stars?"

"He's *the* movie star."

"He's okay," Clove said, wrinkling her nose. "He's not as hot as Brad Pitt."

"Brad Pitt is a tool," Thistle shot back. "If you want a real man, look no further than Johnny Depp. He's artsy, plays the guitar, and looks really hot even if his hair is greasy. He's the sort of man I want."

Aunt Tillie rolled her eyes. "Last time I checked, that one had hair like a girl. You need to stop dreaming about movie stars and live in the real world. I can guarantee that a real man — one who has strength and drive — is far better than those Hollywood bozos you love."

She sounded sure of herself. "Am I going to end up alone?" I was horrified by the thought. I was certain Colin — or someone just as hot — and I would find our happily ever after.

Aunt Tillie heaved out a sigh at my morose expression. "No, you're not. I've seen your future. You're going to do something that shakes this family to its very foundation."

I was officially intrigued. "Marry Colin?"

She shook her head. "Worse."

"Like what?"

"Never you mind." She shook her head and turned toward the door. "Your mothers sent me up here with a mission. Dinner will be ready in twenty minutes. You need to go down and help them set up."

"Wait a second," I protested. "I want to hear who I'm going to marry."

Aunt Tillie smiled. "If I told you, it would ruin the adventure. Trust me. You don't want that."

I was too curious not to pursue. "At least tell me he's hot."

"I'm not telling you anything. You know how this goes. If I tell you what will happen, it won't actually happen — and then where will you be? I'll tell you. You'll be a sad sack and nobody will want to be around you."

"But ... at least tell me one thing."

Aunt Tillie paused by the door. "He'll change your entire world and you'll be better for knowing him."

"Oh, come on! I need more than that."

"That's all I have to give. Now, let's go downstairs so I can tell your mothers how Clove wants to wait for a man to take care of her. That should serve as my entertainment for the evening."

Clove scowled. "You're a horrible old woman."

"And don't you forget it."

# ONE

## PRESENT DAY

"You're not trying!"

Aunt Tillie was edgy, which meant the world was teetering on the head of a pin as she stood in the center of the small clearing, next to the old cabins I used to bunk in during summers camping with my cousins. She drew herself up, armoring herself in her formidable look.

The girl she was trying to help ignored my puffed-up great-aunt.

"I don't even understand why I'm here," Dani Harris complained, sending a pleading look in my direction. For some reason — and I still couldn't wrap my head around why — she'd decided I was the alpha witch in our little group. She would listen only to me, even though the two older witches teaching most of the lessons were ten times stronger. "Why do I have to listen to them?"

I tugged on my limited patience and searched for a way to explain that she would not only understand, but embrace. Her world wasn't exactly normal these days. In fact, that was the last word I would use to describe it. She'd been removed from her home, essentially cut off from her mother and brother, and she had someone watching her twenty-four hours a day. It was not a normal scenario for a teenager ... and yet here we were.

"Because they have a lot to teach," I replied without hesitation, flashing a smile I didn't feel. "You need discipline."

"Why?" Dani had her role as petulant teenager down pat. If they handed out awards, she would definitely take home a shiny ribbon or gold trophy. She was abrasive, whiny, and constantly pushing back on authority. In a weird way, she reminded me of my cousin Thistle when she was that age. Of course, Thistle wasn't responsible for the murder of her father and didn't have plans to terrorize half the town with magically controlled birds.

"Because if you don't control yourself you'll be lost," I replied, matter-of-fact. We'd been over this at least ten times, but Dani continued to push back. I was getting tired of her attitude. "Being a witch is about more than having magic at your disposal."

Dani didn't look convinced. "But ... I'm more powerful than them." She said it with enough earnest energy that I realized she believed it.

"You're not." I was firm. "They're both older than you ... and wiser ... and they can beat the crap out of you if it comes to a magic fight."

Rather than agreeing, Dani shook her head. "They can't. I'm way stronger. I killed people."

The way she said it made me realize she didn't grasp what she'd done. I'd been wrestling with that notion for almost two weeks. Not only did she not understand, she didn't care. We had to break her of that notion and direct her to a different path. Otherwise ... well, otherwise she would turn completely dark and then we would have another decision to make.

"You don't understand about magic," I started, choosing my words carefully.

Dani didn't let me finish. "Oh, that's a bunch of crap." Before I could stop her, she lifted her hands and muttered something in Latin I couldn't quite make out. The sound of screaming birds assailed my ears, and when I looked in that direction I saw flocks of ducks and gulls swooping toward us with clear intent.

"Knock it off!" I gave her a good shake as Aunt Tillie threw up a protection spell to dissuade the birds from attacking. "How many times have I told you to stay away from the birds? You can't call them to do your bidding whenever you feel annoyed with life."

The defiance we'd been trying to smother sparked in Dani's eyes, and I sensed trouble. "I can do whatever I want."

"No, you can't. Everybody lives by certain rules."

"Witches don't have to live by the rules. That's why it's fun to be a witch."

"I hate to break it to you, but witches live by the same rules as everybody else. No matter who you are, rules have to be followed. Nobody gets to live a rule-free life."

Behind me, Aunt Tillie cleared her throat, earning a dark glare from me. "Don't you start," I warned.

"I didn't say anything." Aunt Tillie was the picture of faux innocence. "I'm on your side."

"Uh-huh." I shook my head and turned back to Dani. The look she shot Aunt Tillie was of the "I'm going to pay you back when nobody is looking, old lady" variety and the possibilities made my stomach quiver. "Let's take a break," I suggested, mustering as much enthusiasm as I could. "Dani, why don't you get a soda and sit under the tree and think about what I told you for a change, huh? How does that sound?"

"Boring." Dani was never one to sugarcoat her words. She was blunt, to the point of being rude, and she knew it. She also relished her position of power. She recognized we were trapped in a difficult situation. When we opted to spare her weeks earlier — her murderous aunt was a different story — we knew we were essentially creating a situation that could go very wrong. Unfortunately, that appeared to be where we were heading. Dani didn't want to get better. She refused to see that she'd done anything wrong. If we couldn't break her of her penchant for dark magic, her willingness to endanger (and even kill) others, things would fall apart quickly. Fear of what we'd be forced to do if that happened kept me up late at night.

"Well, you'll look forward to boring afternoons when you're my age," I said, flashing what I hoped would pass as a friendly smile. "You should take advantage of your downtime now."

"Afternoons don't have to be boring," Dani persisted, refusing to let it go. "I know you're old and you've forgotten what it's like to be fun, but we could go out and do things."

I reminded myself that constantly shooting down her ideas was a surefire way to embitter her and adopted my best "I'm a reasonable person and you can trust me" expression. "Okay. What do you want to do?"

Dani shrugged. She seemed surprised by my sudden about-face. "Um ... we could go downtown and cast a spell to make Mrs. Little's unicorns come to life and attack her."

I shook my head. "We're trying to stay away from dark magic."

"Hold up," Aunt Tillie countered, raising her hand. "She might have an interesting idea there."

I flicked my great-aunt's ear, causing her to yelp and glare. "Stop encouraging her. She's getting mixed messages."

"Yes, but Margaret is the Devil," Aunt Tillie insisted. "Tell me the idea of her running from a hundred different pewter unicorns only a few inches tall doesn't sound like fun."

"We're not doing it." I was firm as I rubbed my forehead. "She needs to learn about white magic. That's why you two are spending so much time with her."

I flicked my eyes to Hazel Weller, the other witch in our homeschooling trio, and found her watching the lapping waves as they touched the sand rather than paying attention. She looked lost in thought.

"Hey!" I snapped my fingers in her face to get her attention. I wouldn't have dared act so impudently when I was a kid. I was terrified that she could turn me into a frog or worse when I was younger, but I'd had it. "You guys are supposed to be directing her to safe spells," I reminded them.

"We have been," Hazel protested, returning to the conversation at hand. I'd been dubious when she first volunteered to help us with Dani after the solstice celebration several weeks ago. She'd proven to be gung-ho, though. Unfortunately, she also was ineffective. Dani had zero respect for her, and she wasn't even remotely shy about putting her real feelings on display.

"She's not interested in safe spells," Aunt Tillie explained. She wasn't exactly Hazel's biggest fan, but they were on the same page today. "She gravitates toward the dark ... just like her aunt."

I recognized what she wasn't saying. She thought Dani should've been dealt with in the same manner as her aunt, Diane. They were both technically murderers, though the aunt did the heavy lifting while Dani provided endless power. One of the victims had been Dani's father, so I was still hopeful that she'd get it together and realize that she'd done wrong at the behest of an unstable woman.

So far, I was coming up empty.

"The spells they want me to cast are weak," Dani complained. "I mean ... that one wanted to make me focus on turning the flow of the waves in the lake in the opposite direction." Her scowl told me exactly what she thought of the suggestion as she glared at Hazel. "What good is that?"

"It's not about whether or not the spell is good," I argued. "It's about whether your intentions are good. Bringing Mrs. Little's unicorns to life so they can attack her is pretty much the opposite of good intentions."

"Yeah, but ... she's evil." This time Dani looked to Aunt Tillie for confirmation. "She's a bad person. That means we can do bad things to her."

"No, that's not what it means," I shot back. "There is no Wiccan rule that allows for that."

"You guys have been torturing that woman for years," Dani countered. "Aunt Diane told me so. She told me stories about yellow snow and poisoned food. You just don't want me to have any fun, so you set different rules for me while you do whatever you want."

I wanted to argue the point, but she wasn't exactly wrong. Some of the things we'd done to Mrs. Little over the years made us look like hypocrites. "Listen ... ."

Aunt Tillie stirred before I could come up with a reason that we were exempt from the very rules I was trying to teach Dani.

"The difference is that we don't want to maim or kill Margaret when we mess with her," Aunt Tillie offered evenly. "We only want to irritate her. That's allowed."

Dani wrinkled her delicate nose. "Says who?"

"Says anyone with half a brain," Aunt Tillie, never known for patience, fired back. "We're not talking about us anyway. We're talking about you. We're not the ones who had a hand in your father's murder. That was you."

Dani's expression darkened. "He had it coming. He cheated on my mother."

"Your parents were essentially separated but still living together," Aunt Tillie fired back. "They were sticking it out until you and your brother were out of the house. Then they were going to move on like adults."

"That's not how it works," Dani insisted. "When you get married, it's supposed to last forever." Her eyes moved back to me. "Tell them."

I balked. "Why should I tell them? I'm not married."

"No, but you and that FBI agent are all over each other every second of the day," Dani shot back. "People in town talk about it constantly. I heard Mrs. Little call you fornicators. I looked up the word when I got home. That means you're having sex."

My cheeks burned under the girl's scrutiny. She knew exactly what to say to knock me off my game. It was one of her superpowers.

"They're totally fornicators," Aunt Tillie agreed, not missing a beat. "It's disgusting the way they look at each other. I'm often embarrassed at the way they act. But that's their business. They're not hurting anybody."

"I didn't say they were." Dani's youth made it impossible to turn her back on a fight. Aunt Tillie's stubbornness forced the same outcome. It looked as if they were going to go at each other hard now, and there was no way out of it. "This is about marriage, or at least about relationships. When you're with someone, you're not supposed to cheat on them. You marry forever. That's right in the vows."

I hesitated, unsure what I was supposed to say. I finally went with my gut. "I'm sure when your parents started out they thought they would be together forever. Nobody goes into a marriage convinced it's going to fail."

Dani stubbornly folded her arms over her chest and rolled her eyes, refusing to meet my gaze. She didn't want to listen. I kept talking anyway.

"Sometimes, despite the best of our intentions, things don't work out the way we think they're going to," I persisted. "My parents divorced when I was a kid because things got too difficult for them to stay together. They still cared about one another, but they couldn't stay married *and* be happy. Thistle's parents split up for the same reason ... and Clove's as well. Sometimes it just happens."

"It's not right," Dani insisted. "When you make vows, you should stick to them."

Unsure, I turned to Aunt Tillie. "Do you want to help me here?"

"I agree with her," Aunt Tillie replied. "When you marry, it should be for life. Your mother and father took the easy way out, but I was happy, because I never liked your father. He was always king of the milquetoasts."

I pinched the bridge of my nose. "You're not helping."

"I didn't know I was supposed to be helping." Aunt Tillie was blasé as she threw herself into one of the canvas chairs surrounding the bonfire pit. The camp was run-down. I wasn't sure it was all that safe for Dani and Hazel to stay in one of the cabins that littered the property, but we needed to isolate the teenager. The old camp, which my boyfriend Landon had recently purchased with Aunt Tillie's help, seemed our best option. He wanted to eventually build a house for us on the property.

"You're encouraging her obnoxiousness," I hissed. "She needs to learn balance. All she wants to do is play with dark magic. You know what'll happen if she insists on playing that game."

I hadn't meant to say it out loud. By the time I realized what was coming out of my mouth, it was too late to take it back.

"And what's that?" Dani asked blankly. "What's going to happen if I keep up with the dark magic?"

I couldn't answer her question. Every time I looked at her I remembered the way she reacted when her aunt died. There was no remorse. The sadness wasn't for the loss of a family member as much as for being declared the loser of that particular fight. In truth, one of the things that terrified me most was the idea that, on top of everything else, Dani was a sociopath. She didn't seem to react normally to the small curves life threw her way.

Aunt Tillie had warned me this endeavor was too big to take on. I did it anyway. Hazel volunteered to help, pausing her life because she thought Dani could be saved. Now I wasn't certain either of us believed that. We didn't say it, though, because the minute Dani became a lost cause serious discussions would need to be had — and nobody wanted to go that route just yet.

"She means that we'll have to lock you up in a warded basement for the rest of your life," Aunt Tillie replied, the lie easily rolling off her tongue. "It'll be a lot of work, but that's the course of last resort. Do you want to be locked in the basement?"

Dani looked taken aback. "No. I ... you can't do that." Her eyes flashed hot as they landed on me. "You can't lock me in a basement."

I decided to embrace the lie. "We can do whatever we want," I argued. "Your mother has washed her hands of you. She's afraid after what you did to your father — and what you tried to do to her. She won't complain if we imprison you."

"Yeah, but ... you live with an FBI agent," she argued, refusing to let it go. "He won't allow you to lock me up. There are laws and stuff."

"He's an FBI agent who understands about the paranormal world," I countered. "He knows what you've done. He wanted to find a way to lock you up from the start. We took up for you and suggested we could rehabilitate you. He won't have the slightest problem locking you up if it comes to it."

Dani worked her jaw, looking for a way out. "I'm not a bad person," she said finally.

I wanted to believe her. Badly. I just wasn't sure. "Then you need to try harder," I said. "You're not putting any effort into this. We're doing all the heavy lifting. It can't continue. In fact ... ." I lost my train of thought as a hint of movement across the lake caught my attention.

"Continue," Aunt Tillie prodded. "You were about to put the fear of the Goddess in her. Don't stop now."

I ignored her and pointed to the shore directly across from us. "Do you see someone standing over there?"

Three heads snapped in that direction.

"No," Dani and Hazel said simultaneously.

I focused on Aunt Tillie. "And you?"

She moved her jaw and sighed. "There might be something," she said finally. "The glare from the sun makes it hard to see."

We shared the same witchy gift, so that was all the confirmation I needed. "I have to go over there."

"Why?" Hazel asked, confused. "I don't understand."

"It's a ghost," Aunt Tillie volunteered. "She sees a ghost. And if there's an errant soul hovering over there that probably means there's a body, too. At least that's the likeliest scenario."

"Oh." Realization dawned on Hazel's face and she swallowed hard. "We should go with you. You know, just in case."

Just in case there wasn't a murderer, I surmised, resigned. As if I didn't have enough on my plate. This ghost would probably add a whole other wrinkle. That's the last thing I needed.

# TWO

The quickest way across the lake was by boat, but we only had an old canoe, which I was convinced would start taking on water partway across the lake.

"Stop being a baby," Aunt Tillie ordered, climbing into the canoe and fixing me with an expectant look. "The lake is small. Even if we sink, we'll be fine."

That was easy for her to say. I had a sneaking suspicion I would be doing all the paddling.

"Why can't I come?" Dani whined. Despite Hazel's suggestion that we needed backup, I was leery about taking the teenager, which meant Hazel also had to stay behind.

"It's better if you stay here with Hazel," I replied, refusing to meet her accusatory gaze. I understood that she was grappling with the confinement, but she was dangerous. We couldn't allow her trips into town — or other places for that matter — until we were certain she wouldn't use her magic on some poor soul who happened to accidentally step on her shoe or brush her arm. She was nowhere near that.

"You know, this is cruel and inhumane punishment," Dani snapped as I shoved the canoe into the water. My great-aunt was tiny, didn't top five feet, but she felt as if she weighed a ton when I pushed the canoe. "I'm going to report you to ... someone."

"I suggest reporting us to the authorities," Aunt Tillie said dryly. "I'm sure they'll be sympathetic ... what with you being a murderer and all."

Dani's glare was dark enough to cause a shiver to run down my spine. "You've killed people."

"How do you know?" Aunt Tillie eyed the girl.

"I just do." Dani insisted. "I know she's killed people, because she took out my aunt." She tilted her head toward me.

"Your aunt was trying to kill us," Aunt Tillie argued. "She had it coming."

"Only because you guys wouldn't mind your own business. Maybe you had it coming."

I bit back a sigh. "Dani, there's only room for two of us if we don't want this thing to sink. We don't even know if we'll find anything. Stay with Hazel."

"But ... I want to see."

"Well, maybe we can decide on an outing later," I lied. I didn't want the girl mixing with the unsuspecting residents of Hemlock Cove. We lived in a tourist town. People from all over the state — the country, really — traveled to our small hamlet in northern Lower Michigan because they were witch enthusiasts. The fact that there were real witches on the loose — some legitimately dangerous — would put a damper on the festivities. "You can't come with us now."

I grunted as I gave the canoe a final push, sloshing through the water to keep up and hop in at the last second.

"Head to the east," Aunt Tillie instructed from her perch in the bow of the canoe. "The shore over there is best for hitting even ground. There are few rocks over there."

I growled as I started paddling. I'd provided her with a paddle of her own, but it rested across her knees as she stared at the far shore and let me do all the work. "You could help," I complained as I tried to keep the canoe in a straight line. "It wouldn't kill you to paddle once or twice."

"It might." She was silent for a few moments before glancing over her shoulder. I had the distinct impression she was gauging the distance between us and Dani. That meant she was about to unload her specific brand of wisdom. I wasn't in the mood. "She's not getting any better, Bay."

I was expecting the words. The dark sentiment they were delivered with was another story. "She's ... trying." Even as I made the argument, I knew it wasn't true. The only thing Dani was trying to do was get under our skin, and it was working.

Aunt Tillie's snort was full of disdain. "Who are you trying to kid? That girl isn't capable of growth. She's already been corrupted."

Frustration bubbled up. "She's still young. She could learn."

"You just want to think that because the alternative is too much for you. You're soft."

"And what is the alternative?" I was beyond frustrated. "What are we talking about here? If this doesn't work ... ." I couldn't finish the thought.

"She's a threat, Bay." Aunt Tillie was grave. "You know as well as I do that she can't be redeemed. You're just afraid to take the next step."

"We've been at it barely two weeks," I argued. "She still has attitude over what happened. Seeing Diane die traumatized her. We need to get her over that hump, make her see us as friends rather than enemies. We won't make any inroads with her until she stops believing we're going to turn on her."

"We are going to turn on her," Aunt Tillie said. "She's a danger to anyone she comes into contact with. The cops aren't equipped to deal with her. Listen ... ." She started shaking her head when I opened my mouth to argue. "I know you think your love muffin Fed can do anything — including walk on water — but she could seriously hurt him if he tried to take her into custody."

That had been exactly what Landon Michaels, my live-in love, had wanted to do after the big fight before the solstice celebration. He'd been adamant, attacking me head-on with Chief Terry at his side as they fired constant "rational arguments" at me. I had been equally adamant. I knew he would be at risk if he tried to control Dani. She responded poorly to most authority figures. With men she was terrible. And non-magical men? Forget it. She had no qualms about planting suggestions to jump off a bluff or eat the end of a gun. She didn't understand her own power.

"She can still come back from this," I argued. "I'm not ready to give up on her. We were incorrigible at that age, too. You seem to forget that we misused our magic to go after our enemies. Remember Lila? We made potions that made her hair fall out."

Aunt Tillie let loose an exaggerated sigh. "You are ... being ridiculous. Making a potion to cause that little viper's hair to fall out was general mischief. You didn't try to kill her."

"I might've if I'd had the courage."

"You wouldn't have done anything of the sort." Aunt Tillie's tone was sharp. "You guys liked getting in trouble, but it was the sort of trouble that was funny, not terrifying. You killed Diane because you had to. You still feel guilty about it.

"She would've killed you and laughed, but you're still wondering if you could've done something to save her," she continued. "You don't have it in you to kill with malice. Dani does. That's why she can't be rehabilitated."

"I'm not ready to just wash my hands of her," I warned, struggling with the paddle as I tried to steer the canoe. "We have time."

"I don't think we have as much time as you think," Aunt Tillie countered. "You're not ready yet. There will come a point when you come to the same realization I have. It won't be pretty. You can't fix the unfixable, Bay."

"Just ... focus on the ghost." I could take only so much and I was at my limit. "See if you can catch a glimpse of it."

"Whatever." Aunt Tillie muttered something I couldn't make out. The splashes from my paddle drowned her out, which was probably best for both of us. "Was it a man or a woman?"

"I don't know. I couldn't really see. Does it matter?"

She shrugged. "It might. I've had my limit with women today. I think I need more men in my life or something. The estrogen brigade is becoming a constant headache."

That almost made me smile. "Since when are you a fan of the rougher sex, as you like to put it? Last time I checked, you hated all men."

"Not all men. I like Marcus."

Marcus was my cousin Thistle's boyfriend. They'd recently moved into a converted barn. I was certain they were on the fast track to marriage. Marcus had a delightful ability to blunt Thistle's rough edges — she had many — and he was pretty much the most easygoing man I'd ever met.

"You do like Marcus," I agreed. "That might have a little something to do with the fact that he does whatever you want without question. That includes growing pot ... and clearing a ditch of debris so you can strand Mrs. Little in it this winter."

Aunt Tillie's head snapped in my direction and her mouth dropped open. "How did you know that's what I had planned?"

I smirked. "I didn't until just now. I had a feeling, though. Mrs. Little has ended up in that ditch at least ten times. When I drove by a few weeks ago, there was a downed tree in it. That could've caused a lot of damage.

"Then, two weeks ago, I noticed Marcus out there," I continued. "He had a chainsaw and was clearing the tree. I very much doubt he decided to do that out of the goodness of his heart."

"You don't know. He might've wanted the wood for bonfires this summer."

"We're surrounded by woods. He picked that specific spot because you like stranding Mrs. Little but don't want to damage her car. You know which lines shouldn't be crossed. You're really a good girl at heart."

"That's the meanest thing you've ever said to me."

"You'll live."

"You're on my list."

"I'll still live." I sighed as we drew close to the shore. "Honestly, would helping have killed you?"

"I have delicate hands." She held them up for emphasis. "I don't like blisters."

**I HAD TO HELP AUNT TILLIE OUT OF** the canoe when we finally managed to get to the shore. She didn't want wet feet — though she had no problem with my sneakers getting soaked — and she was back to grumbling as she stood on the sandy expanse.

"That took way longer than it should have," she complained.

"Then perhaps you should've helped." I used my forearm to wipe away the sweat dotting my brow. "Let's look around. Try not to be you and scare away the ghost."

"Yeah, yeah, yeah." Aunt Tillie headed inland so I stuck to the shore, giving the water a long once-over as I slowly trekked to the north.

I'd barely made it thirty feet before something in the water caught my attention. I moved closer for a better look and frowned when I caught sight of a pair of jeans. "Oh, my ... ." I hurried in that direction with every intention of dragging the body out of the water. The closer I got, though, the more I realized it was a wasted effort.

"What is it?" Aunt Tillie asked, appearing at my side. She'd either heard the distress in my voice or sensed it. "Is that ... ?"

"A body," I replied grimly, glancing around. There was no sign of the ghost — I was convinced that's what I'd seen — and we were alone at the satellite camp. When we were kids, this part of the property was a camp for boys. Hazel and Dani were staying at what had been the girls camp. The two camps were allowed to meet only for meals, and only when there were plenty of chaperones on hand. Now Landon owned the property. He had plans for our future, which made me smile, but the discovery in the water eradicated all traces of warmth.

"Well, he's clearly dead," Aunt Tillie noted as she stared at the body.

"How can you tell it's a man?"

She shrugged. "I can't. The body is too ... you know."

The body was definitely in rough shape, which meant it had probably been in the water for some time.

"I'll call Landon," I said, digging in my pocket for my phone. My first call should have been to Chief Terry, but I was rattled enough to want Landon here now. "It's his property. He'll want to see."

Aunt Tillie arched an eyebrow. "You just want your cuddle bear. Admit it."

She wasn't wrong, but I could never admit it to her. "Look around for anything that shouldn't be here. I doubt this guy simply washed up here by accident."

"I'm not your slave."

I pinned her with a harsh look. "Really?"

"Fine." She blew out a sigh. "I'll look, but only because I have nothing better to do."

"Thanks so much for your magnanimity."


**IT TOOK LANDON AND CHIEF TERRY** thirty minutes to reach the camp. They parked behind the old cabins, which were in better shape than those on the other side of the lake.

"Are you okay?" Landon immediately headed for me, his arms already open to pull me in for a hug. He was a tactile man who enjoyed a good cuddle. If you could arrange for a plate of bacon to add to the mix, he was more than happy to rest on top of each other watching movies the entire day.

I nodded. "I wasn't hurt. I just ... thought I saw something over here and we decided to check it out."

"We?" Landon glanced around, frowning when he saw Aunt Tillie using a stick to poke at the ground. "Seriously? Why is she here?"

"I heard that," Aunt Tillie called out. Her hearing was only an issue when she didn't want to listen to something my mother or aunts barked at her. "You're on my list."

"That threat has lost its efficacy," Landon countered, his hand moving up and down my back. He shook his head before turning his attention back to me. "Show me."

I led him to the body, grimacing as he and Chief Terry sloshed in the water for a closer look.

"Well, he's definitely dead," Chief Terry pronounced, his expression unreadable.

"Is that your professional opinion?" Aunt Tillie asked, snark on full display. She'd managed to sneak up on us. The woman had feet like a cat. Sadly, it was one of those cats who preferred peeing on the bed in retribution for some perceived slight.

Chief Terry ignored her. "What caused you to come to this side of the lake?"

"And did you come in that?" Landon asked, pointing at the canoe.

I nodded. "I thought it would be faster." I glared at Aunt Tillie. "Of course, I also thought I would have help paddling. As for why I decided to come over ... ." I hesitated. Chief Terry wasn't always open to paranormal talk. "I thought I might've seen a ghost by the trees, but really I just wanted a break from Dani."

Landon scowled. "Why were you out here with her? I thought we agreed you would limit your visits."

"You agreed," I countered. "I didn't say that. I ... can't ... limit my visits. This isn't Hazel's responsibility. She needs help. That's why Aunt Tillie and I were out here."

"And you just happened to find a body," Chief Terry said. "What are the odds?"

I held out my hands and shrugged. "You tell me. It's possible that whoever this is got drunk, or there was some sort of accident. It's also possible that something else happened. I'm just doing my due diligence as a conscientious resident of Hemlock Cove."

"Cute," Landon muttered, shaking his head. His anger wasn't directed at me. Death offended him on multiple levels, which was probably why he became an FBI agent in the first place. "She's not your responsibility either, Bay."

It took me a moment to realize he was talking about Dani. He was against me helping the girl. Given what had happened with the murderous birds — and her unhinged aunt — Landon wanted me to wipe my hands of the witchy teenager. We'd argued about it multiple times. I couldn't, though.

At least not yet.

"If she's not my responsibility, who's going to make sure she stays on the straight and narrow?" I challenged.

"Um ... how about a prison warden? That's where she belongs. She's not a good girl, sweetie. She's evil."

"That's what I've been saying." Aunt Tillie held up her clenched fist so Landon could bump it. "You and me, it's like we're sharing the same brain."

"Don't tell me that." Landon scowled, ignoring Aunt Tillie's fist. "That means I'm wrong."

His reaction made me smile. "Nobody's wrong," I reassured him. "I just ... don't know what else to do." Whenever talk turned to Dani I felt helpless.

That must've been written across my face, because Landon moved back and hugged me tighter.

"Okay. We'll table this discussion for now. I still think you're wasting your time, but I'll stand by you no matter what. If this is what you want, then we'll figure it out."

That was all I wanted to hear. "Thank you." I pressed a kiss to the corner of his mouth and then glanced back at the body. "What about him?"

"We'll call the medical examiner," Chief Terry replied, already digging for his phone. "As you said, it could've been an accident."

It could've been an accident. But I had a feeling it was something else entirely.

# THREE

Landon suggested we head back before the medical examiner arrived. He didn't want to answer questions about why we were at the old camp. On the surface, it made sense. Unfortunately, I knew the real reason. He wanted to cut down on outside opinions about the situation at the camp.

Nobody knew Dani was with us. I wasn't sure what the people in town believed — if there was a rumor going around, it hadn't yet made it to me. She'd disappeared and nobody had questioned it. If Aunt Tillie and I were present when the medical examiner arrived, he might ask questions ... and lying was always an iffy proposition in scenarios like this.

"I might be a little late for dinner, but I'll be there," he promised as he got me settled in the canoe. He'd agreed to push us out to save my shoes from another dousing. "Just meet me at the inn."

I nodded, searching his face. He'd been acting weird. Well, he'd been acting secretive. I'd caught him on his computer a few times when he thought I wasn't looking, and he became annoyed when I'd sneaked up behind him to see what he was studying. I had a feeling he was trying to find an institution to take Dani, someplace with bars and maximum security. I hadn't come right out and asked because I didn't want to know the answer. It would lead to a very big fight and I simply wasn't up for it.

"I'm sorry about all of this," I offered. "I know this isn't how you wanted to spend your day."

He slid his eyes to me and I read surprise there. "Sweetie, you didn't cause this. You found a body and called it in. That's what you're supposed to do."

"Yeah, but ... this is your land. I'm keeping Dani in one of the old cabins even though you don't want her there. If I hadn't been out here, this might not have happened."

He hesitated and then shook his head. "First, I think of this as our property. The plan is to build a house for both of us to live in together, right?"

I nodded. "Yeah, but ... ."

He pressed a finger to my lips. "This is our land," he repeated. "We needed to know the body was out here. You didn't do anything wrong and I don't like it when you take stuff like this on yourself. You didn't cause this."

"I guess." I forced a smile for his benefit even though my stomach roiled at the thought of what the medical examiner might find. "If you come across anything you think I should know about ... ."

"I'll call you," he promised, swooping in to give me a kiss. "I'll see you in a few hours. Try to get across the lake fast. It'll probably take the medical examiner about twenty minutes to get out here."

I scowled at the back of Aunt Tillie's head. "I'd be faster if I had some help."

"Oh, you're such a whiner," Aunt Tillie muttered, though she lifted her fingers and let loose a definitive snap, causing the canoe to jerk forward as she used magic to propel it in the direction of the other camp.

"Hey!" I cast a desperate look over my shoulder at Landon and found him grinning as the canoe sped across the lake. He looked amused ... and maybe a little intrigued. "If you could do this from the start why didn't you whip out this particular spell when we were coming over?"

"What fun would that have been?" Aunt Tillie asked.

**I SPENT THE REST OF THE AFTERNOON AT** The Whistler, the newspaper I owned and operated. Technically it was a two-person show — with a few freelancers thrown in for good measure — but it was my little kingdom in the middle of mayhem. I loved owning my own business, even if it was a lot of work.

I read over copy and okayed the layout before heading home. Landon and I lived in the guesthouse on the property my mother and aunts owned. I parked there and changed my clothes — I needed dry shoes above all else — and then walked to the inn. I figured Landon would either do the same or drive, so having two vehicles at the inn was a waste.

It was only a seven-minute walk, and the early summer weather was pleasant. I loved this time of year, and I briefly shut my eyes as I inhaled the scents. I never thought of myself as a nature lover until I left Hemlock Cove for the city. I believed at the time that I wanted a bigger life. I learned that life was only as big as you make it. While there were more stories to cover there, I felt rootless and incomplete. Hemlock Cove was my home and, for better or worse, I had no intention of leaving again.

That was a concern when Landon and I first got together. He was stationed in the Traverse City office, which meant he had to live in the city due to residency requirements. The forty-five-minute drive grew tiresome relatively quickly, though he never complained. He kept an apartment in the city, but he started taking longer weekends whenever possible and showing up at the guesthouse in the middle of the week because he missed me. Then he took a promotion that essentially was a lateral move, but part of his agreement with his boss was that he be able to live in Hemlock Cove. He seemed to love the town as much as me.

Still, in the back of my mind, I was convinced he would eventually want to transfer out of Michigan. There was only so much advancement to be had in our location. When I questioned him about it, though, he said that he was home. He even admitted that he might want to leave the FBI at some point, but the idea seemed alien. Part of me was convinced he'd made the decision for me alone, but he seemed perfectly fine with it ... which made me a happy witch.

I couldn't imagine leaving this place again. I was happy here, even if Dani's future weighed heavily on me. Aunt Tillie was right. At some point a decision would have to be made. We had plenty of options until we had to tackle that, though.

"Hey, Peg." Aunt Tillie's teacup pig greeted me at the back door when I let myself in through the family living quarters. The pig was a recent addition. Aunt Tillie had brought her into the fold without asking anyone whether it was okay. Although my mother put up a fight at the start, she'd told me only days before that she preferred the pig to Aunt Tillie.

*Snort, snort.*

Peg greeted me with a wiggling butt. Someone had dressed her in a camouflage tutu. Only one person would bother with that.

"Where is she?" I asked, glancing around. Aunt Tillie's normal spot on the couch was empty. "Is she off getting in trouble?"

*Snort, snort.*

"That's what I figured." I patted Peg on the head and then moved into the kitchen, pulling up short when I realized Mom and Landon were the only ones in the room. They appeared to be whispering. They were near the sink, their heads bent together as Landon showed her something on his phone, oblivious to my presence.

Suspicion is the name of the game in the Winchester household. Everyone is always doing something to mess with another member of the family. That's what I figured they were doing — plotting something to drive me crazy — so I edged closer to try to see the phone without tipping them off.

"Good evening, Bay," Aunt Tillie called from her recliner in the corner of the kitchen. She had a voice that carried, one that might belong to a horrible monster bent on destroying the world. I cringed when Landon swiveled to meet my gaze.

"Hey," I offered lamely, glaring at Aunt Tillie. I hadn't seen her sitting there, which explained why Peg was running around on her own. She wasn't allowed in the kitchen. That was the only rule that seemed to stick where Peg was concerned.

"I was just looking for you." Landon plastered a wide smile on his face as he swooped in to kiss me, sliding his phone into his pocket. I couldn't see what was on the screen before he tried to distract me.

"Well, you found me." I tipped up my chin and accepted his kiss and hug, pinning Aunt Tillie with a dirty look over his shoulder. She just had to open her big mouth. That meant they were looking at something really bad ... like maybe Mom was helping him plot a way to remove Dani from the area without my knowledge. "What were you and Mom doing?" I blurted out, fear suddenly gripping me by the throat. What if Landon tried taking Dani from the camp to protect me and she hurt him in the process? She was capable. And he worried more about me than himself.

"I was showing her a photo of a pig in a combat helmet," Landon replied quickly. "I'm thinking Peg should have one so nobody will be able to tell her and Aunt Tillie apart."

"Oh, please." Aunt Tillie rolled her eyes. "Like I would wear a tutu. Nobody has trouble telling us apart."

Landon smirked. "If you say so."

He hadn't hesitated before responding to my question, but it still felt like a lie. "I want to see the photo."

"What?" Landon's eyebrows hopped. "Oh, well, I closed the window. I'll look for it again later when we get home." He turned away from me and focused on the stove. "What's for dinner tonight?"

"Nothing with bacon," Mom replied. "We're doing tacos because we don't have any guests yet. Clove and Sam are due at any moment. Clove requested tacos. Apparently she's been craving them for days, and now that she's home she thinks she can get us to cook whatever her cravings demand."

I studied my mom's profile for a moment. Clove had returned from her honeymoon only a day earlier. I'd yet to see her — which was difficult, because we'd spent the better part of our lives seeing each other daily — and I was looking forward to a true family dinner. The fact that Clove was pregnant, a condition advanced enough that she was showing, had been a bone of contention during the lead-up to the wedding. My mother and aunts had pretended they were fine with the fact that Clove was pregnant before marriage, but I'd been waiting for the real blowup. So far, I'd been disappointed by the lack of fireworks.

"You're not going to give her grief?" I asked.

Mom's forehead wrinkled. "Why would I give her grief?"

"Because she got pregnant before she got married. When we were kids, you threatened us with death, bloody and terrible, if that ever happened."

"That's because we were trying to keep you girls from throwing your lives away," Mom replied primly. "You're adults now. Clove was going to marry Sam regardless. This was always the path she was destined to take."

I narrowed my eyes. "You're saying all the right things. It would be nice if you meant them."

Mom shook her head. "You have a suspicious mind, Bay. It's one of the things I dislike most about you."

"Really?" Aunt Tillie didn't bother looking up, flipping through a catalog as she kept one ear on the conversation. "I think that whiny thing she does is much worse than having a suspicious mind."

"She gets the suspicious mind from you," Mom shot back. "You can't dislike the trait because you'd have to take a good, long look at yourself."

"No, that's not it." Aunt Tillie finally raised her eyes and met my gaze. "The whining is definitely more annoying."

"I happen to like both the whining and the suspicion," Landon offered, slinging his arm around my neck and tugging me toward the door. "She's perfect."

"That's laying it on a bit too thick," I said dryly. "You're just trying to escape before Mom makes us help with dinner preparations."

"Shh." He grinned and planted a kiss on my lips. "You'll ruin my master plan."

I cast one last look at my mother, debating if I could crack her if I managed to lose Landon in the front of the inn before doubling back, and then opted to let it go — at least for tonight.

"Let's find Clove," Landon insisted as we crossed into the dining room.

"Since when are you so excited to see Clove?"

"Since I like watching you squeal."

That felt like an insult. "I don't squeal."

"Oh, you squeal. In fact ... ." He broke off as two figures moved into the dining room from the opposite door.

"Bay!" Clove broke away from Sam and threw herself at me hard enough that I had to brace myself so I wouldn't fall over.

"Clove!" My voice was shriller than I intended, and when I darted a look in Landon's direction I found him smiling. "That wasn't a squeal," I argued.

"You keep telling yourself that." He squeezed Clove's shoulder before moving behind her to greet Sam. "Congratulations." The two men shook hands — they weren't exactly the best of friends, but they'd grown closer in recent months — and watched us with merry grins. "How was the honeymoon?"

"It was great," Sam enthused. He was sporting a tan that helped him give off a healthy vibe, and he couldn't stop smiling. "It was nice to have two weeks completely to ourselves. The only drama we had to contend with was Clove's rampaging hormones and constant cravings."

Clove's expression darkened as she pulled away from me and focused on her husband. "I don't have rampaging hormones."

Sam was clearly dubious. "Do you want to tell them about crying on the beach when you saw the puppy, or should I?"

Clove's mouth dropped open in mock outrage. "I wasn't crying. I had something in my eye."

"Yeah. Tears."

"No ... it was the sun." Clove's expression was pleading when she turned to me. "I don't have hormone issues."

"Of course not," I reassured her, grinning. I hadn't realized how much I'd missed her until she was directly in front of me. Dani had taken most of my time in Clove's absence. Without her, though, there'd been an empty spot in the family. Now it was filled again, and it caused some of the tension I'd been carrying to ease. "You would never have hormone issues."

"That's right." Clove bobbed her head and glanced around. "Do I smell guacamole?"

Apparently her olfactory senses had kicked into overdrive. "It's taco night. I thought that's what you requested."

"Yay!" Clove clapped her hands and did a little dance. "I texted Mom that's what I wanted, but I wasn't sure she would make it happen. I'm going to eat my weight in tacos."

"That should be impressive," Thistle deadpanned, sliding into the room. She didn't look nearly as happy to see Clove.

"Thistle!" Clove started to throw herself on our other cousin, but she was brought up short when Thistle extended a hand. "Don't you want to hug me?"

Thistle's hair was a bright shade of purple. She'd gotten a new package from Overtone and the last thing she'd said to me before separating the previous day was that she planned to wait at least a week before using the contents. Obviously she hadn't been able to hold out.

"You don't want to hug me, do you?" Clove jutted out her lower lip. "And to think that I missed you on my honeymoon."

"Oh, geez." Thistle rolled her eyes until they landed on me. "I told you she was going to be a pain. We still have three months of this. Now that she doesn't have to hide the fact that she's pregnant it'll be nonstop tears and doughnuts."

"The doughnuts don't sound bad," Landon offered, though he wasn't fixated on the conversation. Instead, his eyes were on the kitchen door, as if he was looking for an excuse to return to the kitchen.

"Is something wrong?" I asked.

"Why would anything be wrong?" He flashed a smile that felt fake. "I was just thinking about something at work. Don't worry about it."

"About the body?" I asked. "Do you know who he is?"

"No. The only thing I know is that someone is dead ... and the body was probably in the water at least a few days."

I pictured the body in the water and shuddered. "That's a horrible way to die."

"We don't have a cause of death yet. He could've died beforehand and fell in the water. We'll have more information — and hopefully an identity — in the morning."

Thistle wrinkled her nose. "Wait. What body?"

"It's a long story."

"And we don't want to hear it," Clove interjected quickly. "We want to talk about something else."

"Speak for yourself," Thistle shot back. "I want to hear about the body. After that, we'll talk about the fact that the store had been completely rearranged when I turned up for my shift today. I'm curious how you managed that when you didn't get back into town until last night."

"You left the lighthouse last night?" Sam challenged. "How did you manage that?"

"I ... ." Clove trailed off, caught. "Um ... the thing is, the doctor says it's perfectly normal for an expectant mother to nest. It should be encouraged."

"Yeah, I'm going to want to talk to this doctor," Thistle said.

"I want to talk to the doctor, too," Sam added. "Now that we're back, I think we should set up an appointment."

"Not until after we tell everybody about our honeymoon," Clove whined. "I don't want to hear about another body. That's normal for this house these days. I want to talk about me."

She batted her eyelashes in such a way that Sam immediately gave in. "Fine. Tonight you can talk about whatever you want. Tomorrow, we're getting serious." He was firm. "We have a lot of things to plan around and not much time to finish them. We need a room for the baby. That has to be our first priority."

Clove blinked several times in rapid succession, her mood shifting quickly. "I changed my mind. The honeymoon was all sex and food. I couldn't have booze, so we don't have any funny stories. Let's talk about the baby's room." She maniacally clapped her hands and hopped up and down.

Landon shook his head. "Nope. No hormone hijinks here. Everything is absolutely normal."

That made me laugh even as my mind drifted to Dani. We had serious issues in this house. For one night, though, the happiness would replace the dire.

# FOUR

Landon was already awake when I wrenched open my eyes the next morning. I'm a slow starter most days — and today wouldn't be any different — and he generally matched my pace. He looked ready to go this morning.

"Morning," I murmured, stretching my arms over my head.

"Good morning." He watched me with a lazy smile, something I couldn't quite identify flashing through his eyes.

"What is it?" I'd felt as if I was walking on slightly uneven ground with him over the past few days. Something was amiss, although I couldn't quite identify what.

"What is what?" he asked, his forehead wrinkling.

"That way you're looking at me."

"Maybe I just love you. Have you considered that?"

He did love me. I was sure of it. There were times in the past I'd convinced myself he would leave over the witchy stuff, because it was easier to brace myself for the worst than accept the best. Now, though, I had trouble believing he would leave me.

Moving on Dani was another story. If he thought that was in my best interests, he would simply swoop into the camp when I was distracted one day and try to remove her without my knowledge. If that happened, and she felt trapped, she would hurt him. The notion made me sick to my stomach.

"What are you thinking?" he asked in a quiet voice.

I balked at being put on the spot. "What makes you believe I'm thinking anything?"

"Because you have a busy brain." He tapped my temple for emphasis. "As long as I've known you, that head of yours has been a tangled place to visit."

"I thought you said you loved my mind," I teased.

"I love everything about you." He wrapped his arms around me and pressed a kiss to my mouth. "Every single thing," he repeated.

"Like what?" I knew the thoughts that were going on inside his head. He was debating if he had time to talk me into a rousing game of under-the-covers monsters before we both had to leave for our respective days.

"I love the way your hair stands on end in the mornings," he said, causing my hands to fly up and check my bedhead situation, which made him laugh. "I love how smart you are. You figure things out faster than I do and I'm a trained investigator."

"I wouldn't go that far," I hedged. "Sometimes I jump to the wrong conclusion. Who has to talk me back from the ledge then?"

"I rarely have to talk you back from a ledge of your own making. Usually, if you fly off the handle, it's because Thistle or Aunt Tillie pushed you in a certain direction."

"I've made myself crazy a time or two, too."

"Oh, I know." He grinned as he kissed the tip of my nose. He seemed to be in a sloppy romantic mood this morning, which made for a fun bout of reminiscing.

"Can I ask you something?" I prodded after a beat.

He nodded as he ran his hands up and down my back. "Always ... unless it's something really serious. I don't want to worry about anything real until I've had my coffee."

I hesitated. Did I really want to ruin our morning? He was adamant he didn't want to talk about anything serious. That probably meant I should take a step back and let him be happy rather than press him.

He sighed when I didn't immediately respond. "You're going to ask me something serious, aren't you?"

I shook my head, making up my mind on the spot. "No. I was just going to ask if you thought I was the prettiest witch you'd ever crossed paths with."

He studied my face, his fingers moving to my cheek as he lightly touched my skin. "That's not what you were going to ask."

"It is. I was fishing for a compliment. That's what I like to do in the morning."

His lips curved but he didn't break into a full smile. "You are the prettiest anything I've ever met," he offered. "I knew the moment I saw you at the cornfield that I wanted to spend time with you."

"Naked time?"

His grin spread. "Pretty much. It was more than that, though. There was always something about you. I don't know how to explain it. I felt this ... pull." He took my hand and pressed it to the spot above his heart. "I love you, Bay. I don't know if I realized that you would become the center of my world the day we met, but I'm not sorry for a single turn we've made, because it brought us here."

That was enough to cause me to warm all over. "You bugged me," I admitted, causing him to bark out a laugh. "The way you watched me made me uncomfortable."

"I wanted you to be uncomfortable. I was trying to scare you away from a dangerous situation. Little did I know you were going to do whatever you wanted no matter what I'd said. Self-preservation isn't always your primary motivation."

And now we were getting to the nitty-gritty. "I need you to promise me something," I prodded.

"I'll love you forever," he said automatically.

"Not that. I've come to the realization that we're tragically co-dependent and attached to one another for life. For the record, I'll love you forever, too. That's not what I want you to promise me."

"Okay. Lay it on me."

I sucked in a steadying breath. "I want you to promise you won't try to approach Dani on your own. If you feel she needs to be moved, then no matter what, you have to get me to help you."

The way he furrowed his brow told me that wasn't the response he suspected. "That's what you're worried about?"

His incredulous expression made me wonder if I'd made a grave misstep. "I just want to make sure you're safe."

"You think she'll kill me," he surmised, shaking his head. "Bay, I don't want you spending any more time with her. You've given it your best shot, but it's a wasted effort."

"I can't just abandon her," I protested. "If I walk away ... then what?"

"Then she goes to prison like she's supposed to. The only reason we didn't arrest her is because you insisted. After what happened with Diane, I didn't want to push you. I gave in and I've regretted it ever since."

I didn't doubt that for an instant. "She's dangerous to you," I insisted. "She could hurt you."

"She could hurt you, too."

"She could." I would never deny that. "That's why I go out there with backup. There's still a chance for her." I believed that to my very core. I had to. "If there comes a time when we all agree that she can't be helped ... ." I trailed off.

"Aunt Tillie already thinks she's beyond help," he pointed out, causing my eyes to flash. "Oh, don't look at me that way. Of course I've talked to her about this." He struggled to a sitting position, the duvet cover falling around his waist. "You're the most important person in the world to me, Bay. I won't risk you for anything. Dani is a concern."

"And that's why you and my mother had your heads bent together last night?"

He cocked his head, surprise briefly flitting through his eyes. "Your mother and I were having a discussion about a few different things. I didn't realize that was against the rules."

"It's not. But you two don't usually talk like that. I know you were talking about Dani."

"We were talking about you," Landon countered. "We both love you. We're allowed to worry about you. Dani is a threat." He pulled me tighter against him and I noted a bit of desperation lurking underneath the tough veneer he always put forward. "Don't let her hurt you."

My instinct was to make him feel better. "I won't. I need you to steer clear of her, though. She might hurt you, because ... well ... just because."

"Let us take her," Landon implored. "Let us lock her up. It's the only way people will truly be safe."

I shook my head. "You won't be able to contain her. Prison won't work for her."

"So, what do you suggest?"

If our intervention failed, there was only one thing we could do to contain her, and I didn't want to think about it. "We have to keep trying." I swallowed hard. "That's our only option. I know you don't want to think about it, but it's true. This is our only shot."

He stared hard into my eyes for a long beat and then sighed. "You have the biggest heart of anyone I know, Bay. Don't let this girl use it to her advantage. She's not a good person. She'll try to twist things so she has the upper hand. Whatever you do, don't turn your back on her."

I nodded.

"Promise me," he insisted. "Don't put yourself in a vulnerable position. I need you too much."

"I won't," I reassured him quickly. "I'm much more careful than you give me credit for."

He rolled his eyes. "You run headlong into danger and don't ever look over your shoulder," he argued, taking me by surprise when he grabbed me around the waist and rolled on top of me. "I think, to be on the safe side, I should handcuff you to the bed and keep you here forever. That way I know you'll always be safe."

"I'll starve."

"I'll feed you ... bacon macaroni and cheese. You'll learn to love it."

I laughed at his grin. "That doesn't sound so bad."

His eyes gleamed. "How about I give you a preview?"

**WE WERE LATE BY** the time we arrived at the inn. Breakfast was on the table, and the look Mom shot us was straight from a bad horror movie.

"You're late," she said primly.

"We're sorry." Landon slid into his usual seat and immediately reached for the coffee carafe. "Our alarm didn't go off."

"Oh, please." Aunt Tillie rolled her eyes as she spooned fresh blueberries on her waffles. "You're both glowing like supernovas. Everybody knows the filthy things you were doing this morning. Let me a guess, did you play a rousing game of 'Officer, I have a different way to get out of this ticket' or did you come up with a new game?"

Chief Terry, who had taken to spending almost every night at the inn now that he and my mother had finally given in and started dating, made a face. "Don't say things like that," he hissed. "You know it makes me uncomfortable."

Aunt Tillie was blasé. "You need to get over it. She's a grown woman. She plays grown woman games."

"Not in my head. There, she's still eight and has pigtails. Oh, and carrying around a stuffed dog and trying to force me into tea parties with her, Clove, and Thistle."

"Hey, those tea parties were never my idea," I argued. "That was Clove's thing. She always wanted to wait on people and make them happy. I wanted to play Monopoly."

Landon arched an eyebrow. "I didn't know you were a Monopoly fan."

"I like winning."

He smirked. "I think that's a family trait." His eyes were serious as he turned his attention to Chief Terry. "Anything on our floater?"

Chief Terry couldn't seem to stop glaring.

"What's your problem?" Landon demanded, attitude on full display. "Did you have a bad night or something? Let me guess, Winnie is as bossy in bed as she is in the kitchen. Maybe you should watch an instructional video or something."

I was horrified by the suggestion, and then I saw the way his lips quivered. He was desperately trying to keep a straight face.

"Oh, you're trying to turn the table on them," I noted, catching on quickly. "It's better that they be embarrassed than us."

"Very good, sweetie." He grinned at me. "You probably shouldn't have said that out loud, though. Now they're on to our dastardly plan."

"I'm going to beat you to within an inch of your life later," Chief Terry warned, turning back to his breakfast. He looked furious. "Ugh. Now I've lost my appetite. I blame you, Landon."

"I'm sorry to hear your stomach is on the fritz." Landon reached for the center platter, where the bacon was piled. "I'll do my best to eat enough for the both of us."

I smirked as he piled at least eight slices of bacon on his plate. "Did you work up an appetite?" I teased.

"You know it." He winked at me and sipped his coffee before turning back to Chief Terry. "Do you have anything on our dead man? I figure that's what we're going to spend our morning on."

"You figured right," Chief Terry said finally, turning to formal business. "It's not a dead man, though. It's a woman."

I was shocked. "Really?"

Chief Terry nodded, grim. "The body was so bloated it threw us all."

"Do we know who?" Mom asked. "Was she a local?"

Chief Terry nodded, causing my stomach to plummet. "Who?"

"Anybody know Valerie Lennox?"

My breath clogged in my throat. "The real estate agent?"

Chief Terry nodded. "One and the same."

"She helped with some of the paperwork when Bay was buying The Whistler," Landon replied. "Another guy in the office was handling the main transaction but she helped with some of the peripheral stuff."

"She seemed nice," I offered as I tried to make sense of what had happened to the gregarious real estate agent. "She worked out of Eric Savage's office. I'm not certain how long she was with his outfit."

"At least a few years," Mom volunteered. "Before you moved back, Bay, we were considering getting an appraisal on the guesthouse. Eric helped us. We ultimately went another way, because we didn't like what he suggested."

"Which was what?" Landon asked, tapping the side of my plate to get my attention. "Eat your breakfast, sweetie. You're going to need fuel to get through the day if you're going to help us."

I was caught off guard. "Seriously? You want me to help you?"

"Of course I want you to help me. We're a team, right? Besides, you saw the ghost. That probably means she's still over there. But we should hit the real estate office first."

"I think that's wise," Chief Terry confirmed. "Once we got confirmation it was Valerie, several people mentioned working with her. I placed a call requesting an appointment with Eric's secretary. Linda at the medical examiner's office — you know the secretary who works at the front desk, right? — she said there was a rumor Valerie was involved with Eric. Whether that's true, I don't know. That body was in the water for several days, though, and we don't have a missing person report filed."

"The real estate office should definitely be first," Landon agreed. "Do we have a cause of death?"

"That's where it gets worse." Chief Terry's expression twisted. "There was water in her lungs and bruising around her neck."

"What does that mean?" my aunt Marnie asked, horrified.

"It means she was held in the water and strangled," Aunt Tillie replied blandly. "This is definitely a murder. You need me if you expect to solve it."

Landon gave her a dirty look. "We've got it under control, thanks." He shook his head. "Eat your breakfast, Bay. It's going to be a long day and I want you with me for at least part of it."

I nodded and focused on my heaping plate of waffles. Something bothered me about this whole thing and I couldn't move past it. "What do you think she was doing out there?"

"I have no idea, but we're going to find out," Landon promised. "That's the first order of business. We'll talk to the boyfriend. He might point us in a direction."

# FIVE

Eric Savage welcomed us into the office with a bright and inquisitive smile. Landon and Chief Terry had warned me to pretend I was merely an interested property owner and nothing more, as if I wasn't used to lying about my witchy abilities. That was one thing they never had to worry about.

"It's nice to see you again." He beamed at me as I sat in the chair behind Landon. I thought it was best to allow them the prime spots. "I'm so glad you're in charge of the newspaper now. I have a few ads I want to run. This is our busy season."

"We'll be happy to run them," I encouraged, keeping my smile neutral. "I never turn down advertising."

Eric sat at his desk and fixed Chief Terry and Landon with a look of curiosity. "I take it this isn't a friendly visit."

"It's not," Chief Terry agreed. "We have some bad news about one of your employees."

"One of my employees?" Eric's eyebrows hopped. "Was there an accident this morning?" His gaze immediately went to me. He didn't ask about my presence, but I could tell he was wondering.

"Not this morning," Chief Terry replied. "I don't know any easy way to tell you this, but Valerie Lennox is dead."

Eric moved to stand and then collapsed back into his chair, his face going white. "I don't ... understand." Oddly enough, he looked to me for answers. "How is this possible?"

"We're not sure." Chief Terry sat straight in his chair. He'd delivered bad news so many times he was used to it. There's no easy way to tell people they'd lost someone but there are a million bad ways. He'd once told me that the key was to keep to the facts, and that's what he did now. "Ms. Winchester is here because she was out at her property on the lake yesterday when she found a body in the water."

"*His* property," Eric automatically corrected, gesturing toward Landon. "He bought it."

"It's *our* property," Landon supplied. "We're going to build a house out there. Bay's name will be on the deed just as soon as we file. I've already made sure the property goes straight to her in the event of my death. That's her property as much as it is mine."

That was news to me. "What? I don't understand."

He slid his eyes to me. "Because the registrar's office moves slow as molasses up here, I wanted to make sure you were taken care of. My parents are well aware that property is yours, but I wanted it spelled out legally.

"My pension and life insurance are going to you, too," he continued. "I don't foresee problems with my parents — they love you — but I'm not taking any chances with your future."

I was absolutely gobsmacked. "But ... ."

"Shh." He pressed his finger to his lips. "We'll talk about this later. We need to focus on Valerie now."

He was right, but my mind was churning. This was the last thing I expected.

"As we were saying, Ms. Winchester was out there looking around with her great-aunt when she thought she saw something in the water," Chief Terry explained. "Upon investigating, they found a body, at which point they contacted us."

"And she was in the water?" Eric rubbed his cheek, not focusing on anyone in particular. I was no drama critic, but if he was faking his reaction, he was very good.

"She was." Chief Terry nodded. "We identified her through dental records early this morning."

"Wait ... ." Eric leaned forward in his chair. "Why couldn't you identify her right away? You've all met her. There should be no reason you wouldn't know who she was unless ... ." He trailed off, leaving the dark thought hanging.

"She'd been in the water quite some time," Landon explained. "We weren't even sure if we were dealing with a man or woman at first."

"She'd just cut her hair," Eric offered absently, his hand automatically going up to his own hair. "This is unbelievable. I don't understand how this happened. Was she swimming?"

"That's unlikely, but not impossible," Chief Terry responded. "You should know that her death has been ruled a homicide."

"But ... how can you be sure?"

"Let's just say there are indications of a struggle and leave it at that for now." Chief Terry was all business. "Several people have mentioned that you and Ms. Lennox were involved."

"It wasn't a secret, but we're no longer involved," Eric explained. He looked dazed. "Er, we *were* no longer involved. We broke up about three weeks ago. That's why she cut her hair. She said she was trying to free herself of things that didn't bring her joy. It was a jab at me."

I pressed my lips together, considering. That sounded like something a woman would do after an emotional breakup. Clove had gotten more bad haircuts than I could count on both hands. Before Sam, she had bleeding tragic taste in men. Heck, when she first hooked up with Sam we were convinced he was another in a long line of disastrous choices. We turned out to be wrong, for which I was grateful. Sam was going to be a wonderful husband — he was infinitely patient — and a terrific father.

"Why did you break up?" Chief Terry asked in anticipation of jotting notes.

"Because ... we grew apart." It was a lame answer, something Eric must've realized because he quickly tried to fill the silence in the room with a better response. "I thought we were compatible when we first started dating, but that didn't turn out to be the case. Valerie was ... I don't know how to phrase this without sounding like a jerk, but she was a defeatist."

That was an interesting take on the woman. I revisited some of my interactions with her. Now that he'd pointed it out, I could see it.

"I don't understand what that means," Landon prodded.

"She never saw the bright side of life," Eric volunteered. "She was never excited about anything. Even when something good happened, she immediately started in on the, 'Well, it won't last' stuff. Occasionally it's okay to celebrate."

"I think that's just a woman thing," Landon countered, causing me to frown.

"I'm not a defeatist," I muttered, earning a sidelong look from him. He almost looked amused at my discomfort, but he returned his attention to Eric.

"Women do have a tendency to see the bad in things depending on their moods," he agreed. "Valerie always took it to the extreme. She would see the absolute worst in every situation — and person, for that matter — but never look for ways to fix things. She was happy just to accept that things were crappy and move on from there. It became frustrating."

"So you broke up with her," Chief Terry said. "How did she take it?"

"Not well, and that wasn't the only reason I broke up with her," Eric hedged. "I planned to break up with her but was looking for the right time. Then something happened that made me realize I couldn't wait any longer."

"And what was that?"

When Eric didn't immediately respond, I did it for him. "He met someone else."

"Is that true?" Landon asked.

"If you're asking if I cheated on Valerie, that's technically true," Eric said. "It wasn't a conscious decision. I didn't even know I was developing feelings for this woman until it had already happened. It was ... quick."

"I see. Did you tell Valerie you'd met someone else?"

"I tried not to. I didn't want her blaming this particular individual. She tends to hold a grudge. If she was going to be angry with someone, I wanted it to be me. She kept pressuring me after the breakup. I held her at bay as long as I could — but then she started following me."

I straightened in my chair. Now we were getting to the meat of the story. "She saw you with this other woman," I supplied. "Did she interrupt a date or something?"

"She followed me to Heather's house. We were inside having dinner when a rock came through the front window. I went outside to check, assuming it was kids, but it was Valerie. She absolutely melted down."

"Did she threaten this Heather?" Landon asked. "Do you think she was dangerous? I ask because it's possible she attacked Heather and there was a struggle. Maybe Heather was simply trying to protect herself and panicked."

"I can't see Heather doing that." Eric was firm. "She's the gentlest person I know. She felt bad for Valerie. She suggested we ignore the behavior. That Valerie would lose interest in hounding us."

"That was probably sound advice," Landon acquiesced. "It's my understanding Valerie was still working for you. Is that correct?"

"Well, technically." Eric looked increasingly uncomfortable. "I thought she'd quit after the rock incident, just didn't offer any notice. There was a lot of yelling that night. I didn't fire her, but I told her that respect was expected in a professional setting.

"She was ranting when she left," he continued. "She swore she was going to get revenge on both of us. When she didn't show up for work the next day, I just assumed she wasn't coming back. I had her things packed and I was going to have one of the other agents drop it off at her house."

Chief Terry rubbed his chin. "And who is this other woman you've been dating? You mentioned a first name but not a last name."

Eric balked. "I don't want her dragged into this."

"There's no way around that. We need to question her. It sounds as if she has nothing to worry about, but we have to talk to her."

Eric looked resigned. "Heather Castle."

Landon looked to Chief Terry for explanation but received only a head shake. "I don't know that name," Chief Terry said.

"She bought the old Lakin house out on the lake," Eric said. "She's recently divorced and moved from a suburb down south. She bought the house with her settlement."

"Ah." Realization dawned on Chief Terry's face at the same moment some of the cobwebs cleared from my mind. "She's rich."

"That's not why I care for her," Eric countered hurriedly.

"Maybe not, but I'll bet Valerie jumped to that conclusion," Chief Terry argued. "Heather lives on the lake where the body was found. We definitely need to talk to her."

"You're looking in the wrong direction." He was insistent. "Heather doesn't have it in her to murder anyone."

"Because she's such a good person?" Landon challenged.

"Because ... she doesn't like getting dirty." Eric's expression turned petulant. "She's an indoor girl. That's a regular joke between us. She likes the view of the lake, but she doesn't like the woods or anything. She's really turned off by that camp. She says it reminds her of a horror movie. I said you planned to tear it down, but she doesn't think you're moving fast enough."

Landon arched an eyebrow and I could tell what he was thinking. He had no intention of spending money to tear down the old buildings just to appease a neighbor. "Well, we'll do our best to accommodate her," he said dryly, shaking his head. "Does Ms. Castle work?"

Eric hesitated and then shook his head. "She doesn't have to. She made out quite well in the divorce."

Landon tilted his head and pursed his lips. "The medical examiner believes Valerie went into the water about thirteen days ago. We're going to need you to account for your whereabouts for that time."

Eric was incredulous. "I ... don't know. I'll have to look at my date book."

"That's fine. What about at night? Were you with Heather that night?"

"Thirteen days ago was about the time Valerie threw the rock. I'm pretty sure that was the same day, because I was just thinking earlier that it had been almost two weeks."

"So ... you were at Ms. Castle's house," Chief Terry prodded.

"Until about eight o'clock," Eric replied.

"Where did you go after that?"

"Home. There was a game on I wanted to watch."

"Can anybody corroborate your alibi?"

"I didn't know I was going to need an alibi." Eric sounded exasperated. "Should I get a lawyer?"

"That's up to you." Chief Terry stood, causing Landon and I to follow suit. "Have you talked to Ms. Castle since that night?"

"Yes. I told you we're seeing each other. We talk several times a day."

"Have you seen her?"

Eric hesitated, then nodded. "Yes. We've eaten in town several times since then."

"But you haven't been back to her house?"

"Um ... not that I can think of. We both agreed we didn't want to antagonize Valerie and cause her to return there. We've been meeting in town so Valerie would have no reason to return to the house."

"It looks like she never left," I murmured.

"Yes, well, I don't know that."

Chief Terry glanced at Landon and then motioned for the door. "Thank you for your time, Eric. We'll be in touch."

Eric was flabbergasted. "Wait. That's it? You have to tell me what you think happened to Valerie."

"We don't know yet. You'll be the first to know when we do."

**BACK IN CHIEF TERRY'S VEHICLE,** opinions started flying fast.

"This situation is messed up," Landon said. "It's possible Valerie attacked this other woman and Heather Castle killed her in self-defense."

"It's also possible this woman got fed up and went after her," Chief Terry noted.

Landon slid his eyes to me. "What do you think?"

"I think it's weird that you think you're going to die," I answered without thinking. "How could you leave all that stuff for me and not bother to give me a heads-up?"

"Oh, geez." He stared out the windshield. "I can't believe we're having this conversation in front of an audience."

"I'm mildly curious, too," Chief Terry admitted. "Isn't that something you should talk about?"

"The possibility of me dying on the job?" Landon shot back. "No. Call me crazy, but I don't want to think about that. I just want Bay taken care of in case it happens. I don't see how that makes me a bad guy."

"It doesn't make you a bad guy," I argued. "I just ... don't want you to die."

"Sweetie, I have no intention of dying. You're the most important thing in the world to me. I need to make sure that you're taken care of. I also don't want to talk about it. As far as I'm concerned, we're going to have decades together ... at a house we build on the lake. Don't go getting crazy over this.

"Every year, all my paperwork with the bureau comes up for review," he continued. "Last time I changed the beneficiary on everything to you. That's what you do when you're in a relationship with someone."

He sounded so reasonable and still ... . "What if you change your mind?"

"I'm not going to change my mind."

"But ... ."

"I'm done talking about this." Landon tapped the steering wheel to get Chief Terry's attention. "This is not funny," he said when he caught the older man smiling. "I want Bay taken care of. That's it. End of story."

"I didn't say anything." Chief Terry stuck his key in the ignition. "I think it's a sweet gesture."

"Yes, well, it's what I wanted." Landon turned to look at me. "Don't read anything into this. I don't think I'm going to die. You are the single most important thing to me, and this way your future is guaranteed.

"I can't control everything," he continued. "I know in the Winchester world that's unheard of, but in the real world horrible things happen. I'm going to make sure they don't happen to you. Is that so terrible?"

I shook my head, momentarily overcome by emotion. "I just wish you would've told me."

"I didn't realize it was important. I'm sorry."

"It's okay." I turned to the window to blink back tears. "Thank you."

"Oh, good grief." Landon sounded aggrieved. "I knew this was going to turn into thing. Let's go," he prodded. "I want to talk to Heather Castle before Eric warns her that we're coming."

"I guarantee that's what he's doing right now," Chief Terry said.

"And you." Landon turned back to me again. "Don't turn into a weepy mess. You and I will be together forever. I did this because it made sense. That's all there is to it."

"I know." I forced a smile for his benefit. "It's just ... a big step."

"Not really. You only think that because your mind goes to strange places. Everyone else will find it reasonable. Mark my words."

# SIX

I tried to push Landon's bombshell — whether he believed it or not, that's exactly what it was — out of my mind as we headed toward the lake. I was in my own little world, gazing out the window when we turned into the driveway of the house.

"This is set pretty far back," Landon noted. "I didn't even know this house was out here."

"Yes, you did," I countered, forcing myself back into the conversation. "It's the house with the big balcony that overlooks the water. We saw it the day we took the canoes out to see if they would float."

"Really?" Landon turned to look at me. "I never thought about it. This must be a long driveway."

"It is," Chief Terry confirmed. "This house is a pain to get to in the winter. I'm surprised she moved here full time. Before, the house was only used during the summer."

"Well, we're going to build a house that puts that one to shame," Landon said, grinning. "I do like that balcony, though. We need a huge balcony like that so we can sit and stare at the stars without having to worry about naked witches dancing around us."

I smirked. He talked big but he liked the naked dancing — though he made a point to look anywhere but at my mother and aunts when the gyrating started.

"And when are you going to break ground on this mansion?" Chief Terry asked.

"Not for a few years." Landon turned sheepish. "I make a decent living, but we need to put money away. If we put our heads together we can come up with a five-year plan."

"Five years, huh?" Chief Terry looked amused. "Are you going to be happy living on the Winchester land until then?"

Landon shrugged. "I'm used to it. I don't even think about it now. I'm fine with our living arrangements."

"What about you?" I asked, directing my attention to Chief Terry. "Are you going to be happy living at the inn?"

Chief Terry jolted at the question. "What do you mean?"

"You spend every night there," I pointed out. "It's only a matter of time before you decide to pin down your living arrangements. Mom isn't going to leave. She can't, really, because she's the only one Aunt Tillie listens to."

"Tillie won't be around forever," Chief Terry said.

"I guess." As much as Aunt Tillie drove me crazy — and she did — that wasn't something I wanted to think about. She was in her eighties and still spry, but no matter what she declared, she couldn't live forever. "Have you talked to Mom about moving?"

"No." He met my gaze in the rearview mirror. "I didn't mean to upset you. It's possible Tillie will outlive us all. She has plenty of good years ahead of her."

"That's truly frightening," Landon muttered. "She really could outlive us all."

I smirked as Chief Terry crested the final hill that led to the house. Landon let out a low whistle when he saw it for the first time.

"Wow," he intoned, shaking his head. "This is even better than I expected. What we see from the lake is nothing compared to this. Maybe we won't have the best house in the area after all."

"We don't need this," I reassured him as Chief Terry parked and I unbuckled my seatbelt. "A smaller house is fine. We basically live in a closet now."

"No, we'll have a big house." Landon was firm as he met me outside of the truck. "It'll be a great house. I just don't see ever being able to afford something like this."

That made two of us. I glanced around. "So how mad will you get if I start looking around for a ghost?"

"Mad," Landon replied without hesitation. "Stick close. We'll question

Heather and then look around ourselves. I don't want you wandering off unattended."

"If she's with you I'll be perfectly safe."

"Unless she's not our killer and there's some wacko running around out here."

He had a point, but I didn't want to admit it. "Okay. I'll stick with you."

"Thank you."

Chief Terry knocked on the door. We waited a good two minutes — he had to knock twice more — before someone finally answered.

The woman who stood on the other side of the threshold looked fresh off the pages of a magazine. She was striking, to the point of looking fake. Her cheekbones were so high they looked to be chiseled from marble, her hair so blond the sun glinted off it. Her makeup was absolutely perfect and her eyes were a vibrant blue that made me think of the beaches of a tropical island.

"Hello," she practically purred as she came face to face with Landon. "Are you delivering something? If so, I'll have to order more of it."

Her flirtation raised my hackles. "He's delivering law and order," I volunteered.

Landon pinned me with an admonishing look, but it was obvious he was amused by my reaction. "I'm with the FBI, ma'am." He held up his badge for proof. "My name is Landon Michaels. This is Terry Davenport. He's the police chief here in Hemlock Cove. We're here to discuss a serious matter with you."

"I see." Heather's gaze moved to me. "Is she your secretary?"

I'd barely met this woman and I already wanted to shake her. "Only when he's feeling really dirty," I replied with faux sweetness.

"What?" Heather's forehead creased in confusion.

"This is Bay Winchester," Landon replied. "She owns The Whistler in town."

"Oh, is that the advertorial thing?" She beamed at me. "That's kind of cute, the way you guys try to come up with news for the town every week. I absolutely loved that story about the woman who was trying to grow pumpkins in June. You're very gifted."

I felt patronized but flashed the smile I knew was expected of me. "Thank you."

"She is very gifted," Landon agreed. "She's also a property owner here on the lake."

"Really?" Heather brightened considerably. "That's great. I didn't know anyone else lived out here. We should hang out when you have some free time. Where is your house?"

TO LOVE A WITCH

I shifted from one foot to the other, uncomfortable. "We own the old campground. We're going to build a house on the property eventually. We just bought it."

"Oh." She nodded her head. "That's you. I heard someone had bought that property. I'm glad something is going to be done with it. Nobody wants an eyesore like that around."

"It's not so bad," I argued. "I went to that camp as a kid. I enjoyed it."

"Well ... that's nice." Her smile never wavered, but it was obvious she was quickly losing interest in being best friends. "You said 'we.'"

"Excuse me?"

"We," she repeated. "Are you married?"

"Oh, no. My boyfriend actually purchased the property."

"Well, at least it's a step in the right direction." She turned her full attention to Landon. "Would you like to come inside?"

"That's fine," Landon replied, "but don't you want to know why we're here?"

"You can tell me inside." She led us into an ornate foyer. The ceilings were so tall it would've been hard to make out the intricacies of the light fixture — if it was a normal fixture. It was so large I was fairly certain it wouldn't fit in the guesthouse.

"This is a beautiful home," Landon noted.

"Thank you. I'm very fond of it." Heather acted as tour guide as she led us through the main floor of the house. It was an impressive showpiece, but her attitude grated. Once we were in the living room, I made sure to snag the spot next to Landon on the sofa because I had a feeling she would gladly take it. He raised an eyebrow but remained silent.

"We don't want to take up much of your time, but there's been an incident on the lake," Chief Terry started. "Yesterday, in the afternoon hours, Ms. Winchester was checking her property when she discovered a body in the water at the camp on your side of the lake."

"That's horrible." Heather's hand went to her heart as she feigned shock. I was convinced it was an act. Unlike Eric, who was either a very good actor or honest, Heather wasn't. "What happened?"

"I'm pretty sure Eric already called you," I volunteered, earning a scathing look from Chief Terry that I ignored. "I bet we weren't even out of the parking lot before he tipped you off."

Heather's eyes flicked back to me, and for the first time I saw something dark there. She couldn't hide it. "I ... well ... he might've called," she admitted, sheepish. She batted her eyelashes and turned back to Landon. "He thought I should know. We weren't trying to put one over on you or anything. That's probably impossible anyway. I mean ... you are an FBI agent."

I kind of wanted to punch her.

Landon replied evenly, "It would behoove you not to lie to us. This is a very serious situation. Ms. Lennox's death has been ruled a homicide. Our understanding is that her relationship with you and Mr. Savage was ... less than amiable."

"He means you guys hated each other with the fire of a thousand suns," I offered helpfully.

Heather briefly pinned me with a dark look. Her smile, however, remained firmly planted when she focused on Landon. "I didn't hate Valerie. You mustn't think that. I was frightened of her."

"Because she threatened you?" Landon asked.

"Because ... she was obsessed with Eric. She was stalking him. Did you know she followed him out here and threw a rock through my window?"

"Mr. Savage related that story to us about an hour ago," Landon replied. "Can you show us the damage?"

"I've already had it repaired." Heather leaned forward, giving Landon a clear view of the cleavage packed into her skintight tank top. "I live alone. I didn't want a hole in my window inviting anyone to come inside and try to have his way with me."

"No one blames you for wanting to protect yourself, ma'am," Landon said. "Just give us the name of the glass repair company you used and we'll confirm it."

"Oh, um ... I don't remember." Heather chewed her bottom lip, taking on a far-off expression. "I need to think. I paid the gentleman who came out in cash because he worked so quickly."

She was full of crap. I didn't believe anything she was saying. It was hard to determine if Landon and Chief Terry agreed. Of course, they were more likely to believe her because she was playing the helpless female and they fancied themselves righters of wrongs when it came to damsels in distress. In the Winchester household, they were fresh out of damsels.

"We still need to know who came out here." Landon was firm. "I need you to tell me what happened with Valerie."

"She was ... frightening," Heather replied. "I didn't even realize anything was wrong until the rock came through my window. We were just having a quiet night, enjoying dinner and wine, when I heard this terrific crash.

"We ran into the other room, and it took me a few minutes to realize what I was looking at," she continued. "I had no idea that Eric's breakup with her had been harsh. He didn't tell me about it. I wasn't even aware he was involved until after we'd already gone out a few times. I thought about ending things, but when he told me that he hadn't formally broken up with her because he was worried about her mental health ... well, I took pity on him. He was trying to be a good man."

I could think of a few other ways to describe him. "When was the last time you saw Valerie?" I asked. I could feel Landon's eyes on me and knew he was agitated that I was inserting myself in the question-and-answer portion of the day's events.

"The night she broke the window, Eric went outside, tried to reason with her. She took off. I was shaken, and Eric helped me tape the window until I could get someone out to fix it the next day. I haven't seen her since."

Landon pursed his lips. "Thank you for your time. If we have further questions we'll be in touch. Before we go, we need to look around your property."

"Absolutely. I'd be happy to show you wherever you want to go."

**I'D ABOUT HAD** my fill of Heather. She'd insisted on giving us a guided tour of the property, which meant we couldn't talk openly. I had a few things I wanted to say about her behind her back, none of them pleasant.

Chief Terry and Landon walked with Heather to the water's edge, leaving me to trudge behind. I felt like the fourth wheel on a three-person date and it was making me grouchy.

"She's the worst, isn't she?" a snarky voice said from behind a tree to my right. When I looked around, I found an ethereal ghost watching the show with an angry sneer.

"Valerie," I said in a low voice, keeping my eyes on Heather should she look in my direction. She hadn't paid me more than a second's attention since heading outside. She was much more interested in talking to Landon and Chief Terry. That was probably to my benefit, but it still grated.

"I wish she would just die." The ghost momentarily solidified and the atmosphere sparked as she spewed her vitriol. Then she went transparent again.

I'd seen the phenomenon before, and it made me nervous. "Do you know what happened to you?"

"Yeah. I got dumped by a jerk for that piece of walking silicone."

Her reaction almost made me laugh, but I held it together. "I mean do you know what happened to cause you to end up here?"

"I got dumped."

"Beyond that."

"I ... ." For a moment, fear flitted through her eyes and I thought she was going to bolt. She calmed and recovered enough to smile.

"I probably lost my job," she said. "I should've seen that coming. I didn't think Eric would go that route, because he didn't want to risk a lawsuit. But I guess I'm not that lucky. Man, I don't want to find another job. This sucks."

I swallowed hard and risked a glance at Heather. She'd completely forgotten my presence and had continued down the shoreline, Chief Terry and Landon paying rapt attention.

"You didn't lose your job," I countered. "Well, I mean ... you did. That's not what's important. Why are you still here? Did something happen to keep you here?"

She looked confused. "What are you talking about?"

I hated it when they didn't realize they were dead. Talking to ghosts was difficult enough without having to drop the big death bomb on them. Some didn't take it well, and I had a feeling Valerie would be one of them.

"So ... what day do you think it is?"

"I don't know. No, wait, it's ... Saturday." She was obviously taking a wild guess.

"It's at least a week and a half later than you think it is. Most likely two weeks. You never left this place."

"What do you mean?"

I sighed. "You never left this place." I didn't know another way to tell her, so I just blurted it out. "I found your body in the water yesterday. It had washed down to the campground. I'm guessing you never left here after what happened two weeks ago. Whether Heather or Eric had a hand in what happened to you I can't say. I only know that you're dead."

Valerie's mouth dropped open and she fixed me with a look of pure shock. It was quickly replaced with anger. "That's not true."

"I'm afraid it is."

"Well, it's not." As if to prove it to herself, she took a swipe at my arm. Her hand passed through me. "I ... ." The stark white of her features made me distinctly uncomfortable.

"It's okay," I said in a gentle voice. "I can help you. We just need to figure out what happened and go from there."

"No." She jerked away from me as if she'd been scorched, although I knew she wasn't feeling anything, at least on a physical level. "This isn't right. I'm ... dreaming. That's what it is."

"You're dreaming of me?" I sent her a rueful smile. "How likely do you think that is?"

"I'm not dead!" She practically screamed, causing the leaves above to whip hard.

I stared at them, worry coursing through me. When a ghost was powerful enough to affect his or her surroundings, the outcome was never good. I had to be careful with Valerie, but I had no idea how to stop the transformation I was certain would eventually overtake her.

I licked my lips, debating what I should say. When I glanced back to where she'd been floating only seconds before, she was gone. Obviously the news had been too much for her.

"Are you okay?" Heather asked, causing my shoulders to jerk as I forced my attention back to her. She stood too close, and the expression on her face was unreadable.

"I'm fine." I flashed a smile I didn't feel, wondering how long she'd been watching me. "I was just admiring your property. It's truly lovely."

"Thank you." She beamed at me. "It's a work in progress, but I love it. Come along. You don't want to fall behind."

"Definitely not."

# SEVEN

"What do you think?" Landon asked when we were back in Chief Terry's vehicle and heading to town.

"She's ... interesting," Chief Terry replied after a few seconds, his focus on the road. "I'm not sure I believe everything she's selling, but looking at her, it's difficult to believe she could kill someone."

I snorted. "Excuse me? She's totally capable of killing someone. She spent the entire time we were there lying."

"How do you figure that?" Landon asked.

"Well, if you two had bothered to focus on anything other than how tight her pants were — or how low the vee in her shirt dipped — you would've realized she couldn't come up with the name of a window repair place. That means their story about Valerie throwing a rock through the window is bull."

Amusement flitted across Landon's features. "She said she was going to find the name of the contractor and call us."

"Which means she's going to conveniently forget to call you because she's so upset about Valerie's death happening so close to her property," I shot back. "You're going to be calling to remind her in twenty-four hours — that is if you don't find an excuse to stop out there. She's going to run a sob story on you."

"Tell me how you really feel," Landon drawled.

"That is how I really feel."

He was silent a moment. "Are you really that jealous?"

I found the question insulting. "I'm not jealous. Why do you think I'm jealous? I don't get jealous. Besides, she's fake. There's nothing to be jealous about. I'm real."

"You are definitely real," Landon agreed, his expression hard to read. "You know you have nothing to be jealous about, right?"

"Of course not. I'm the prettiest witch in all the land," I drawled.

He smirked. "I also love you so much I've become blind to all other women."

That was a huge load of crap. "Uh-huh."

"It's true." Landon faced forward. "All I see when I think of beauty is you."

"I think I'm starting to smell something," Chief Terry noted. "It's a distinctive smell. It kind of reminds me of dog crap."

Landon refused to be drawn in further. "Make fun of me all you want, but Bay's too pretty and sweet for me to ever look at another woman."

Chief Terry met my gaze in the rearview mirror. "You're not buying this, are you?"

I knew Landon was laying it on thick, but I couldn't stop from smiling. "It's likely crap," I agreed.

"It is."

"I still like hearing it. I guess that makes me a girl after all."

Landon smirked and reached back to squeeze my hand. "I meant every word. Now, tell me what you and the ghost talked about. I knew you'd found her the way you were hanging back and avoiding Heather."

"I was trying to avoid Heather because she's annoying," I replied. "As for Valerie ... I don't know." I sobered as I thought back to the way she'd sparked. "I'm a little worried."

"About what?" Chief Terry pressed. "She's dead. What more could happen to her?"

"She seems consumed by rage."

Landon looked curious. "And?"

"When a ghost is consumed by rage, things can ... happen."

He feigned patience, but I could tell he was agitated. "I need more than that, Bay. Give me a for instance and we'll go from there."

"Okay, for instance, do you remember when Floyd's ghost went nuts and started throwing dishes in the dining room of the inn because he wanted to kill us? That's what happens when ghosts are consumed by rage."

Landon worked his jaw. The memory of dealing with Floyd Gunderson probably hadn't fallen out of his head, but it happened so long ago that it was unlikely still at the forefront. At the time he'd been melting down because I was thrown from a horse and his family was in town for a formal meet-and-greet with my family. Since then, we'd faced off with a number of enemies, most far more terrifying than Floyd.

"He was a poltergeist," Landon said. "I remember you explained that to me. Are you saying that Valerie is a poltergeist?"

It was a tricky question. "She showed signs of going that route," I said. "I have no proof that will happen, but she was agitated, to the point she might finish the journey and turn completely bad."

"What does that mean?" Chief Terry asked. "If she turns into a full-fledged poltergeist, is Heather in danger?"

"You would worry about that first and foremost," I muttered, shaking my head. "I'm so telling Mom."

He didn't fly off the handle or admonish me to keep quiet. Instead, he remained calm and fixed me with a pointed look. "While I don't want to spout ridiculous sonnets and look like a wimp like Landon here, you know darned well I have no interest in that woman. She is a resident and it's my job to keep her safe.

"I'm serious," he continued. "Do you think she's in physical danger?"

It was a straightforward question. Unfortunately, I had nothing but convoluted answers. "I don't know." I held out my hands and shrugged. "Valerie could be dangerous. The thing is, she didn't know she was dead. To her it was perfectly normal to be hanging out in the woods by Heather's house. When I told her the truth, she freaked out and took off. I'm not sure what to believe about her."

"Well ... maybe I should send one of the uniforms out there to watch the house," Chief Terry said after a few moments of contemplation. "I can use the excuse that we're trying to keep Heather safe in case there's a killer on the loose."

"It might not be a bad idea," Landon agreed.

"We don't know that Valerie is dangerous," I argued, annoyance bubbling up. "She obviously has an attitude where Heather is concerned, but can you blame her? She thought things were fine with Eric and then she got dumped for a Barbie doll with money."

"Wow." Landon shot me a sidelong look, his lips curving. "You really are worked up about her. I can't help being surprised. You've never struck me as the jealous type."

I didn't return the smile he lobbed in my direction. "I'm not jealous. Stop saying that."

"Then what are you?"

"I don't know." That was the truth. I was frustrated and yet I couldn't identify why. "If you want to know the truth, I think I'm picking up on Valerie's emotions. Or, it's conceivable that now that Clove is back she's affecting my emotions again. But she seemed perfectly happy last night.

"I guess it's possible that she was covering," I continued, babbling on for my benefit more than theirs as Chief Terry navigated toward town. "She pinned everything on that wedding, kept saying that she would be fine once they were married and could focus on the baby. Maybe now that she's back, she realizes that it's more than she can handle."

Landon's expression was grave. "What?" I asked. "It's possible."

"It is possible," he agreed, "but I don't like either of those options — especially because they didn't occur to me."

"Well, I'm sure there's nothing to worry about," I offered, forcing a smile for his benefit. "Clove's emotions will be a rollercoaster for the remainder of her pregnancy, but she waited so long to tell people that it won't be long until we reach the end of the ride. Three more months and we're home free."

"I still don't want you upset." He was thoughtful. "Between Clove's inability to control her own magic and your powers growing every time I turn around, I don't know what to believe."

His concern wiped away the remnants of my annoyance. "It's going to be okay," I reassured him. "If it's something weird, we'll deal with it. We always do."

He reached back and linked his fingers with mine. "We will," he agreed.

It was only then that I realized he was providing the pep talk for his own benefit and not mine.

**CHIEF TERRY PARKED AT THE DINER** so we could compare notes and discuss the case over lunch. Landon and I shared one side of a booth while he got comfortable across from us. His eyes darkened when Landon slid his arm around my shoulders and snuggled me close to his side.

"Do you have to do that?" he complained, making a face. "We're in public. Nobody wants to see you two all over each other like that."

"That's not true," Landon countered, grinning at the waitress, Sarah Butler, as she halted at the edge of the table and handed us a specials menu. "You want to see us all over each other, don't you, Sarah?"

I'd known Sarah for as long as I could remember. The diner was her baby. She was often persnickety like Aunt Tillie, but without the magic to back it up. She never failed to make me laugh, and today would be no exception.

"I happen to love watching you two fawn all over each other," she drawled.

"Do you want to know why? I'll tell you why. It's because it drives certain members of this community insane." She pointedly inclined her head toward a corner booth, where Mrs. Little sat with a few of her gossipy cohorts. "As long as they're unhappy, I'm happy. That means I want you two to basically go at it on the table."

"Oh, my ... ." Chief Terry slapped a hand over his face and shook his head as he made a disgusted sound deep in his throat. "Don't encourage them. They'll do it just to irritate me."

Sarah chuckled and shook her head. "We have fish and chips, steak quesadillas, mushroom BLTs with tomato bisque, and stuffed cabbage rolls on special," she started. "Do you all want your usual iced tea?"

"I do," Landon replied. "But a question: Why would you ruin a BLT with mushrooms?"

Sarah shook her head. "It's a house favorite. If you don't like the mushrooms, you can have a regular BLT."

"You had bacon for breakfast," I reminded him. "Maybe you should get something healthier. All that bacon is going to start catching up with you."

Landon looked horrified at the prospect. "Is this because I teased you about being jealous of Heather? I take it back. You would never be jealous. Now, leave my bacon alone."

My lips curved as I stared at the menu. "I'll have iced tea ... and the stuffed cabbage rolls. They sound really good."

"Fish and chips for me," Chief Terry said, leaning back in his chair. "Just out of curiosity, have you met the new woman living by the old campground out at the lake? The one who bought the Lakin house?"

Sarah wrinkled her nose. If she was bothered by the conversational shift, she didn't show it. "I've met her a few times. She's been hanging around town, trying to get to know people. She mentioned opening a store a few days ago because she's in love with Margaret's shop."

I pinned Landon with a triumphant look. "I told you she was nuts."

He held up his hands in a placating manner. "I stand corrected."

Sarah smirked. "She claims to have a bunch of money from her divorce. She's not ashamed to brag about it. I heard her trying to entice Margaret into a conversation, but she wasn't having much luck. I think that's because Margaret tried to buy the house before Heather. Financing slowed things down and by the time Margaret worked things out Heather was already two days from closing."

"Thank you so much for spreading my private business all over town," Mrs. Little drawled from the other side of the diner, her expression dark. I was surprised she could hear from so far away, but, like Aunt Tillie, her hearing was only an issue when someone was spouting something she didn't want to hear. "You have no idea how much I appreciate that, Sarah."

For her part, Sarah was unbothered by Mrs. Little's admonishment. "It was my pleasure." She winked at us and gathered the menus. "What about you, handsome? You're the only one who hasn't ordered."

Landon blew out a sigh. "I can't have mushrooms on a BLT. That completely ruins the sandwich. And you don't pair tomato soup with a BLT. It goes with a grilled cheese."

"You're being awfully picky about your food," Sarah pointed out. "Are you having sympathy cravings with Clove now that she's pregnant? That's the only reason I can see whining the way you are."

Landon scowled. "I'll have a cheeseburger with everything and an order of fries."

"Hold the onions on that cheeseburger," I ordered, poking his side. "He doesn't need the onions."

My attempt at flirty banter had the desired effect on him, because Landon's smile was back as he squeezed me close. "Hold the onions," he agreed, his eyes drifting to Mrs. Little, who watched us with unveiled annoyance. "Why were you interested in that house?" he asked. "I get that it's pretty, but that's a haul for you. It doesn't seem practical given the fact that you're in town eight times a day."

"Why do you care?" Mrs. Little shot back. "You have your property on the lake. Mind your own business."

Something occurred to me. "That's why she wants it," I offered. "We bought the property she wanted and now she's determined to get out there through other means."

"That doesn't make much sense," Landon argued. "She said she wanted the old campground because she wanted to lease the property to the town for satellite festivals. You can't do that with the property Heather bought."

He had a point. I pursed my lips as I regarded Mrs. Little, who suddenly found something fascinating on her plate to steal her attention. "I guess I don't know."

"I know." Chief Terry looked smug as he glanced between Landon and Mrs. Little. "How much will you give me if I tell you?"

Landon frowned. "Are you trying to blackmail me? What do you want?"

"I want you to stop feeling up my sweetheart over lunch because it's giving me indigestion."

Landon snorted. "No deal. There's nothing you have to offer that will stop me from enjoying my time with Bay. Besides, you're going to tell us regardless."

Chief Terry looked offended. "How do you know that?"

"Because you're just as chatty as the women you spend all your time with," Landon replied without hesitation. "Just tell us what you know."

"Fine." Chief Terry shot one more dark look at the hand Landon was using to rub the back of my neck. "You two are officially gross. I want you to know that."

"We're willing to accept our lot in life," Landon replied. "Why did Mrs. Little want the Lakin house? I mean, other than the obvious. It's gorgeous, but I'm pretty sure she doesn't have the money to buy it."

"That wouldn't be a problem if she found the treasure," Chief Terry said, his eyes sparkling.

"Treasure?" Landon shifted his gaze to me. "Do I even want to know what he's talking about?"

I hesitated. "I'm not sure," I admitted. "What treasure are you referring to?"

"The treasure of Arlen Topper."

The name sparked something deep in the recesses of my mind. "I'm not sure I know what you're talking about," I said. "I feel like I should know that name, but I can't remember the story."

"I'm disappointed in you," Chief Terry chided, wagging his finger. "You should remember better than anyone given the fact that Tillie took you out hunting for the treasure every single day for three months straight when you were a kid."

"She did?"

"Who is Arlen Topper?" Landon asked.

"He was a local folk hero in these parts about a hundred and twenty years ago, but his story didn't make it to other parts of the state."

"Yeah, I need more than that," Landon prodded.

"He was a pirate." Chief Terry smirked as confusion caused Landon's eyebrows to knit. I, on the other hand, finally remembered where I knew the name from.

"Oh." I bobbed my head, grinning. "I remember now. But the story is a bit fuzzy. Arlen was a pirate and he supposedly stashed his booty somewhere around Walkerville. People thought it was out by the lake because he had a house somewhere out there."

"Nobody knows exactly where the house was," Chief Terry said. "It supposedly burned down, and because Arlen was the ornery sort, he was the only one on the lake at the time."

I nodded. "I want to research that story when I get back to the office. I completely forgot about it."

"I'm still confused," Landon countered. "How can you have a pirate in an inland state? Pirates sail the oceans."

"He was a Great Lakes pirate," Chief Terry explained. "Believe it or not, there were pirates on the Great Lakes. He got rich attacking ships and stealing their freight."

"And he ended up in Walkerville?" Landon didn't look convinced. "Why?"

"The secret port," I volunteered, grinning as the memories flooded back. "That inlet by the lighthouse has a storied history. Boats can't be seen by patrol ships and the cove was a secret for a long time. Only locals knew about it. That made it an enticing place to hide from the authorities."

"Huh." Landon rubbed his chin. "And what does Arlen Topper have to do with Valerie Lennox's death?"

"Nothing," I reassured him. "It just explains why Mrs. Little wanted the property. There's a rumor that Arlen buried his money out there. If that's true and someone manages to find it, they'll be set for life."

"Wait ... does that mean if the money is on our property we can use it to build our house?" Landon's eyes lit up. "That might be fun."

I chuckled. "It might, but I'm pretty sure Aunt Tillie went over every inch of our property years ago. If she couldn't find it, I guarantee it's not there."

"I guess." Landon's lips curved down. "It's still fun to dream about."

He wasn't wrong. "Keep dreaming then." I patted his knee under the table.

"I already have everything I want," he reassured me, briefly resting his forehead against mine. "The money would be a bonus."

"Don't make me come over there," Chief Terry barked. "I will throw water on you if I have to."

That made me laugh.

"You have to get over it," Landon admonished, shooting an annoyed glare in Chief Terry's direction. "We're not going to change."

"We'll just see about that."

# EIGHT

Research on the Walkerville Wanderer — that was Arlen Topper's pirate name, which was a bit of a disappointment — was slow going. I would've preferred tapping The Whistler's resident ghost Viola for information, but she was nowhere to be found. The one time I actually needed her, I couldn't find her.

After two hours of poring over old copies of the newspaper and painstakingly flipping through old records, I was frustrated. I decided to take a break and picked up coffee from the local shop to take to Hypnotic, the magic store Clove and Thistle owned. I expected to find them arguing about Clove's redecorating attempt when I walked through the door.

Instead, they were arguing about something else.

"I'm not babysitting that kid," Thistle supplied, the obstinate tilt of her chin telling me this argument had been going on for some time. "It's simply not going to happen."

"Of course you're going to babysit." Clove sat on the couch, her feet propped on the coffee table, and paged through a catalog. She looked relaxed, happy even, and she beamed at me. "Hey, Bay. You're going to babysit for me, right?"

"Probably not." I placed the drink carrier on the center of the table. "I've got your caffeine fixes. You can thank me with information."

Thistle arched an eyebrow. "Maybe I don't want to share information. Have you ever considered that?"

"You like to gossip with the rest of us." I flopped into the open chair at the center of the furniture configuration. "So, does anybody want to hear about my day?"

"We're talking about me right now," Clove replied. "I'm feeling sad because no one wants to take care of my baby to give me a break. It's horrible feeling unloved." She rubbed her rounded stomach, making me think she was talking to the baby rather than us. "It's enough to make me depressed."

"Oh, geez." Thistle rolled her eyes. "This is going to be the longest three months of our lives. You realize that, don't you?"

It took me a moment to realize she was talking to me. "It's going to be an adventure," I said with a smirk. "Seriously, though, don't you want to hear about my day?"

"I want to talk about the baby," Clove countered, waving the catalog for emphasis. "Sam says we can start picking out stuff for a nursery. I need help."

"And nobody but you cares," Thistle shot back. "I want to hear about Bay's day."

"Since when do you care about other people's feelings?" Clove asked suspiciously.

"Since it has to be better than listening to you wax poetic about salmon pink versus baby pink," Thistle said, pinning me with a desperate look. "Please tell me there's an evil witch out to kill us. I'll take any distraction to get away from Clove right now."

Amusement rolled through me as I glanced between them. I'd missed this while Clove was on her honeymoon. Thistle and I enjoyed arguing as much as anybody else in the family — which was saying something, because the Winchesters could all medal if arguing was an Olympic sport — but if we didn't have a third person to create uneven teams it wasn't nearly as much fun. "Well, they identified the body we found at the camp."

"I heard." Thistle grabbed her coffee and sat in the chair across from me. "Valerie Lennox. I didn't know much about her. She always seemed nice."

"I think she might've been a bit of a nut." I told them about what I'd learned, leaving nothing out. When I got to the part about Heather, Clove was appropriately annoyed on my behalf.

"I can't believe Landon flirted with her," she said, her expression dark. "That is just ... the worst. He did that right in front of you?"

"He wasn't really flirting with her," I hedged, feeling foolish now for sharing that part of the story. I'd probably exaggerated a bit ... or a lot. My dislike of the woman was on full display and I was starting to project emotions that might not have been based in fact. "She was flirting with him, but it wasn't exactly sexual. It was more 'I'm too cute to be a murderer' than anything else."

"She sounds like an idiot," Thistle noted. "Is it possible she's not smart enough to have carried out a murder? I mean, she doesn't sound as if this is in her wheelhouse to plan."

"Unless it was all an act."

"Do you think it was an act?"

"I don't know." It was hard for me to differentiate fact from fiction given how much I disliked the woman. "I mean, considering where we found Valerie's body, I'm not sure we're dealing with a smart individual."

"She would have to be an absolute moron to think she could get away with killing Valerie with what was going on with Eric," Thistle argued, leaning back in her chair. "What do we know about him?"

I shrugged. "He was a few years ahead of me in high school. We never hung out or anything."

"I remember him being hot," Clove offered. "Is he still hot?"

"His hair is starting to go gray," I replied.

"That means he could turn into a silver fox. I happen to like a silver fox."

"Oh, geez." Thistle looked disgusted. "Are the pregnancy hormones kicking in or something? I think this is about the tenth time today you've talked about hot dudes and silver foxes."

"I'm pretty sure I haven't mentioned any other silver foxes," Clove fired back, indignant.

Thistle was defiant. "George Peterson."

Clove cringed. "I didn't say he was a silver fox. I said I bet he was ... like twenty years ago. He's eighty now."

I was curious. "Why were you talking about George Peterson?"

"We were trying to find a date for Aunt Tillie now that she seems to have given Kenneth the boot for good," Thistle replied. "There aren't a lot of options, so we thought a deaf guy who was also half blind might be our best bet."

I could see that. "Let's go back to talking about me," I said. "I think there's a very real chance Valerie is turning into a poltergeist."

I expected exclamations of worry — at least from Clove — but they both merely stared.

"A poltergeist," I repeated. "That's a really bad ghost."

Thistle snorted. "We're not idiots. We've seen poltergeists before."

"We've also seen you and Aunt Tillie beat the crap out of them," Clove offered. "I'm the first to worry — we all know it's true — but I can't get worked up over this. If she's a poltergeist, we'll just send her over and call it a day."

I was flabbergasted. "Since when aren't you afraid of ghosts?"

"Since you're now the ghost whisperer," Thistle replied simply. "Not only can you talk to ghosts, you can control them. I'm assuming it's the same for poltergeists. If she's bothering you, just order her to knock it off. Easy-peasy."

That hadn't occurred to me. "You know I don't like controlling them," I said. "It feels somehow ... wrong."

"Yes, but we're not talking about some random ghost minding its own business," Thistle pointed out. "We're talking about a potential poltergeist that could turn violent. You don't have to do anything until you figure out exactly what's going on with Valerie. Nobody is saying you have to banish her to another world right this second or anything. We're simply saying it's an option should things get out of hand."

And another point for my cousins. I was starting to regret my visit. "Do you guys remember the story of Arlen Topper?" I decided to change the subject.

"Is he the guy who is talking about rebuilding the blacksmith shop?" Clove asked.

"No. He's the pirate who supposedly buried treasure up by the lake."

"Oh, him." Thistle smirked. "I knew I recognized that name. Aunt Tillie used to take us up there all the time looking for treasure. She said that because we always found her wine stash even though we were too young to drink it, we were uniquely qualified to find buried treasure. She was ticked off when the only thing we found was someone's secret pot field."

"I'm pretty sure that was her pot field," I said. "Once we blabbed about it, there was no reason for her to hide it so far from the property. That's why it's magically cloaked but easily accessible now."

"Oh, you're right." Thistle bobbed her head. "She did move the field to the inn not long after that. Aunt Winnie was so mad. It was hilarious."

I didn't particularly remember that as a happy time in the house. It was hardly important, though. "Mrs. Little let it slip today that she tried to buy the Lakin house before Heather Castle did."

"How could she possibly afford that?" Clove asked. "She had to jump through hoops to get the financing for the camp and that probably cost only a quarter of what that house went for on the open market."

"I don't know. Chief Terry thinks she wanted the house because she wants to look for the treasure."

Thistle practically choked on her coffee when she started laughing. "You cannot be serious. That's a ridiculous town legend with no basis in fact. Arlen Topper wasn't real."

"I don't know about that," I countered. "I have found mention of him in land deeds from back then. I'm guessing his exploits were exaggerated. If he really did have money buried up there, someone would've found it."

"Or it's gone forever," Thistle agreed. "Are we sure Mrs. Little wanted the property for that reason? Maybe she just wants to retire on that lake or something. She might've had a plan in place and is still miffed that Landon swooped in and bought it out from under her."

I'd considered that, but something felt off about the scenario. "I don't know. I just find it odd. I spent the afternoon researching Arlen out of curiosity."

"That seems like a great way to waste your time when there's a murder to cover," Thistle said.

I managed to rein in my temper enough to refrain from barking at her — just barely. "When I told Valerie she was dead, she seemed confused and took off. It could be days before she shows up. I have nowhere to focus when it comes to the murder, so I'm not really wasting time."

"Except you can make her show up," Thistle reminded me. "You're a necromancer, Bay. You control ghosts. If you have questions for Valerie, force her to come here and answer them. You have the power to do it."

"Yeah, but ... ." The notion made me feel icky.

"Bay doesn't want to do that," Clove said. "She's afraid if she starts using that magic for every little want and whim that she'll turn dark. Given what's going on with Dani, that's a line she doesn't want to cross. Give her a break."

I worked my jaw. "Since when are you a mind reader?"

"I've always been intuitive," Clove replied. "Now that I'm pregnant, I find my senses are keener. *All* my senses, including my sense of smell, which is why Thistle needs to get rid of anything that smells like mint. It makes me gag."

"I'm not getting rid of the mint," Thistle fired back. "We've talked about this. The mint is important for rituals. A lot of rituals. It stays."

"Well, then I don't want to hear a thing about the constant vomit you'll be cleaning up."

"Why will I be cleaning it up?"

"Because I'm pregnant and my sore back won't allow me to do it."

I chewed my bottom lip and avoided Thistle's murderous stare. She wanted me to side with her, but I found Clove's newfound backbone — however manipulative — entertaining. I cleared my throat to draw their attention before we could be indefinitely sidetracked. "Speaking of Dani, for all we know, she could have killed Valerie. She's out there at the camp."

Thistle slowly dragged her gaze from Clove, her forehead wrinkling. "Dani? Why would she want to kill Valerie?"

I shrugged. "I don't know. I don't have any proof, but I'd be lying if I said the possibility didn't occur to me. She's not getting any better. I keep telling people she is, but that's just wishful thinking. If anything, she's worse. I'm not sure she can come back from this."

Thistle clucked her tongue, sympathetic. "I know you don't want to hear this, but it's probably time we start coming up with a contingency plan. If she can't be tamed we're going to need an alternative. It's not as if Hazel can live out at that camp with her for the rest of her life."

"I know. And Landon is making noise about me going out there. I don't know what else to do." I dragged a hand through my hair. "We were raised to believe that actions have consequences. Dani doesn't believe that. She still doesn't think she did anything wrong. She has no remorse whatsoever regarding the death of her father."

"Then maybe that's your answer," Thistle said. "Maybe it's time to give up."

"And do what?" I practically exploded. "We're not capable of keeping her under lock and key forever. Human cops aren't either. I've repeatedly warned Landon about going out there because I can see her hurting him for kicks. If we turn her over to law enforcement, someone else will die. They won't be able to contain her."

"So, what options do we have?" Clove looked genuinely curious as she rubbed her stomach. "If we can't contain her, do we have to eliminate her?"

"We're not the dudes from *Goodfellas*," I groused, annoyed. "We can't just kill her."

Thistle opened her mouth and I sensed she was going to argue that point. Wisely, though, she changed her mind. "We'll all put our minds to it," she promised. "We'll figure something out. This isn't simply your problem. We all need to deal with her together."

She was trying to make me feel better, but it was a wasted effort. The more I thought about Dani, the more my insides constricted. "Thanks. I just don't know what to do. I ... ." A furtive form flew past the front window. When I turned to get a better look, I recognized Aunt Tillie.

She was moving so fast she couldn't be walking — or even running. Even though I couldn't see it, I was convinced she was on her new electric scooter. The cape she'd had made for her outings streamed behind her, and underneath the combat helmet she wore for safety was a determined expression.

"What is she doing?" Clove asked.

"I'm almost afraid to look," I admitted, getting to my feet and moving toward the window. "I haven't seen her on that thing for a few days. I thought she'd lost interest."

"Winnie hid it from her," Thistle volunteered, sliding in at my side and peering through the window. "She was sick of Aunt Tillie riding it around the inn. Aunt Tillie was threatening to get a basket to put Peg in so they could both enjoy it together. I think that was the final straw that made Winnie snap."

The image of Aunt Tillie in her offensive leggings with a pig in a basket riding a scooter made me smile. "I don't see why it's such a big deal. It's good for her. She gets a workout while riding it."

"That's my philosophy," Thistle agreed. "Winnie says she's broken three vases."

"Then put up the vases."

"You're preaching to the wrong Winchester," Thistle said. "That scooter has been a great investment. Aunt Tillie has barely been around since she got it."

"What has she been doing on it?" Clove asked. Apparently the sight of Aunt Tillie on her scooter was enough to motivate her off the couch.

"That." I inclined my head toward the corner, to where Mrs. Little stood with another woman. They looked to be having an intense conversation and weren't paying attention to their surroundings, which they would live to regret in about five seconds.

"I still don't understand," Clove said.

"Watch," Thistle said, her lips curving as Aunt Tillie appeared on the sidewalk behind Mrs. Little and the other woman. "Here it comes."

"Oh, this looks bad." Clove chewed her lip. "Shouldn't we stop whatever she's about to do?"

"No," Thistle and I answered in unison.

"It's funny," I added. "Compared to all the other things she's done to Mrs. Little, this is mild."

"But ... ." Clove trailed off when she realized Aunt Tillie was building up speed. "Oh, I'm so afraid."

She barely got the sentence out before it happened. Aunt Tillie invoked her magic, causing a small tornado to form next to her, and as she sped past Mrs. Little and her friend, the force of the cyclone started pulling on clothing and hair.

"What the ... ?" Clove's mouth dropped open as Mrs. Little's hair, which had always been a helmet of hairspray and curls, flew off and landed in the gutter. "Holy crap!" Clove's eyes were so wide I swear they almost popped out of her head. "Mrs. Little wears a wig?"

I smirked when the screaming on the corner started in earnest. Mrs. Little was stomping her feet and making a scene. "Apparently so. We were surprised when we found out, too."

"How could you not have called and told me this?" Clove screeched. "This is the biggest news since ... well ... we found out that her pewter was really cheap tin and she was selling knockoff unicorns."

"Aren't you glad you're back?" Thistle clapped her on the shoulder. "One thing you can say about Hemlock Cove, life here is never dull."

Clove cocked her head to the side. "Is she putting that filthy thing back on her head?"

"Yeah. I think Aunt Tillie wiped out her entire wig collection over the past two weeks," Thistle replied. "That scooter really is worth its weight in gold."

# NINE

Thistle and I went outside to continue watching the show. Mrs. Little's fury was on full display as she strung together a group of curse words I wasn't even aware she knew. Her face fired crimson as her friend did her best to help tug the wig back into place.

"What are you looking at?" Mrs. Little barked when she realized Thistle and I were on the street and staring.

"We're debating the meaning of life," Thistle drawled. "I think that happiness is the most important thing, but Bay thinks it's good hair. What do you think?"

I cringed at the look she cast in my direction. "Good manners are the most important," she sniped.

"Really? I never would've guessed." Thistle snickered and tugged on my arm. "We're going to take a walk. It's a lovely day for it. Beautiful sun, a mild breeze just strong enough to tickle the ends of my hair."

Sensing the conversation was going to completely fly off the rails, I grabbed Thistle's wrist and pulled with all my might. Even though she tried to remain planted in her spot, it was no use, and she gave in.

"You're no fun," she complained as we rounded the corner in search of our wayward great-aunt. "How often do we get a chance to mess with her?"

"Every single day of our lives. We grew up with Aunt Tillie."

"It's still fun."

"I don't think Mrs. Little agrees."

"Like I care what that hateful old bat thinks," Thistle grumbled. "That woman has made it her life's mission to mess with us at every turn. Do you remember when we were kids and she called our mothers and told them we were at the town picnic passing around a bottle of Aunt Tillie's wine?"

"We *were* at the picnic with the wine."

"That doesn't matter. She enjoyed ratting us out."

"We were also all under the age of sixteen," I reminded her.

"So? We weren't drinking it — at least not that day. We were selling it. And we made a killing."

I remembered that little business venture well. "We all got new summer sneakers out of it." I smiled at the memory as we turned another corner. There, sure enough, was Aunt Tillie. She looked to be having a grand time as she cackled and cavorted. Hazel was with her, and the two seemed oblivious to their surroundings as Aunt Tillie reenacted her wig attack.

"You should've seen it," she enthused, leaning against her scooter and tipping her combat helmet back so her gleeful face was visible. "The wig flew off as if it was a bat or something. It landed right in the gutter. It was awesome."

I cleared my throat to get their attention. Hazel, clearly distressed at being caught celebrating Tillie's torturing of Mrs. Little, had the grace to be ashamed. Aunt Tillie was another story.

"Whatever you think I did, you're mistaken." She was the picture of innocence as she met my gaze. "I was just out riding my scooter — at my age you have to enjoy life to the fullest because you don't know when you're going to go to sleep and never wake up. Whatever that old biddy says I did, she's lying."

It took everything I had not to laugh.

"We saw the whole thing," Thistle offered. "We're not angry. It was funny. Well, actually, Bay might pretend to be angry, but she's really not. We were laughing so hard we fogged up the window."

"Oh." Aunt Tillie straightened. "Then what's the problem?"

"What makes you think we have a problem?" I asked, my eyes drifting to Hazel. She didn't say anything, but I guessed what she wanted most in the world was to find a rock to crawl under.

"You have that look." Aunt Tillie's lips curved into a sneer. "Listen, I'm an adult. I'm allowed to do whatever I want. That includes riding my scooter and minding my own business — which is exactly what you saw me doing a few minutes ago. You're not the boss of me."

"Believe it or not, we were trying to find you to congratulate you," I offered. "We thought you would be alone."

"Hey, we're playing nice." Aunt Tillie held out her hands. "She's still not my favorite person in the world or anything, but she's better than Margaret."

"We don't care about that," I stressed.

"We don't," Thistle agreed, leaning closer to me. "What do we care about again?"

"The fact that Dani is apparently at the camp alone," I answered loudly enough for Aunt Tillie and Hazel to hear, my gaze pointed. "She's never supposed to be alone. We agreed on that."

"We did." Hazel straightened her shoulders and met my gaze head on. "I'm not shirking my duties. It's just ... she's a lot of work. Occasionally I need a break. She was taking a nap and I thought it was a good time to take a breather and regroup. I'm sorry if that makes you unhappy."

The weariness she wore like a blanket caused me to reconsider what I wanted to say. "You know what? It's probably good that you're here. We rarely get to talk when Dani isn't around eavesdropping. We should go into Hypnotic, have some coffee and tea, and discuss a few things."

Hazel nodded. "That's probably best."

"You should come, too," I said to Aunt Tillie, my tone no-nonsense. "You're involved in this as much as we are."

"I've already told you my feelings on the situation," she sniffed. "I think we should dig a hole, toss her in it, and leave her for the animals to scavenge. That's just me, though."

She was a big talker, but I knew she was just as worried as I was. "You're part of this. We need to come up with a new plan. Obviously Hazel can't spend every waking moment with Dani."

Aunt Tillie worked her jaw, giving me the distinct impression that she might continue arguing. But she threw up her hands. "Fine. Have it your way. We'll talk about Dani. I'll have you know that I was going to circle the block and give a repeat performance. You've totally ruined my fun."

"You'll live."

Thistle tugged on my shirt sleeve. "She could meet us at the store after the repeat performance," she suggested.

Frustration bubbled up. "Since when are you a fan of giving her what she wants?"

"Since it will drive Mrs. Little crazy. She's the Devil. We all agreed that you have to shout at the Devil. This is Aunt Tillie's version of shouting."

I was going to argue but realized it ultimately didn't matter. Aunt Tillie would find a way to get what she wanted no matter what. "Fine. One encore." I held up my index finger for emphasis. "But just one. After that, we have serious issues to discuss."

"Yeah, yeah, yeah." Aunt Tillie gripped the handlebar of her scooter. "You really need to learn to lighten up. You're far too young to be this stodgy."

"I'll keep that in mind."

**HAZEL MADE A BEELINE FOR CLOVE WHEN** we entered Hypnotic through the back door. She knew darned well that Clove would be the most sympathetic to her plight. In truth, I felt bad for the situation we'd placed her in. Unfortunately, I was fresh out of ideas on how we could go about fixing it.

"She can't stay out there with Dani twenty-four hours a day," Thistle noted in a low voice as we moved back to the window. We craned our necks to see the front of Mrs. Little's store. She was still outside, her lips flapping as she complained, but I couldn't yet see Aunt Tillie.

"I know that. I'm not angry as much as worried."

"Okay, but we're all swimming in uncharted waters here. She's doing the best that she can. You're doing the best that you can. If Dani fails, then Dani will have to face the consequences."

What she said made sense. I was still uneasy. "We need to come up with a plan. There could be someone dangerous in those woods for all we know ... and I'm not talking about Heather. Dani could take Heather, no problem."

"I hate to break it to you, but Dani could take almost anyone, including us. I'm sure she's fine."

"I hope so. Wait, did Aunt Tillie change her outfit?" I narrowed my eyes as I tried to make out the figure on the scooter. It was definitely Aunt Tillie, but the cape she'd been wearing five minutes before had disappeared. In its place she looked to be wearing a fuzzy onesie, complete with hood and fin.

"Oh, she's a land shark." Thistle hopped up and down, clapping her hands. "I knew when she ordered that outfit that it would be worth it."

"You knew she ordered that outfit?" I was incredulous — and a little impressed. Somehow Aunt Tillie looked right at home in what should've been the world's geekiest ensemble.

"She was going for the adult size, but I told her the ones for kids would be more durable." Thistle wiggled her hips as Aunt Tillie started barreling down on Mrs. Little again. "Oh, this is the best day ever. Somebody start filming."

"I'm on it." Clove already had her phone out and was sliding through the door. "What do you think she's going to do for water?" The question was barely out of her mouth when I heard an odd sound, like metal grating against metal.

Thistle and I crowded the door for a better look. It took me a full five seconds to realize what was about to happen.

"Oh, geez." I grabbed Clove's arm and spun her back toward the store. "Get inside."

"Why?" Clove pouted as I shoved her with all my might. "I want this on video."

"Trust me." I thought about grabbing Thistle, who was so busy waiting for the land shark to make contact with her prey that she hadn't noticed the valve on the fire hydrant spinning without human help. I was more worried about Clove and the force of the water than I was about Thistle, though. She was on her own.

I slammed the door at the exact moment the valve opened. A torrent of water barreled into Mrs. Little, flattening her against the wall of her store as Aunt Tillie started humming the shark theme from *Jaws*.

I noticed the stream of water spurting intermittently. My elderly great-aunt — who always swore age was just a number — smoothly slid between the pulsing blast, her pace never changing. At some point she must've seen Thistle, because she added a little extra something to her spell and the water started funneling off the building and heading straight for the grumpiest Winchester in the world.

I squeezed my eyes shut when I heard Thistle hit the door. It was hard to make out exactly what was happening thanks to all the water, but when I regained some semblance of where the parties landed, I figured out two things quickly: Aunt Tillie was completely dry and Thistle looked as if she'd been through a tsunami.

"I'm going to kill you, old lady," Thistle screeched once she'd spit out the water she'd ingested, lurching toward Aunt Tillie. "You'd better start running."

Clove snickered as she took in the scene. "I'm so glad I'm back."

I grinned at her. "Me too."

**IT TOOK ALMOST FORTY-FIVE MINUTES FOR** Thistle to calm down enough to be in the same room with Aunt Tillie without threatening to end her life in the vilest manner possible. She'd been shouting potential ideas —

including death by Kardashian marathon and drowning in a lake of boiling chocolate — but Aunt Tillie didn't appear bothered.

"This isn't my fault," she explained to me as she sat at the table and claimed the coffee Clove hadn't touched from my earlier delivery. "I think I've made it very clear that it's every witch for herself when I'm executing a plan. Bay and Clove didn't get wet. That's because they knew to stay off the street."

"Actually, we went out there," Clove supplied. "Right before it happened, Bay dragged me inside. She said I would thank her." Her eyes glistened with unshed tears as she faced me. "You were right. You saved my life. Thank you so much." She moved to throw her arms around me, but Thistle used her hip to intervene.

"What's up with that?" Thistle barked. The water had caused her eye makeup to run. She looked like a deranged raccoon. "Why did you save Clove? I thought we had an agreement. We save ourselves first, and then, if we have time, we save each other. Clove is always third on the list."

Clove's eyes dried almost instantaneously. "What? You guys have an agreement that puts me third? You're dead to me. I don't want to know either of you."

It shouldn't have been necessary to explain myself, but obviously Thistle wasn't going to let it go. "I was afraid that the baby might get hurt if the water hit her. She could've been knocked down. If she wasn't pregnant, I would've left both of you out there."

"Hey!" Clove's eyes flashed.

"I don't know that I can accept that response," Thistle argued. "I need to think about it. The odds of that baby being hurt by water are slim."

"I was playing it safe." I heaved a sigh and turned my attention to Hazel, who appeared amused by the argument. It was time to get serious. "So, how often do you leave Dani out there alone?"

"Not often," she replied, sobering. "Maybe once every couple of days — and only for a few hours. You have to understand, there are times I need a break."

"I understand." I rubbed my forehead, debating what I should say. "The thing is, I don't know that Dani should ever be alone. She's not showing any sign of understanding that what she did was wrong."

"She's not," Hazel agreed. "I'm not sure what the answer is."

"I already told you the answer," Aunt Tillie interjected.

"And I told you that we're not there yet," I shot back. "There must be another way. She's a teenager. We can't kill her." There. I'd said it. The mere thought made me sick to my stomach, but it was out there.

"Of course we can't kill her." Hazel sent me a sympathetic look. "I don't know that we can change her either. In situations like this, someone has to want to get better. Dani doesn't. She thinks everything she did is perfectly okay."

"She's power-hungry," Thistle said. "She thinks just because she uses dark magic that she's more powerful than those unwilling to use it. Maybe the key is to show her the opposite."

I glanced at my cousin, intrigued. "Meaning?"

"Meaning she needs a lesson in white magic. And not a fluffy one in which she learns to grow plants or change the water flow in the lake. She needs a hard lesson, one that makes her the loser. If she has actual fear — something she's not feeling despite what happened to Diane — she might realize that adjusting her attitude is the way to go."

It was an interesting thought. "Do you have any ideas on exactly what sort of lesson we should teach her?"

Aunt Tillie's hand shot in the air.

"I wasn't talking to you," I said, though further thought made me wonder if it wasn't best to unleash Aunt Tillie on Dani. We weren't quite there — at least not yet.

"I'll give it some thought," Thistle replied. "Until then, you're right. Dani can't be alone."

"We have to come up with a schedule," I said. "Even if it means I spend time out at the camp working remotely. Hazel needs time off. Dani is too much for any one of us."

"We can take shifts," Clove volunteered. "I can go out there a few afternoons each week. Now that I'm back from my honeymoon I have free time before the baby comes."

Thistle and I shook our heads in tandem.

"Absolutely not," I said, firm. "You can't go anywhere near her."

Hurt flashed across Clove's face. "Why not?"

"You're pregnant," Aunt Tillie interjected. "If Dani wants to go after us, you would make an easy target. You can't go out there. It has to be the three of us helping Hazel."

"We might be able to talk Mom and the aunts into going a time or two," I added. "We have to come up with a plan. That cabin is warded from top to bottom. Maybe it's time to ward the property, too. It will take a lot of power, but it might be our best bet."

"I have books that might help us with that back at the inn," Aunt Tillie offered. "I'll do some reading. For now, we just have to watch the kid and make sure she doesn't fly off the handle again. That's the best we can hope to do."

It was a sad realization, but she was right. We were out of our depth with Dani, and the truly frightening thing was that the teenager knew it.

# TEN

I met Landon outside the police station just as his shift was ending.

"Did you miss me that much?" he asked, breaking into a grin as he wrapped his arms around my waist, dipping me low for a kiss. "That's kind of sweet. I missed you too."

I accepted the kiss because I thought it was best to play along. Plus, well, he was a really good kisser. The only reason we stopped is because Chief Terry started making throat-clearing sounds that weren't exactly conducive to romance.

"You really know how to ruin a fun time," Landon complained, shooting him a dark look. "I mean, seriously, is there a reason you have to make those noises?"

Chief Terry's smile was serene. "I have no idea what you're talking about." His eyes flicked to me. "Your mother is making pot roast for dinner. You guys are coming to the inn, right?"

One of my favorite things about Chief Terry was that he enjoyed family dinners. He knew going in that there would be drama, but it didn't matter. As long as he got to spend time with Mom and me, he was happy. Unfortunately, he was going to be disappointed tonight.

"I've already been on the phone with Mom," I hedged, darting my eyes to Landon. "She's going to pack a picnic basket for Thistle and me to take. That way we'll have dinner at the ready."

Landon's eyes narrowed. "And where will you and Thistle eat this dinner?"

I didn't blame him for being wary. He'd obviously put together the fact that I wasn't waiting for him at the end of his shift because I missed him.

"The camp."

His frown grew more pronounced. "Why are you going to the camp?"

"Because Hazel can't possibly take care of Dani twenty-four hours a day." I calmly related the tale of my afternoon. I threw in Aunt Tillie's terrorizing of Mrs. Little because I knew that would serve as a source of entertainment. When I finished, he seemed frustrated, but resigned.

"One person can't do this alone," I explained. "She needs a break."

"So, naturally that means you have to do it," he muttered, shaking his head as he turned his attention to Main Street. He was trying to rein in his temper and not say what he was really feeling. He believed Dani was a lost cause. He knew I wasn't ready to accept that, which meant a fight if he wasn't careful. That was the last thing he wanted.

"Thistle and I are taking the night shift," I said. "I talked to Mom and she thinks that she, Marnie, and Twila can take one or two afternoons during the week. Hazel cannot do everything herself. It's not fair to expect her to."

"She volunteered," Landon pointed out.

"She did, but this has to be a group effort." I was firm. "I'm sorry you're upset, but I feel this is what I need to do."

His eyes momentarily flashed with annoyance, but he collected himself. "You don't have to apologize." He held up his hand. "You're doing what you think is right for that girl. It's just ... how late will you be?"

This was the part he was really going to hate, and I braced myself. "Thistle and I are spending the night."

"What?" Landon's eyebrows practically flew off his forehead. "Why do you have to spend the night?"

"Hazel occasionally needs more than two hours of downtime." I refused to back down despite his obvious annoyance. "Dani has to be watched at all times. Hazel needs at least two nights a week away from her."

"So ... you and Thistle are trading off on the nights?"

I shook my head. "I think both of us should be there in case Dani tries something. We're backup for each other against her magic."

Chief Terry stirred. "Do you think she'll try something?"

"I don't know." I held out my hands and offered him a neutral smile. "It's hard to say. We need two of us to be safe, though. Dani will sleep in the warded cabin and we'll be by the bonfire."

Landon made a sound I couldn't identify as he scuffed his foot against the ground. The slope of his shoulders told me he wanted to argue but was fighting the effort.

"I'm sorry," I offered. I meant it. "Maybe you and Marcus can have a guy's night or something."

"I don't want to have a guy's night with Marcus." He turned petulant, which made me smile. "I want to have a Bay and Landon night in front of the television — with popcorn and hot chocolate." He was a very food-oriented individual. "Since that doesn't appear possible, I guess I'll be camping with you."

He surprised me. "You want to go with us?"

"Um, yeah. You guys are going to need to sleep sometime. I'm sure Marcus will head out there, too. We'll all take turns watching to make sure the kid doesn't do anything evil."

"You don't have to."

"Maybe not, but I'm not being separated from you." He smiled. "It's tragically co-dependent, but now that we live together the idea of spending a night away from you irritates me. I know we did it for a long time, but I would rather sleep on the hard ground with you than on our soft mattress without you."

I found that an absurdly romantic statement. "Are you sure?"

"Yeah." He cupped the back of my head and gave me a quick kiss. "It's time we whip that kid into shape. You're not going to let this go, so we've got to come up with a plan to contain her."

"It's not going to be that easy."

"When has that ever stopped us?"

**DANI WASN'T HAPPY WITH THE CHANGING** of the guard. Even when she found out it was only one night, her attitude was on full display.

"I don't understand why I need a babysitter," she complained, making a face when Thistle indicated she should sit at the picnic table. "I'm an adult. Nobody needs to watch me."

"Obviously that's not true," Landon countered, responding before I could decide what to say. "You were involved in the murder of several people — including your own father — and that means you're incapable of making good decisions. Until you prove that's changed, you need a babysitter."

The look Dani pinned him with was dark. "My father was a bad man who was cheating on my mother. He deserved what he got."

Landon didn't as much as flinch at the vitriol Dani spewed as he calmly helped Marcus unpack the picnic basket. "Your father and mother had an understanding. They were both seeing other people. They wanted to stay together for you and your brother, until you were adults. They managed to carve out a harmonious living situation that benefitted everyone, including you.

"It doesn't matter if your mother was brokenhearted," he continued. "Nobody deserves to die at the hands of another person. You don't have the right to kill because you feel like it."

"Bay killed Aunt Diane." Dani refused to let it go. "Why doesn't she need constant babysitters?"

"Your aunt was a menace who was using your magic to further her own agenda," I replied, finally finding my voice. It was going to be a long night if the arguing continued. "I'm sorry if that's difficult for you to understand, but it's the truth. Your aunt was a user."

This time Dani's unhappy glare was aimed at me. "She was strong. You're just saying bad things about her because you didn't like how strong she was."

"Bay was obviously stronger," Thistle countered. "She had no problem taking out your aunt."

I pinned Thistle with a quelling look, silently admonishing her. Let's not go there. I cleared my throat and drew Dani's attention back to me. "I know it's frustrating to be in your position," I started, searching for the right words. "Your aunt warped your worldview. It's not fair ... or right ... or even your fault in some respects. You're paying a price for her actions now.

"The thing is, you refuse to admit you did anything wrong," I continued. "Acceptance is the first part of the process. You'll be stuck in neutral until you acknowledge your wrongdoing and try to make amends for it."

"And how am I supposed to do that?" Dani challenged. "My father is dead."

"He is. You can still apologize to him. Sometimes ... sometimes spirits remain behind. It's possible he'll be able to hear you." In truth, I knew that wasn't true. Adam Harris, Dani's father, remained behind in his ghostly form until his murder had been solved. Then he quietly crossed over. Our last conversation revolved around what would become of Dani. He was fearful but knew he could no longer dictate what happened in the realm of the living. He belonged with the dead.

"My mother and brother are no longer at our house," she persisted.

My shoulders stiffened. "How do you know that?"

"I went looking for them." Either Dani was too stupid to deny her actions or she wanted me to know she'd been off the campground property. The former would've been preferable, but odds were we were dealing with the latter. "Everything has been packed up. The furniture is still there, but all the clothes and my brother's books are gone. They left."

I wasn't expecting to have this conversation for a bit, but apparently I had to prepare myself for a difficult topic. "You frightened your mother and brother." I was matter-of-fact. "They were well aware of what you planned to do to them. Do you blame them for not wanting to be around you?"

"Um ... yeah. You're supposed to love your kids no matter what."

"You can love your children without liking them," Landon pointed out, using the plastic ladle my mother had provided to start dishing out dinner. "Your mother still loves you. She does not, however, like you. Can you blame her after what you did?"

"I did it for her."

"Really? You were going to kill her for her?"

"That was Aunt Diane." Dani jabbed a finger in Landon's direction. "I didn't want to hurt my mother. That was her idea."

"And you went along with it," Thistle pointed out. "You want to blame her for everything that happened, but you were a willing participant. That's exactly why you need a babysitter. You might not like it, but there it is."

"Except you've picked a babysitter who takes off for long walks in the afternoon to get away from me," Dani fired back. "She goes off for hours, leaving me here alone. I can wander away whenever I want. Nobody can stop me. Nobody could stop me even if they were here." There was defiance in her eyes as she met my gaze. "I do what I want, when I want. The fact that I'm still here means I've earned a little trust. I don't see why you can't just loosen the reins."

She really couldn't see why. She was too far gone to grasp the things that she'd done ... or the real-world ramifications associated with her deeds. "We know that Hazel has been struggling with the weight of her responsibilities," I acknowledged. "That's why we're here tonight. She needs a break."

"And you think the four of you can watch me?" Dani almost looked haughty. "Have you considered that maybe I'm better than all four of you combined?"

"You're not." A voice from the trees caused me to jolt.

Landon's hand immediately swept in front of me as a protective measure. He relaxed — if only marginally — when he realized it was Aunt Tillie. "What are you doing here?"

Aunt Tillie ignored the question, her focus on Dani as she joined us. "I know you're at an age when you think that you're all-powerful and unable to be contained, but nobody has that power, Dani." She was grave, reminding me of a few conversations she'd had with us when we were kids. "You're not more powerful than my girls." She gestured to Thistle and me. "You're not smarter than them either. You might think you are, but that's pretty far from the truth."

"My aunt told me that I'm stronger than anyone," Dani persisted. "I believe her. She said I could do anything I set my mind to."

"Just because you can doesn't mean you should," Aunt Tillie argued, plopping down in the open spot next to Landon and shooting him an expectant look. "Where's my dinner?"

Landon scowled. "There's not enough for you."

"Oh, please." Aunt Tillie rolled her eyes. "Winnie packed that picnic basket. That means there's enough for twice this many people. You just don't like sharing. It's not as if I'm asking you to share your girlfriend. Chill out."

Landon's scowl deepened. "Why are you even here?"

That was a good question. The truth was, I was so happy to see her I didn't care. The odds were now three-to-one when it came to magical beings. Dani would be contained overnight whether she liked it or not. That was the important thing.

"I thought I would share my joy and light with you guys this evening," Aunt Tillie replied breezily. "You're welcome."

Thistle snorted. "In other words, our mothers got annoyed and told you to amuse yourself elsewhere."

"That shows what you know, Mouth," Aunt Tillie fired back. "They begged me not to go. That's how popular I am up there."

She was full of it. On all counts. She slipped out of the inn to offer us backup. She didn't want people to know she had a heart, though. It was easier for her to spar with Thistle than admit to being worried about Dani.

"It doesn't matter," I interjected before they could launch into a full-scale war. "We're all together. Let's make the best of it."

"Yes," Aunt Tillie drawled, shooting me a withering look. "After dinner, we'll host a sing-along and hold hands while gazing at the stars and sharing our hopes and dreams."

I glared at her, which made Landon laugh.

"I'll sing to you later," he whispered, giving me a wink.

I turned back to my dinner, my stomach growling in anticipation. We were eating an hour later than normal.

"What is this?" Dani asked when we passed her a plate. Her nose wrinkled in such a manner that it was obvious she was about to say something snarky.

"Food," Aunt Tillie shot back. "Eat it and shut up."

Dani's eyes darkened. "Maybe you should shut up," she grumbled under her breath.

Either Aunt Tillie didn't hear the snarky comment or she opted not to put on a magic display so early in the evening, because she didn't say anything. Landon, however, seemed desperate to keep things pleasant.

"It's the best pot roast in the world," he said. "Seriously, the gravy is so good I want to take a bath in it."

The image made me smile. "What about the bacon? I thought you wanted to take a bath in bacon grease."

"Oh, gross!" Dani shifted on her seat. Even though she was being a typical teenager and running her mouth, she almost looked as if she was suddenly enjoying the conversation. "That's the most disgusting thing I've ever heard."

"I bet I would glow after taking a bath in bacon grease," Landon argued. "I would also smell divine."

"Yes, every man in town would be questioning their sexuality if you did that," Thistle agreed, making me laugh.

Landon bumped me with his shoulder, encouraging the reaction. "You'd like it if I smelled like bacon twenty-four-seven, wouldn't you?"

"I would prefer you smelled like cookies," I admitted.

He made a face. "No. That's a chick scent. I'm a manly man."

"How can chocolate chip cookies be a female scent?" I argued.

"Because women bake cookies," Dani answered. "He's sexist. Get him, Miss Tillie!" There was no doubt this time. She was definitely enjoying herself.

"It's not sexist," Landon argued. "I just think bacon is a more manly scent."

"And yet you rub yourself all over Bay whenever Aunt Tillie curses her to smell like bacon," Thistle noted. "You think bacon smells manly, so that must mean Bay reminds you of a man."

Landon glared. "Don't you start."

"It's a fair point," Aunt Tillie argued, mischief flitting across her face. "Maybe we should test a few things. For example, next time you tick me off — which will certainly happen before bed this evening — I can curse you to smell like cookies. I'm all for experimentation."

Landon shook his head. "Whatever. You act like that would be punishment, but if Bay is rubbing herself all over me it's a win for us all."

"And what happens when you go to work tomorrow and everyone notices you smell like cookies?" I asked.

He shrugged. "I'll say I used some of that body spray you have that makes you smell like cookies."

"Cake," I corrected.

"It's the same thing."

"Not even remotely."

"Whatever. The point is, if you want me to smell like cookies, I'm fine with it."

"Actually, doughnuts might be better," I mused, mostly to myself.

"Doughnuts, cookies. I'm fine with either." Landon was blasé as he forked up his pot roast.

"I think you're just saying that so Bay will be willing to walk around smelling like bacon three days a week," Thistle countered.

"No, I'm not." Landon was firm. "I'm fine smelling like cookies without any payback."

Aunt Tillie's lips curved into an evil sneer. "Challenge accepted."

## ELEVEN

Dani's attitude waxed and waned throughout the evening. She seemed to bristle under authority — any authority — but there were times she forgot her teenage angst crap and engaged. Those were the moments I clung to, because I was desperate for her to embrace that part of her personality. The glimpses were rare, though, leaving me agitated.

"Do you want to tell me what's bothering you?"

Landon found me by the lake shortly before dark. He and Marcus had built a roaring bonfire, something they claimed was a "man's job." It took them three times as long as it would've taken Thistle and me. We left them to their shenanigans, though, because they seemed to be having such a great time.

I studied his face for a long moment and then shrugged. "Why does something have to be bothering me? Maybe I'm just thinking."

"You're definitely thinking," he agreed, lowering himself to the ground next to me, resting his back against the same fallen tree and plucking my hand from my lap so he could study it. "You know I love you, right?"

The question seemed to come out of nowhere. "I'm well aware. You whisper sweet nothings into my ear about bacon every night. You also put up with Aunt Tillie daily. If that's not love, I don't know what is."

He smirked. "The bacon is a game ... it really is the epitome of goodness and light in our world."

"It is," I agreed automatically.

"Aunt Tillie is an extension of you. I love her, too, even if she is ... difficult ... at times."

"That's a nice way of putting it."

His smiled. "What I feel for you is completely beyond anything I ever thought possible." His voice was low but clear. "Before you, I wasn't sure I would ever find ... this." He moved his finger between the two of us. "I wasn't sure it was really possible. I figured it was some construct of romance movies and something I was programmed to believe was true but wasn't attainable."

I had no idea where he was going with this conversation, but I was intrigued. He wasn't shy about professing his feelings. This felt somehow different. It was almost as if he was building to something — and I had a sneaking (and sinking) suspicion I knew exactly what that something was.

"I think I knew from the first moment I saw you that we were supposed to end up here."

"Sitting next to a log, staring at a lake, and wondering if the teenager in our midst is going to try to murder us in our sleep?" I decided to get to the heart of matters. There was no reason to meander.

"Here as in here." He linked our fingers and lifted them. "When I'm with you I feel whole."

The naked emotion on his face caused my heart to stutter. "I love you too."

He grinned. "I know. Just wait until Aunt Tillie makes me smell like cookies. You will love me even more then."

His excitement over that possibility made me laugh. "It's not nearly as much fun as you imagine. I mean ... what are you going to do when all the women in town start following you around like lost puppies?"

He arched a mischievous eyebrow. "You make that sound like a bad thing."

"Oh, so you want other women to chase you?"

"It's always nice to be wanted." He poked my side, letting me know he was kidding. "Of course, I would explain to them in no uncertain terms that I'm a one-witch guy. Leaving a trail of crushed and broken women in my wake isn't the ideal situation, but I'm willing to take one for the team if it keeps you happy."

I shook my head. He was in an odd mood. I couldn't quite identify the emotions fueling it, but I wasn't complaining. If he was feeling playful, that might bode well for the rest of the night. "Do you know where Dani went?" I asked, craning my neck for a better look at the campsite.

"She's following Aunt Tillie around," Landon replied, his smile slipping. "Apparently Aunt Tillie is strengthening the wards on the cabin and Dani is complaining about it. She says the wards make her feel weak."

"They should. We've warded that thing to the freaking studs. She can't do anything evil in the cabin."

"That doesn't stop her from doing something evil outside of it," he pointed out.

"I know." I averted my gaze and went back to staring at the lake. "Aunt Tillie plans to ward as much of the property as possible after Dani goes to bed, but that's not as easy as warding a cabin."

He squeezed my hand insistently, until I turned my eyes to him. "I want you to know that I admire what you're doing here." He hesitated before continuing, as if he was trying to pluck up the courage to say something difficult. "I think we need to start coming up with contingency plans, though."

My stomach constricted. "Landon ... ."

"Hold up." He lifted his free hand to quiet me. "I am not trying to dictate to you. I know it's difficult for you to believe, but it's true. I don't want to tell you what to do in this situation. I'll be the first to readily admit that I'm out of my depth here. I don't know what to do with an out-of-control teenage witch.

"That doesn't mean my opinion should immediately be discarded," he continued, earnest. "You're the single most important thing in the world to me, Bay, and I don't want anything bad to happen to you. If I lose you ... ." He trailed off and exhaled heavily, as if evening out his emotions.

"You won't lose me," I reassured him. "I was just thinking about that."

"About dying on me?" His eyes flashed.

"About contingency plans for Dani. Did you watch her tonight? There were times she still found great joy in being with us. She has attitude and seems to really enjoy irritating Aunt Tillie, but that's a teenage thing. It's not an evil witch thing."

"Baby ... ." Landon looked frustrated.

"What are we going to do with her if this fails?" I asked, genuinely conflicted.

"We'll send her to a hospital or something. We'll get her professional help."

"And what happens if she uses her magic on the people in the hospital?" I was deadly serious. "She could torture those people and nobody would be the wiser. She might get joy in it."

"And that's exactly why I don't want you hanging around with her," Landon argued. "I don't want her getting joy in hurting you."

"She won't."

"You don't know that. Of everyone here, she has the most attitude with you. I know you might not see it, but it's true. When she looks at you she sees an enemy. You took her aunt out. You stopped what they thought was a foolproof plan. You're the one she wants to topple, and it would kill me if something happened to you. I'm not joking about that."

"You love me more than bacon, huh?" I was going for levity because his demeanor made me nervous.

"I love you more than anything." He held my hand tighter. "She's not your responsibility, Bay. It's okay to let her go."

"You're talking about making her someone else's responsibility."

"I am."

"And when she kills someone else, how am I supposed to live with that?"

"I ... don't know." Frustration bubbled up as he dragged his hand through his hair. "I can't see beyond keeping you safe. If that makes me selfish, well, I'm not sorry. You're essential to me. I won't be able to breathe without you. I just ... don't want you around her."

"I get it." I did. "The day we decided to take her on after what happened with Diane, she became my responsibility. I don't know what the answer is, but we can't put innocent people at risk. We have to figure out a way to reach her on an emotional level."

"And if she turns on you?" Landon held my gaze. "If she tries to hurt you with her magic, will you be able to protect yourself without feeling guilty? Will you be able to take her out?"

It was a fair question. "I'll do what I have to do." I meant it, but my stomach hurt at the prospect. "I'll protect the people I love by any means necessary. I just don't want to give up on her yet.

"I remember what it was like being her age," I continued. "I once read a study that said you can't run personality tests on teenagers because the vast majority of them could be diagnosed as sociopaths. She's at a weird age. I'm sure you would've hated me at that age too."

"No. I always loved you."

I snickered. "You didn't love me as a teenager."

"I did. Something inside of me knew you were out there and I loved you. You'll never be able to convince me otherwise. This was destined."

He was being so sweet all I could do was nod and sigh. "I'll be careful, Landon. I promise. I'm just not ready to wash my hands of her."

"Fine." He was resigned. "You need to do what you think is right. But you need to start planning for what happens if this fails. We need a backup plan in place if things go south, because it's far more likely they will than you'll get the happy ending you want."

I swallowed hard at his words. "There are different kinds of happy endings."

"There are," he agreed. "You and I will get our happy ending regardless. But Dani ... sometimes people are truly lost causes, Bay. You need to prepare yourself for that possibility."

"I'm not ready yet."

"That's what terrifies me most. You have to watch your back whenever she's around. She's like a snake. She'll wait until your guard is down to attack. Don't let her beat you."

"I won't."

He lifted our joined hands, pressing a kiss to my knuckles. "I love you, Bay. Don't you ever leave me. I couldn't take it."

"Right back at you."

He smirked. "We're quite the pair, huh?"

"Quite the schmaltzy pair."

"Yeah. Do you want a s'more?"

That put a smile on my face. "You know the way to my heart."

"And don't you forget it."

"DO YOU THINK LANDON IS ACTING WEIRD?"

Two hours later, my stomach mildly upset from too much chocolate and marshmallows, Thistle and I toiled in the woods surrounding the camp. We were setting ward traps — spells that picked up on intent and doled out retribution accordingly — while Landon and Marcus kept an eye on Dani. With no women present to agitate her, Dani was a bundle of flirty (and sweet) energy with the men. It was an interesting development.

"You need to be more specific," Thistle replied, her fingers busy as she laid down invisible lines of magic. "I've always thought he was weird."

"I just mean that ... he seems different." I looked to the bonfire, to where Landon and Marcus were sharing a story and Dani was laughing hysterically, as if she were watching a *Saturday Night Live* skit play out in real time.

Thistle followed my gaze. "He seems pretty normal to me. He's sitting over there holding court while we're out here doing the work."

I made a face. "How do you suggest he lay down wards? Should he use the witchy powers he's been hiding since we met?"

"You know what I mean." Thistle leaned back on her haunches to study her work. "Why do you think he's acting weird?"

I hesitated, briefly wondering if I should've left the topic for another time. It was too late now. The serious nature of our earlier conversation had stuck with me. "He's afraid ... and he's hiding something."

Thistle's eyebrows drew together. "What is he afraid of?"

"Dani. He believes she'll turn on us."

"I hate to break it to you, but I believe that too. I'm pretty sure Aunt Tillie does as well. If you're gauging weirdness on that particular belief, you might be the odd witch out."

"It's not that I trust her," I said hurriedly, moving to another spot so I could add a ward to the mix. We were trying to fill the woods with traps, something of a last resort should Dani lose her mind and decide to go on a rampage. The wards weren't guaranteed to work because we couldn't cover every spot, but I figured they were better than nothing.

"So why are you surprised he's worried?" Thistle asked, her gaze drifting across the lake to the other campground. "Do you think we should do the same thing over there?"

I shrugged. "Maybe. We can't do it tonight. If we decide it's necessary, we'll stop by in the morning before heading to town. The only way across is by canoe, and I'm far too stuffed from the s'mores to paddle."

"You and me both." Thistle turned back to me. "Bay, Landon is a weird guy. He once told Marcus his idea of the perfect day is you, him, a hammock, and a plate of bacon. He wasn't joking. He was deadly earnest."

"That's my idea of a perfect day," I admitted. "Well ... I don't need the bacon. We might have to add some doughnuts to the mix."

She smirked. "If Aunt Tillie makes him smell like baked goods, I will never stop laughing. That has the potential to be one of the funniest things ever."

I didn't disagree. "He really is acting odd," I pressed. "I think ... I think there's something on his mind he doesn't want to tell me about."

Thistle studied my face and then shrugged. "Like what?"

"You were going to call me crazy and then changed your mind, weren't you?" I challenged, instantly suspicious.

She shrugged. "Your instincts have been right more than wrong the past few weeks. I figure you've earned the right to be paranoid if you want."

"I'm not paranoid."

"Then how is he acting odd?"

I debated and then plowed forward. "Last night I caught him in the kitchen whispering with Mom."

Thistle waited a moment and then held out her hands. "And?"

"And they were whispering."

"So what?"

Frustration bubbled up. "They acted like they weren't having some secret conversation when I showed up. They tried to change the subject and distract me. They were obviously talking behind my back."

"Well, I hate to be the bearer of bad news, but everyone in this family gossips about one another," Thistle argued. "That's just the way we are."

"I don't gossip."

She rolled her eyes. "Please. We spent the two weeks Clove was on her honeymoon debating how much weight she would put on during her pregnancy. Then we started a betting pool as to how whiny she'll be during labor. If that's not gossip, I don't know what is."

I balked. "We were worried about her. That conversation came from a place of love."

"If you say so."

"It's true."

"Oh, it is not." Thistle lost all semblance of patience and planted her hands on her hips. "Nobody can live a life without secrets, Bay. Did it ever occur to you that Landon and Winnie were talking about Dani? I hate to break it to you, but everyone is worried about this situation. We're all afraid that you're putting yourself in danger by refusing to see the truth."

"And what's the truth?"

"That she's beyond being saved. You see it but don't believe it."

"You're right. I don't believe it. I don't see it either." I gestured toward the fire. "Look at her now. She's having a good time. She's not being manipulative ... or threatening anyone ... or even acting surly. There's a still a chance for her."

The look Thistle shot me was full of pity. "Right now, she's playing it up for their benefit because she thinks they'll be easier to manipulate. They're not magical. Therefore they're nothing but pawns to her.

"She pushes boundaries with us because she wants to see how we'll react," she continued. "She'll soon grow sick of pushing boundaries and decide to punch across them entirely. You need to prepare yourself for that."

This was the second time in the same night I felt as if I was trapped in the world's most uncomfortable conversation. "I have everything under control."

She shook her head and looked away. "Until you're willing to see the truth, this conversation is a waste. Landon is worried about you because of Dani. If you want him to stop having quiet conversations with your mother, don't give him anything to worry about."

I pressed the heel of my hand to my forehead and fought to keep from starting an argument. I needed to vent, but if I started now things would spiral out of control. We needed to work together, not splinter. Dani would pick us off one by one if we didn't stand united.

"I'll think about what you said," I promised after a beat. "I know you're worried. I don't want that. I don't want any of you to worry." I focused on the far back, narrowing my eyes when I caught a hint of movement. "I can't give up on her yet. I'm doing the best that I can."

"I know." Thistle sounded sad. "It's just ... when you can't save her you're going to blame yourself. This was never your responsibility."

"You sound like Landon."

"Yeah, well for once I don't have a problem with that. He loves you to distraction. He wants what's best for you. He sees you going down a dangerous road. He has to fight to protect you the only way he knows.

"Sure, we would all prefer that our boyfriends not talk to our mothers because it freaks us out, but he is trying to be the best man he can be — for you," she continued. "You can't hold the fact that he loves you against him. He wants you safe. That's not an unreasonable demand."

"I know." I felt inexplicably sad. She was standing up for Landon, something she would never do unless she was absolutely terrified. I'd created an untenable position for my family and I didn't know how to fix the problem. "I'll think about what you said."

"That's all I ask." She patted my shoulder and then moved on to set more wards. "Let's finish this up. My stomach is upset from too many s'mores."

That made two of us, but there was more where I was concerned. I could feel eyes watching me from a distance and the feeling drew my gaze to the other side of the lake. "Yeah."

"You shouldn't have let me eat so many."

"I'll try to wrestle you down and take the s'more away next time," I said dryly, my gaze still on the ghost watching us from beyond the water. The figure was too far away, but I had no doubt it was Valerie. She was still hanging around the woods. That couldn't be good.

"I'll hit this side of the trees with another three wards," she offered. "You do the other side. Then we'll head back together."

Valerie's appearance made me uneasy, but I nodded. "Sounds like a plan."

# TWELVE

It was almost ten o'clock when we decided to call it a night.

"You should hit the hay," I instructed Dani. "You need your rest."

Her expression was dark when she turned her gaze from Marcus to me. "I'm not a little kid. I don't need a bedtime."

"Maybe not," Landon replied, "but we're old. We're going to bed ... which means you have to go to bed."

"Since when is that the rule?" Dani argued. "When Hazel is here, I'm allowed to stay up as long as I want. In fact, there are times she heads out for walks and I get tired of waiting for her so I turn in before she even gets back."

I frowned. That was the second time Dani had brought up Hazel's penchant for taking walks. I couldn't decide if she was trying to get us to turn on Hazel, or if she was simply speaking because she liked the sound of her own voice. One possibility was more troubling than the other.

"Well, Hazel isn't here tonight," I pointed out, calm. "She's taking a break because she's earned it."

"Maybe I want a break." Obstinate to the point of being obnoxious, Dani folded her arms across her chest and pinned me with an unreadable look. "I'm an adult. I don't have a bedtime. Only babies have to go to bed at a certain time."

She was testing me. She wanted to see exactly how far I could be pushed. It was time to lay down the law.

"Last time I checked, babies didn't work with outside forces to kill their fathers," I replied evenly. "Babies don't plot against their mothers. That means babies deserve more freedom than you."

"That's not entirely true," Thistle hedged. "I'll bet there are evil babies out there who would totally kill their parents if they could. Like when Ted Bundy was a baby, I bet he still had murderous urges. You can't say all babies are innocent."

I pinned her with a look. "Is that really the point right now?"

She shrugged. "I was just saying that babies can be evil."

"She's right," Aunt Tillie offered from her spot next to the fire. She looked as if she was one s'more away from lapsing into a sugar coma. "When Thistle was a baby, I knew without a shadow of a doubt that she was evil. I tried telling Twila, but she refused to listen. Now we're stuck with her."

Thistle narrowed her eyes. "I'm not a baby any longer. I can sneak up on you and smother you with your sleeping bag the second you fall asleep and nobody will be the wiser. They'll assume that you just died in your sleep because you're so old."

Aunt Tillie's eyes were glittery slits. "You're on my list."

The argument might've been entertaining under different circumstances, but there was nothing amusing about the interplay now, especially when I was trying to exert control over Dani.

"You made poor choices, Dani," I offered. "That's the point. Until you can prove that you're over making those choices, you have to bend to our will. That means it's time for bed."

"And what if I don't?" Dani puffed out her chest, defiant.

"Then I guess we'll have to make some hard choices." I kept my voice even despite the fact that I was suddenly feeling weak in the knees. "Is that what you want?"

For a moment, I thought she was going to push the matter. At the last second, though, she shrugged and wrinkled her nose. "Oh, don't be a big whiner. I was just saying that I don't want to go to bed. If you're going to make a thing out of it, I guess I'll go in there and read or something. There's no reason to fight."

"It's not about a fight," I replied. "We're tired. It's been a long day. We all have jobs to report to tomorrow."

"Yeah, yeah, yeah," Dani grumbled, slowly getting to her feet. "I get it. I don't have a job. I'm not important."

"If you weren't important, we wouldn't be here," Landon argued. "But you need to start putting in some effort. If you're unwilling to meet us halfway we will start questioning whether we should even make the effort."

"Is that supposed to frighten me?" Dani demanded. "Are you going to threaten me with freedom because I'm no longer worth the effort?"

Landon didn't shift his gaze. "Not freedom. That's not on the table."

She initially looked taken aback but recovered quickly. "I'm going to bed. I'll be a good little girl."

Landon's expression never wavered. "We're not congratulating you for doing the right thing. You need to want to do it. That's why we're here."

"Great." Dani scuffed the soles of her shoes against the ground on her way to the cabin. "I guess I'll see you in the morning."

"That's the plan," I agreed, watching her slink off with some level of trepidation. "We should set wards around where we're sleeping," I said once I was certain she was out of earshot. "You know, just to be on the safe side."

"I've already handled that," Aunt Tillie said. "As long as we stay in the square around the fire, we're safe. I marked the lines with little stakes."

I looked at the wooden pegs. "That's smart, but what if someone has to go to the bathroom in the middle of the night?"

"I guess that means you'll have to go before then and hunker down for the night," Aunt Tillie said. "That means no funny business tonight."

"Oh, and I was looking forward to dressing up like a clown and honking Bay's horn all night," Landon drawled, earning a glare from Aunt Tillie.

"We've got it," I reassured her before an argument erupted. "We'll make our bathroom runs before bed."

"Should we keep watch?" Marcus asked. He might not have understood all the hoopla surrounding Dani, but he was a master at reading moods. He knew Dani made everyone edgy, and that made him wary. "That way, at least we'll know what she's doing."

"She's warded in the cabin," Aunt Tillie argued. "She can't leave until we say it's okay. She's in there for the night. There's no reason for anybody to miss sleep."

"Fair enough." Marcus bobbed his head before collecting the sleeping bags we'd stacked near the picnic table. "I guess that means it's time for bathroom breaks and then bed."

"I look forward to sleeping under the stars with you," Landon teased, lowering his forehead to mine. "There's little I like more than cuddling in the same sleeping bag with you."

"It will be nice," I agreed, faltering when I realized Aunt Tillie was watching us with a dour expression. "Not that we're going to do anything," I hurriedly added. "It's going to be a quiet night, involving just sleeping."

"It had better be," Aunt Tillie warned, shaking a finger. "If I hear any hanky-panky, you'll be dealing with Mulder and Scully."

"Why Mulder and Scully?" I asked after realizing she was naming the fists she was holding up.

"She's been watching old reruns of *The X-Files*," Thistle said. "I caught her a few days ago. She was explaining to Mulder through the television what he was doing wrong. When I asked why she watching it, she said she was exploring ways to take down 'The Man' from the inside." Her gaze was pointed when it landed on Landon. "If I were you, I'd be afraid."

Landon was blasé. "And somehow I think I'll survive. Come on, Bay. It's bedtime. I'm ready to pass out and put this day behind us."

He wasn't the only one.

**I THOUGHT FOR A FEW SECONDS** that the screaming I woke to was part of a dream. Landon and I had zipped our sleeping bags together so we could sleep wrapped around one another. His jerk swiftly brought me back to reality.

"What is that?" Thistle asked, jerking up her head.

"It's coming from across the lake," Landon replied, glancing around the campground. His gaze immediately went to the cabin, where he sought out Dani. She stood in the window, seemingly intrigued, but didn't move to exit the cabin. She couldn't without permission from one of us. That's the way the wards were set up.

"It's Heather's house," I said, rolling out of the sleeping bag and searching for my shoes. "It sounds like she's in trouble."

"It's probably faster to drive over there, right?" Marcus asked. He was much more alert than Thistle. "It will take too long to go by canoe."

I shifted my eyes to Aunt Tillie, who was already heading toward the shore. "Not necessarily." I glanced around the campground. "We can't take Dani with us and we can't leave her here without someone to release her should it become necessary."

Marcus hesitated. "You want it to be me, don't you?"

"I think we might need as many magical people as we can get," I offered, apologetic. "Also, Landon has a badge if it becomes necessary."

"We're wasting time," Aunt Tillie barked. She was already using her magic to push one of the canoes into the water.

"Maybe you should stay with Marcus," Landon suggested to Aunt Tillie. "We can cross the lake faster without you."

AMANDA M. LEE

Aunt Tillie turned haughty. "Except you need me to power the canoe. Thistle and Bay don't know the right kind of magic. Do you want to know why? They spent their lives as dabblers. They've only recently shown interest in becoming a true witch."

"Great story," Landon drawled. "We still need to get across that lake fast."

"Do you believe this guy?" She turned to me, incredulous. "I'm going to save the day. He's the one who will slow us down. And who, may I ask, is being threatened?"

I was already tired of the bickering. "We need to go." I hesitated before fixing Marcus with an apologetic look. "I am sorry, but we need someone to stay here in case something goes wrong."

He nodded without voicing a word of argument. "Just keep me posted." He leaned over and gave Thistle a quick kiss. "Be careful. Don't get in any trouble."

"I'm with Bay and Aunt Tillie," Thistle pointed out. "What could possibly go wrong?"

"You don't really want me to answer that, do you?"

**AUNT TILLIE USED HER MAGICAL PROPULSION SPELL** and we were across the lake in four minutes. We went so fast, in fact, that I felt mildly sick to my stomach when we beached on the opposite shore.

"Stick close to me," Landon hissed.

"Maybe you should stick close to me," Aunt Tillie countered.

"I'm the FBI agent," he fired back.

"And I'm the witch."

I ignored both of them and started for the house. The closer we got to Heather's mansion, the sicker I felt. Something was terribly wrong on this side of the lake, and I felt that even before the screams had abruptly stopped during our trip across the lake.

"Are we going to break in?" Thistle asked, struggling to keep up with me. Her legs were shorter, and usually it took her a good fifteen minutes to fully wake up. Right now, though, she was alert and ready.

"Probably," I replied grimly, looking up at the second-story windows for movement. There was nothing. "We have to go in." I looked over my shoulder, searching for Landon. He was almost directly on top of me.

"We do," he agreed. "I have probable cause. You guys should wait here."

That wasn't going to happen. "We need to stick together," I insisted. "You're not going in there without us."

"She's right," Thistle said. "You need us to watch your back."

Landon didn't look convinced but he relented. "Okay, but I'm in charge. Do what I say."

"Oh, you've been waiting for this moment since you met us, haven't you?" Aunt Tillie chortled. "This must be an exciting day for you."

Landon ignored her and tried the door handle. It was locked. He raised his foot to kick it in, but I stopped him by extending a hand.

"There's no reason to destroy it," I said. "Just ... let me." I whispered a spell and the door slowly opened.

"You're feeling pretty good about yourself, aren't you?" Landon shook his head but there was a slight curve to his lips. "Be quiet," he instructed as we stepped into the house. "I'm not sure what we're dealing with here, but I can't believe it's good given the hour."

I agreed with him wholeheartedly.

Once inside, Landon cocked his head and listened to the sounds of the house. It was quiet — eerily so. He seemed to be debating which direction to go when something whispered in the back of my brain.

"This way." I headed for the stairs, not even looking over my shoulder to see if the others followed.

"Bay," Landon growled, giving chase. "You can't just wander around the house without invitation. Besides, I said I was in charge. That means ... ." Whatever he was going to say died on his lips as we hit the top of the stairs.

There, things happened rapidly. It was difficult to wrap my head around what I was seeing.

Valerie's ghost floated in the middle of the hallway, her eyes glowing red. When she turned to face me, the hatred flowing through the room caused my stomach to shrivel.

"Is that a body?" Thistle asked from somewhere behind me.

"Heather Castle," Landon said grimly. "She owns the house." He moved to step closer to the body, and that's when I realized he didn't understand the danger was still present. He couldn't see Valerie's ghost. Even if he could feel the chill, his instincts would take over and he'd want to check on the woman to see if she was still alive.

"No!" I blocked him before he could cross the threshold. I was desperate to keep the others safe even as I wanted to determine what had happened. "Why did you do this, Valerie?"

"Is there a ghost here?" Thistle asked suddenly, freezing.

"It's more than a ghost," Aunt Tillie offered. "It's ... something more."

The wind in the room picked up. I kept my eyes on Valerie rather than letting the rattling picture frames hanging on the walls serve as a distraction. "What did you do to her?" I asked. "Is she still alive?"

Valerie's eyes flashed brighter. She was completely consumed by ... something. I didn't even know what to call it. I'd never seen a phenomenon like this, and fear pervaded my heart as I tried to gain control of my emotions.

"You don't belong here," Valerie intoned.

"We heard her screaming from across the lake. We had to come and see."

Valerie shook her head. "You don't belong here." She was firm. "I don't belong here either. This was supposed to be my life — but she took it."

"But she didn't," I argued. "She might've taken Eric, but this life was never meant to be yours." I was uncomfortable with the way she looked at me, but I couldn't stand around doing nothing. If Heather was still alive, she needed help. There was no time to waste. "I'm going to move closer."

"I don't think that's a good idea," Landon hissed, his lips close to my ear. "I can't see that ghost, Bay, but I can feel her. It's not a good feeling."

"We have to check on Heather." I took a long stride forward. "Just let me check on her."

Valerie watched me with curious eyes as I tentatively crossed the room. I thought she would allow me to help the prone figure — right up until the last second. When I reached out to check for Heather's pulse, Valerie grew enraged.

"I said no!"

A wall of ghostly energy smacked into me as the irate specter lost her grip on reality and attacked. Instinctively, I lashed out with my necromancer powers. I intended to shred the spirit even though that was always the choice of last resort as far as I was concerned. She surprised me enough to make it necessary, but it failed. She continued forward, the magic glancing off her as my eyes widened.

She hit me hard, dark magic pulsating from her, and I found myself flying back toward the stairs. I thought I would tumble to my death, images of my neck snapping as I fell end over end flooding my mind, but a pair of strong arms caught me before I could fall.

"I've got you," Landon grunted, his arms encircling me. "You're okay."

For the moment, that was true. Valerie's rage grew more pronounced when she realized I wasn't about to fall victim to her power.

"You don't belong here," she bellowed, the room reverberating as her anger took shape. "This was supposed to be mine. I'm taking it back."

Her magic was so great that the skylight above us shattered when she screeched again, shards of glass cascading down upon us.

Aunt Tillie was the first to react this time. She sent up a wall of magic to collide with the glass, causing it to fly in thousands of directions rather than rain down on us.

My breath came in ragged gasps as Landon held me tight and protected my face.

"What was that?" he asked when he finally found his voice.

That was a very good question.

# THIRTEEN

Chief Terry was furious when he arrived at Heather's house.

"Do I even want to know what happened here?" he demanded as he took in our faces. His hair was a mess, making me think he'd been woken from sleep, and I couldn't help but wonder if my mother had been running her fingers through it as they ... completely tainted my dreams for the rest of my life.

"We were at the camp," Landon volunteered. He'd insisted I sit and collect myself before trying to walk down the stairs. I was convinced it was an elaborate plot to keep me close so he wouldn't have to worry about me, but I was too tired to argue any point, let alone that one. "We heard screaming and came to check it out."

"You drove?" Chief Terry's forehead wrinkled. "I didn't see any vehicles outside."

Landon hesitated. "We came by canoe."

"You responded to a scream across the lake by canoe?"

"Aunt Tillie made it go so fast," Thistle offered from the spot on my right. "We were here within five minutes."

"Oh, well, that will be fun to explain to the medical examiner," Chief Terry barked. "Why can't you guys ever have an outing that doesn't end in us having to come up with an elaborate lie? Is that too much to ask?"

"Apparently so," Aunt Tillie replied as she studied the art on the wall. She seemed unbothered by the body on the floor, but the look she shot me was full of curiosity — and a bit of concern. "How are you feeling, Bay?"

The question caught me off guard. "I'm fine." I forced a tight-lipped smile. "Don't worry about me. I'm okay."

The shift in subjects threw Chief Terry. "What happened to Bay?" He moved in my direction, concern lining his features. "Are you sick, sweetheart?"

"Oh, now you care," Thistle muttered, earning a grin from me.

"I cared," Chief Terry argued, hunkering down in front of me. "Why are you so pale? Did something happen?"

Landon, who flanked me, ran his hand down the back of my head. "I can't say I'm sure what happened."

"She was attacked by a ghost," Thistle offered helpfully.

"A ghost?" Chief Terry made a face. "I don't want to hear that. Ghost stories give me indigestion."

"It wasn't just a ghost," I argued, my mind rushing back to Valerie. "She was ... different."

"It's a female ghost?"

"Valerie Lennox," Landon volunteered. "Bay saw her when we were out here yesterday, tried to talk to her. When we arrived tonight, apparently Valerie was hovering over Heather's body. Bay tried to talk her down, but it didn't go well. Valerie did ... something ... and basically threw Bay down the stairs."

Chief Terry straightened, all signs of weariness vanishing from his well-worn features. "She was thrown down the stairs? Why aren't we taking her to the hospital? That's a long drop. She could have internal injuries."

"I didn't get thrown down the stairs," I argued. "She tried, but I never made it that far. Landon caught me. I'm fine."

Chief Terry looked to Landon for confirmation.

Landon nodded. "She didn't hit the ground," he said. "That doesn't mean I'm not worried. I just ... I thought you were supposed to be able to control ghosts, Bay. I don't want to call your powers into question, but it didn't seem you had control of anything."

I scowled at him. "What a weird way to kick me when I'm down."

"I'll make him smell like cookies tomorrow," Aunt Tillie offered. "But oatmeal raisin so he won't benefit from it. That should be good payback."

Landon shot her a look. "Oh, no. It's too late for that. You could've made me smell like chocolate chip cookies three hours ago, when it benefitted me, but you've lost your chance."

Aunt Tillie snorted. "We'll see about that."

"We will," he agreed, firm. His eyes came back to me. "Do you know what happened? Is Valerie a poltergeist, like Floyd?"

I held out my hands, unsure. "She's stronger than a normal ghost," I replied finally, searching for the right words. "She's different. She could affect her surroundings without expending much effort, and there was ... evil ... in her. I don't know how to explain it."

Landon switched his attention to Aunt Tillie. "You must know what happened."

"Why would I know?" Aunt Tillie shot back.

"How many times have you told me you know everything?"

"Well, that's true." She flashed a smile but it didn't make it all the way to her eyes. "I don't know what it was. It was hard to see from my spot on the stairs. I had a big, beefy FBI agent in front of me, which made it difficult to figure out what was happening. I thought I saw at least one thing of interest, though."

"The red eyes?" I prodded.

Aunt Tillie nodded. "Yeah. I've never seen that before. There was something else fueling her. Bay is right, she's more than a poltergeist. And the fact that Bay couldn't control her ... well, that makes me think we're dealing with something else entirely."

"Oh, well, that's always what I want to hear in the middle of the night," Thistle said. "There's nothing better than a new monster to fight. What's to stop this thing from popping into houses all over town and killing people for the fun of it?"

"Nothing," I answered. "The thing is, it still had Valerie's memories. It seemed propelled to act because of her feelings. I thought I saw Valerie watching us from across the lake earlier. I wasn't sure, so I didn't say anything, but she looked normal a few hours ago."

"You said that she was acting weird at the house earlier," Landon said. "You were convinced something was going on with her."

"She didn't know she was dead. That's not uncommon."

"But you said you sensed something different about her." Landon refused to let up. "Don't second-guess yourself now. Something clearly happened, and I want to figure out what it is before we run into this ghost again."

"What could it be?" Chief Terry asked, his eyes moving back to the body on the floor. "Do we know what killed Heather?"

"Her neck is broken," Landon replied. "That's pretty obvious. I didn't know ghosts could do things like that — but it seems that's what we're dealing with. It's a murderous ghost."

"Or enhanced poltergeist," Thistle argued.

Landon pinned her with a look. "Same thing."

"Not even close," Aunt Tillie said. "It doesn't matter. This ... thing ... is definitely different from the other ghosts we're used to going up against. It had a lot of power. Given the fact that Valerie has been dead for two weeks at the most, she's either lying about not realizing she was dead or something else is fueling her."

"And what could that be?" Chief Terry asked.

Aunt Tillie shrugged. "I have no idea, but we'd better figure it out. If we don't, someone could get killed during our next meeting of the minds."

Landon's eyes flashed with fear as he turned back to me. "Is there a way for you to gain control of her? I ... I know you were caught off guard this time, but you're a necromancer. I thought you were more powerful."

"I am more powerful," I supplied, wearily rubbing my forehead. "But I'm not omnipotent. Nobody is."

Aunt Tillie raised her hand and cleared her throat. I didn't give her a chance to speak because nobody was in the mood for that particular diatribe.

"You're not omnipotent," I argued, shaking my head when she looked as if she was about to argue the point. "Nothing is. No one. This magic is still new to me, but I tried exerting power over her. It was a reflex, to protect myself. It didn't work. Not even a little.

"It wasn't that I briefly gained control and she shook me off," I continued. "I never had control. She didn't have to listen to me, which means I've either lost my necromancer powers — which doesn't seem likely — or we're dealing with something else entirely."

"Well, great." Landon's expression was sour. "I can't tell you how happy I am to know we've got some new, fresh horror killing off people to deal with. That fills me with such joy."

Aunt Tillie rolled her eyes. "Suck it up. This is the life you chose when you took us on."

Landon blew out a sigh and then leaned over to press a kiss to my forehead. "You guys need to get back to the camp. Chief Terry and I will take it from here. In the morning, go straight to the inn for breakfast. We'll meet you there."

My heart dropped. "You think you'll be here all night?"

He nodded, grim. "We have to explain this somehow."

I hadn't considered that. "I'm sorry."

"You didn't cause this, Bay. You have nothing to be sorry about."

The words made sense, but things still felt off. I might not have been to blame, but I couldn't help thinking I'd missed something.

"YOU GUYS LOOK TIRED," MOM announced when Thistle, Marcus, Aunt Tillie and I filed into the dining room the next morning. We'd stayed at the camp, watching the house across the lake for signs of movement, until Hazel returned with the sun to take over Dani duty.

For her part, the young teenager seemed annoyed that we'd gone on an adventure without her. She complained bitterly as we made coffee and cleaned up our mess. She was angry — her emotions were close enough to the surface that I could feel them rippling — but she held it together when she realized we were too tired to put up with her crap. After that, she sat in her chair and glowered until Hazel returned. She didn't even bother saying goodbye.

"We had a long night," Thistle said, immediately reaching for the coffee carafe as Twila pressed a hand to her daughter's forehead. "I'm not sick. I'm just tired."

"And crabby," Marcus added, sliding into his regular seat.

I was morose as I took my spot, flanked by empty chairs because Landon and Chief Terry hadn't arrived. "Any news from them?" I asked, gesturing toward the chairs.

Mom's expression was hard to read as she shook her head. "No. I'm sure they'll be here soon. Landon can smell bacon from ten miles away."

"The lake is farther than that."

"Terry didn't say where he was going." Mom's furrowed brow made me uncomfortable enough that I refused to make eye contact with her. "He just said something happened and he probably wouldn't be back. I didn't realize it had anything to do with you guys."

"Yes, he was thrilled when he found out," Thistle drawled.

"We still don't know what happened," Marnie reminded us. "Was it bad?"

I heaved out a sigh and rubbed my forehead. "You could say that." I launched into the tale, leaving nothing out. When I got to the part about Valerie's ghost attacking me, my mother sucked in a breath and immediately looked at Aunt Tillie.

"I thought that wasn't possible," she challenged, unable to hide her annoyance. "You said Bay could control ghosts now and it would make her more powerful than the rest of us combined."

That was interesting. Aunt Tillie had never said anything of the sort to me. "What?"

Aunt Tillie kept her focus on Mom. "I said that in secret. *Secret!*" Her eyes flashed with annoyance. "You can't say things like that in front of her. Now she'll get a big head. We already have this one pretending she's queen of Hemlock Cove." She jerked her thumb toward Thistle. "We don't need to add an overblown Bay ego to the mix."

I was offended. "Hey!" At least I thought I was. "I just don't understand. How is being a necromancer going to make me more powerful than you?"

Aunt Tillie's eyes narrowed. "Nobody is more powerful than me! I'm the queen and you're all my subjects."

That was the moment Landon and Chief Terry strode into the room. If they thought there was anything strange about the declaration, they didn't show it.

"Hey." I immediately turned to Landon. He looked exhausted. "Did you get any sleep at all?"

He shook his head, his eyes roaming my face. "It doesn't look like you did either." He sat down and pressed his hand to my forehead, exactly as Twila had greeted Thistle. "You're not warm."

I offered him a half smile. "And here I thought you fell for me because you found me hot."

"Oh, you're definitely hot." He gave me a quick kiss and did his best to appear happy. I could see the trouble lurking in his eyes, though. "You should take the day off."

I found the suggestion ludicrous. "Because I'm tired?"

"Because you were almost thrown down a flight of stairs by a crazy ghost. You need a recovery day. You should go back to the guesthouse, put on those fuzzy pajama pants you love so much, make some tea, and watch old movies."

"Why would I do that?"

"You need rest."

"What about you?"

"I have a job to do. If I could, you can bet I would be right there with you ... perhaps without the fuzzy sleep pants. I'm convinced they're only cute on you."

Part of me thought I should be angry with him because he thought I was too weak to make it through the day on limited sleep. The other part was touched he cared enough to keep talking as if it were something I would actually do.

"I have work," I said. "I can't just take the day off. The Whistler can't run itself."

"It's a weekly and you have days before the next edition," Landon argued. "I think you can take the day off."

"That's not going to happen." My tone turned icy. "I'm fully capable of making it through a day on only a few hours of sleep. I'm not fragile."

"I didn't say you were fragile." The tilt of his head told me he wasn't in the mood to argue. "I just don't like it when you're this pale. I apologize for suggesting you get rest. Obviously I'm an ogre."

His passive-aggressive response only annoyed me more. "Did you find anything important at the house?" I asked Chief Terry, who sat in his regular chair.

"Nothing much to speak of," Chief Terry replied. "Landon was right about her neck being broken. There were no signs of forcible entry, including the door you all came through. That wasn't easy to explain, by the way."

"Why not just say she didn't bother to lock the door?" Thistle asked as she poured a glass of juice. "That seems an easy enough lie to come up with."

Chief Terry frowned. "Not now." He jabbed a finger at her and turned back to me. "The only thing we have going for us right now is that we're in control of the investigation. If another department had jurisdiction, we'd be in a world of hurt."

"So what happens now?" I asked. "You can't blame a ghost in your report."

Chief Terry took a deep breath. "We'll question Eric, make sure he's aware of Heather's death, and go from there. We'll handle it like a normal investigation even though it looks like a ghost is our culprit."

"That's probably smart." My mind had been so busy when we returned to the camp that I could barely shut it off. I'd come up with a hunch. "We might be looking for someone human after all."

"What do you mean?" Chief Terry asked.

"Valerie is different. I think the reason I couldn't control her is because someone else already was. That means we're dealing with someone with magical powers."

Landon stirred. "Someone like you?"

"Maybe not exactly like me, but close."

"How sure are you that we're dealing with another magical being?"

"Fairly certain. It makes sense."

He nodded. "Okay, we'll go with that. Now we just have to figure out who hated Valerie and Heather enough to kill them. Eric is the obvious suspect, but that almost feels too easy."

I had to agree. "I think we're missing part of the puzzle."

"Then we'll work together." Landon moved his hand to my back, not caring in the least that I was still agitated with him. "We're a team."

"I thought you wanted me to take a nap."

"I do, but I'm willing to hold off until we can nap together. That will be better for both of us."

I studied his face for a moment and then smiled. "So you're coming to my office to pass out for an hour at lunch?"

"Do you have a problem with that?"

I shook my head. "Nope. It's a date."

# FOURTEEN

I stopped at the guesthouse long enough to shower. I wasn't alone. Landon had seemingly lost interest in trying to get me to stay home — which still struck me as weird — and we had a round of fun before separating for the morning. He promised to keep in touch with any developments and I did the same.

By the time I made it to The Whistler, the lack of sleep was catching up with me. The couch in my office was inviting. I had work to do, but I figured a short nap couldn't hurt. I meant to close my eyes for twenty minutes.

Two hours later, I woke to someone shuffling in my personal space and I almost jumped out of my skin as I swiveled to scan the office.

"If you're going to sleep in here, you should lock the door," Mrs. Little announced, her prominent nostrils flaring. "Someone could just walk in off the street if you're not more careful. Do you want random people to walk in off the street?"

My mind was muddled from the heavy sleep and it took me a moment to wrap my head around the situation. "Aren't you a random person who just walked in off the street?"

She fixed me with a haughty look. "I'm the head of the Downtown Development Authority, president of the Hemlock Cove Festival Committee, chairman of the Friends of Hemlock Cove Community Outreach Program, and the single most influential businessperson in town."

I blinked several times in rapid succession. "And?"

"I'm pretty far from a random person."

"Oh, well ... ." I swung my legs to the side of the couch and tried to force myself to wakefulness. I'd been in the middle of a particularly lovely dream — one that involved Landon, a picnic, and the campground all to ourselves — when she burst into my reverie. Now I was awake and stuck with her.

"What do you want?" I asked. I expected her to announce her intentions, but she seemed content wandering my office.

She stopped at my desk and lifted one of the framed photos. It was Landon and me after a night of drinking on the bluff that overlooked the inn. He had his arm slung around my shoulders and boasted one of the widest smiles I'd ever seen. I was particularly fond of the photo, though I had no idea who had snapped it. My memory of that night was hazy thanks to copious amounts of Aunt Tillie's homemade wine.

"When was this taken?" she asked.

"Last summer," I replied, forcing myself to stand so I could snatch the photo from her. "What do you want?"

"That's not a very friendly greeting, Bay," she chided. "You're a business owner now. You should be gracious to other business owners."

"I'll keep it in mind." I returned the photo to its spot, taking a moment to wipe the smudge she'd put on the glass before giving her my entire focus. "Do you need something?"

"Information." She turned prim. "I understand that you were out at Heather Castle's house last evening and might have information regarding the tragedy that befell her."

This felt like a dangerous conversation, especially since I wasn't quite yet awake. "I was at the campground last night," I corrected. "We thought we heard a scream. It was hard to ascertain exactly where it was coming from. Heather's house is the only other structure in the vicinity, so we decided to check it out in case she needed help."

"And you found her dead, correct?"

I didn't understand how she already had that information. "Who told you that?" I was suspicious of her intentions and didn't want to give too much away.

"Larry Boggs was out there this morning because the ambulance carrying Heather's body got stuck in the ditch. That driveway is treacherous, and if you're not used to it, then it can lead to problems. She should have had it widened before she took over occupancy."

"Well ... that seems like the perfect thing to worry about given her death," I said dryly, shaking my head. "I'm not sure what that has to do with anything."

"I'm not here about the driveway. That's a problem for another day. I'm here about Heather. You saw her after the fact, right?"

"I ... we went in when nobody answered." I chose my words carefully. It probably wasn't wise to own up to anything in front of Mrs. Little, but I was worried that she would start sniffing around if I wasn't forthcoming with what should've been considered easy information. "Landon was with us, so he made the call. The screams were loud and frightening. We didn't want to walk away when no one answered the door. If she was in trouble, we wanted to help."

"Yes, yes. I figured all that out myself." She impatiently waved her hand. Apparently Heather's final moments weren't all that important to her. "I'm more interested in the house. It wasn't destroyed in the attack, was it?"

The question caught me off guard. "I ... what are you asking?"

"The house," she repeated. "Was it damaged? Someone said there was no damage to the house, but I'm not sure I believe the guy who drives the ambulance part time for a living when he says there was no damage. He also thinks that crappy truck he drives looks okay."

"I feel like I'm still asleep or something and not understanding what you're asking. I apologize, but why are you worried about the house?"

The sigh she let loose was long and drawn out. It was obvious she thought I was being difficult. "This isn't rocket science, Bay. I'm asking about the house because it's important. Was it damaged in the attack last night? If so, how much damage would you estimate?"

"I didn't really look around. I had other things on my mind — like the dead body on the floor."

"Yes, absolutely tragic," Mrs. Little agreed, drawing her shoulders straighter. "That poor woman was barely in town and she's already gone. Terrible." She made a tsking sound. "I'm simply worried about the house. That's quite the showplace up there and I want to make sure it wasn't damaged so it won't take too long for it to go back on the market."

It was only then that I remembered the story of her being interested in the house. "You think you can waltz in and buy it."

She was suddenly the picture of innocence. "I didn't say that. Did you hear me say that?"

"No, but you were trying to buy it before Heather came to town and beat your offer."

"She didn't beat my offer. She got priority because she had the cash."

"I'm pretty sure that's the same thing."

"And I'm pretty sure you know nothing about real estate because you've never owned anything before," she shot back.

"I own this place." I gestured toward my office. "Landon bought the campground with the express intent of building a house for us out there."

"Yes, but you didn't buy either of those." Mrs. Little was snotty on a normal day. Apparently my attitude had her feeling extra salty, because the look she shot me was full of warning. "Landon took care of that for you, correct? He bought the newspaper. He bought the campground. You're very lucky to have stumbled across him. Most women would kill for a man who wants to take care of them in that manner."

Anger grabbed me by the throat. "First, we take care of each other," I snapped. "Second, I bought this place. He gave me a small loan for the down payment, but I've already paid him back. This is my business."

"How wonderful for you." Her smile was bland. "Back to the house, though. Did Terry say what he expects to happen now? How soon do you think it will be before it's back on the market?"

Heather had been dead less than twelve hours and Mrs. Little was trying to steal her property. The realization made me sick to my stomach — and furious. "You'll have to take that up with Chief Terry."

"I would but he's asked that I limit my visits to the police department to once a week unless there's a genuine emergency. And he gets to deem what constitutes an emergency."

I almost laughed. He'd failed to mention that development. It would've been funny on any other day. What happened last night, though, left me sad and puzzled. "Then I don't know what to tell you. I'm not a real estate expert."

"But you could find out," she wheedled. "All you have to do is call Terry. He's very fond of you, though I've never understood why."

"I could call him," I agreed. "But he's busy with other things. A murder takes precedence over your real estate needs."

"Oh, don't take that tone with me. I'm not unsympathetic, but that property is very important to the town. I want to make sure it's handled correctly."

"You want to find out if there's any wiggle room for you to step in and claim it because Heather had barely taken possession."

Mrs. Little's eyes flashed with hatred. "I don't need your attitude, Bay. It's a simple question. If you don't know the answer, just say so."

"I don't know the answer."

"Fair enough." She made an annoying sniffle and started toward the door. "It would probably be best if we kept this conversation confidential. You know, just so there are no misunderstandings in town."

"I have no interest in sharing this information with anybody." Even as I said the words, I was lying. I knew at least five people who would be interested in the information.

"Great. I'll see you soon." She gave me a faux cheery wave and disappeared through the door, leaving me with nothing but annoyance and a dim memory of the happy dream I'd lost thanks to her visit.

"That was weird," I muttered, my brain finally kicking into high gear. "She's up to something."

**I WAS RECHARGED AFTER MY** visit from Mrs. Little so I headed to the second real estate office in town, the only one that competed with Eric's office.

Wayne Lawson went to school with my mother. He fancied himself a town big shot, even though he had a shady reputation. Most everyone looking to buy property went to Eric or independent agents because Wayne's reputation wasn't lily white. It was gray, which is why certain business owners — including Mrs. Little — utilized his services. He was known to cross ethical boundaries, which is why I decided to visit him first.

If Mrs. Little was trying to pull a fast one, she would go through Wayne.

"Bay Winchester," he boomed when I walked through the door. He didn't bother getting to his feet, instead remaining in his chair and offering one of those smiles that makes you want to punch someone in the face rather than return it. "I haven't seen you in a bit. This is a nice surprise."

"Yes, well, I was walking by and had a few questions," I said.

"Questions?" He winked, but he couldn't do it right; one eyelid closed halfway while the other closed completely. "I think you just got a hankering to see old Wayne. You always were fond of me. I think you had a little crush on me when you were a kid."

That was the most absurd thing I'd ever heard. "Yeah, I had a crush on Mike Proctor. He was the guy who served under Chief Terry when I was ten. I'm pretty sure I couldn't have picked you out of a lineup."

Rather than be offended, Wayne gestured to the chair across from his desk. "Have a seat. Are you here to talk about the bad deal your boyfriend got on that campground? If you're looking to unload, I might be able to scrounge up a buyer for you — but I don't know that he'll recoup all his money."

"Actually, we're quite happy with that purchase," I countered, taking the chair and crossing my legs as I tried to get comfortable. "In a few years, we're going to tear down the old cabins and build a house. Landon has a five-year plan."

"He's going to build a house on a cop's salary? How is he going to manage that?"

"He's an FBI agent."

"Same thing."

"Not really. But that's not why I'm here. I want to talk about the other house. The one Heather Castle purchased a few weeks ago."

All jocularity left Wayne's features as he clucked his tongue and shook his head. "I heard what happened out there last night. That is a tragedy."

Apparently news had spread faster than I'd anticipated. I blamed Mrs. Little. I blamed her for everything I possibly could because she was a horrible old wench. "It's definitely a tragedy," I agreed.

"Are you looking to buy that house? No offense, but I don't think you can afford it. I heard you had trouble putting together the money you needed for the newspaper. This would be substantially more than that."

The fact that everybody knew my financial situation was a nuisance, but I managed to keep my face neutral — barely. "I'm not interested in buying it. I want to know what happens to the property now that Heather is gone."

"I don't know the specifics of Ms. Castle's will." He sent me an odd look. "Is this for an article?"

"Research," I lied. "Now that Heather is dead, the property will be up for grabs. I believe there was something of a bidding war the last go-around. You and your client against Eric and Heather Castle — and they won."

"Ah." Understanding dawned on Wayne's face. "This is about Margaret."

"I have no idea what you're talking about," I lied again.

"Oh, don't bother." His lips curved into a smug smile. "I'm not surprised that she's already sniffing around. She was furious that she lost that property. I tried to explain why cash was more motivating to a seller, but she was irate."

"I'm not quite sure I understand why she wants that property," I admitted. "It's a haul to and from town."

"And yet you plan to live out there."

"Yes, but she's older ... and already has a house. Landon and I would most likely raise a family out there before growing old together."

"You assume," Wayne countered. "If you don't marry you'll have no claim to that property. But as for the house, I'm not sure how things will go. I'll probably put it on the market again by the end of the day — just in case there are interested buyers passing through. But I don't expect any nibbles for at least a week or so."

I was flabbergasted — and a little disgusted. "How can you put that house on the market without knowing who owns it?"

"The owner is dead."

"Yes, but she probably had a will."

"She was divorced. She won't be leaving the house to her ex-husband. It's likely she had no heirs."

"That doesn't mean you get to sell her house," I argued. "Everything has to go through probate. That will likely take six months. You can't just sell the house ... or try to renegotiate a deal that didn't close."

"It's possible that Heather's heirs — if she has any — might want to reverse the sale. If so, someone else can swoop in and buy it from the bank."

"But you have no knowledge of that."

"I plan to by the end of the day."

He sounded sure of himself and yet something felt off. "You know something. What is it?"

Now he feigned innocence. "I have no idea what you're talking about."

"You're lying."

"That's not a very nice thing to say."

I thought about hurling a few more insults, but it wouldn't matter. They would simply bounce off him because he had no sense of shame. "Fine. I don't have time to dig for whatever you're hiding. I'll put someone else on the job."

Wayne's smirk was pronounced. "Should I expect a visit from your beloved FBI agent in the near future?"

"Oh, no. I know everybody in this town thinks he does everything for me, but I have a different interrogator in mind for you."

"Terry? I'm not afraid of him either."

"Chief Terry is tied up in the same investigation Landon is knee-deep in right now. I wasn't thinking of either of them."

"Well, don't keep me in suspense."

I had no intention of doing anything of the sort. "Aunt Tillie."

He swallowed hard, some of the color fleeing his cheeks. "I don't understand."

I had him now. "Aunt Tillie," I repeated. "She's never liked you and she hates Mrs. Little. This little mission sounds right up her alley."

"And what do you think?" he challenged, finding his backbone. "Do you think I'm going to crumble in the face of ... well, whatever odd things she comes up with?"

"That's exactly what I think."

"You should probably brace yourself for disappointment."

"We shall see."

# FIFTEEN

People sniffing around Heather's property when she was still laid out on the autopsy table in the medical examiner's office gave me pause. I had no idea the land was considered so valuable. Of course, I'd never given it much thought. The people who owned the property before Heather had it for years. I almost never saw them, because they were uber-rich and only used the house as a weekend getaway in summers.

"You look like your head is about to start smoking," Clove noted when I wandered into Hypnotic several minutes after leaving Wayne's office. "Are you in the middle of an epiphany or something?"

"What?" I shook myself from my reverie and focused on Clove. "Um ... no. I was just thinking about something."

"I believe that's what she suggested," Thistle said from her spot on the floor. She was rearranging shelves in the candle department, and she didn't look happy. "Where have you been all morning?"

"I took a nap for two hours."

Thistle smirked. "Without Landon? He's going to be miffed. He told Marcus one of his favorite things to do is to sneak over from the police department when he's supposed to be working and nap with you. He says it feels illicit and dirty."

I wrinkled my nose. "It makes him feel dirty to sleep in the middle of the afternoon?"

Thistle shrugged. "Don't ask me. I thought it sounded weird too. Marcus thinks it's funny."

"Well, I didn't mean to fall asleep, but I was tired."

"We had a late night," Thistle confirmed. "I slept for an hour at home this morning."

"Yes, you had a late night," Clove said shrilly, her eyes flashing. "You two, out by yourselves. Without me. You had a late night together."

"You didn't miss anything," I reassured her.

"Really? I heard I missed s'mores ... and lots of talk about Dani ... and a nice bonfire. You know I love bonfires."

"You also missed crossing the lake in a magically powered canoe in the middle of the night and watching Bay almost get thrown down a flight of stairs by a crazy ghost," Thistle pointed out. "Did you really want to be part of that?"

Clove jutted out her chin and nodded. "I did."

I stared at her for a moment and then started laughing. "You did not. You just have fear of missing out. Trust me, you were better off far away from what happened last night."

Clove protested. "I don't like being left out. We're supposed to do stuff as a unit. The three of us. We've been together since we were kids. Now you guys are constantly going off without me. It's not fair."

"Hey, we're not the ones who can't figure out how to read the instructions on a birth control packet," Thistle fired back. "We're not the ones who changed the dynamic of this trio. That would be you. You insisted on getting engaged and then pregnant and then married. That's on you."

Clove's expression turned dark. "I've always wanted to get married. You know that. You two are purposely cutting me out because I got married, and that's not fair."

"We're not purposely cutting you out," I countered, making a face when my stomach constricted. "By the way, you need to stop that. Your emotions are riled up again and you're making things difficult for Thistle and me. You need to learn to rein that in."

Clove rolled her eyes. "I can't always help it. I have hormones and they're off the charts."

"I get that, but we have responsibilities," I fired back. "There are times you're around and I can't get through a meal without wanting to cry."

Clove was obviously miffed. "Try being me. Everything makes me want to cry. Hallmark movies? I sob like a baby."

"So don't watch them," Thistle fired back. "They're crap anyway. If you're going to watch something and affect our moods, go for the horror. At least that way we'll be in butt-kicking mode."

"Actually, I don't think we will," I countered. "Think about it. We feel emotionally overwhelmed when she's watching a sappy movie about a prince falling in love with his fair maiden, even though we'd be angry because it borders on sexual harassment if we watched it. We're feeling her feelings."

Thistle tapped her bottom lip, considering. "Ugh, you're right," she said after a beat. "I never really considered it, but you're totally right. If she watched a horror movie, we would spend the next eight hours terrified because she's afraid of slasher villains."

"I'm not afraid of them," Clove argued defiantly. "I just think they're ... stupid."

"Really?" Thistle didn't look convinced. "That wasn't you who insisted we sleep with the light on for a week after watching *A Nightmare on Elm Street* when we were, like, eighteen and nineteen?"

Clove balked. "That doesn't count. He's creepy. The others aren't creepy."

"I seem to remember you refusing to go into the woods for almost a month after we did a *Friday the 13th* marathon in middle school," I volunteered.

"He carries a machete and is deformed under that mask," Clove practically screeched. "He's terrifying."

"But you would make us strong after watching a horror movie." Thistle shook her head. "Crap! This means we have to confiscate her television until she's no longer pregnant so her fear doesn't overtake us at the worst possible time."

Clove stomped her foot. "You'll pry that television out of my cold, dead hands. I need my cooking shows."

"Which probably explains why I've been hungry for two months straight and have to lay flat on the bed to zip my pants lately," I said. "She watches the shows and we eat the calories."

"Oh, that's just crap!" Thistle stewed. "You're banned from watching cooking shows."

Clove was having none of it. "Then what am I allowed to watch? I need to entertain myself when you two are off having adventures without me. That's only fair."

Before the argument could devolve further, the chimes over the door jangled to signify someone entering. When I snapped my head up, I found Landon watching us with speculative eyes.

"Do I even want to know what you are fighting about now?" he asked, his gaze busy.

"Clove has been watching cooking shows and making us feel her emotions," Thistle snapped. "Now we're eating extra calories because of her. In essence, she's making us fat."

"Oh, well, things could be worse," Landon offered. "She could be watching horror movies and you guys could be quaking under your covers. Now that I think about it, I like that idea. You should go home and watch the entire *Halloween* series, Clove. That way I know Bay will be safe for the foreseeable future."

I shot him a quelling look. "How am I not safe? You see me standing here, right? I'm totally safe."

"Yes, well, you almost flew down a flight of stairs yesterday." He moved closer to me, his hand automatically moving to my forehead to check for a temperature. "You scared the crap out of me."

I grabbed his wrist before he could pull away. "I'm sorry. Now we know that Valerie's ghost is something to fear and we'll adjust our approach. You have nothing to worry about."

He held my gaze for a moment and then his expression softened. "I can't help worrying. I'm kind of fond of you." He leaned in and gave me a quick kiss. "Suck it up, because I can't help but worry. It is what it is."

"I guess." I exhaled heavily to center myself and then wrinkled my nose. "Did you just come from the bakery?"

"What? No." He shook his head. "Why?"

"You smell like ... ." I leaned forward and inhaled the heavenly aroma.

"Oh, he smells like warm doughnuts," Clove volunteered. She'd moved closer to Landon and was now practically plastered across his back. "And not just warm doughnuts, warm doughnuts with chocolate frosting and sprinkles."

"You can smell the sprinkles?" Landon pinned her with a warning look when her hands went to his back. "You can't rub yourself all over me like that."

"What? Oh, right." After what seemed a monumental effort, Clove snapped out of it. "I'll just be over here ... staring at the bakery." She moved to the window. I was almost positive she was salivating. "We should head over and get a snack or something," she said to Thistle.

"I just found out you've been making me eat empty calories for months," Thistle argued. "I can't have a doughnut now."

Clove whined. "The baby is really hungry. Do you want her to starve?"

Thistle rolled her eyes and shook her head before focusing on me. "Do you believe this? We have months of this to go."

I was barely listening because I couldn't get my mind off Landon. "Aunt Tillie must've decided doughnuts were better than cookies," I murmured, pressing close to Landon to sniff his neck. "I just ... think she might be the most brilliant woman in the world."

Landon arched an eyebrow, his lips curving. "She just might be," he agreed, switching course quickly. "Do you want to go back to your office and take a nap with me?"

"Sure," I answered automatically. All I could think about was the marvelous smell.

"She already took a nap," Thistle volunteered as she threw herself in the chair three feet away. She eyed Landon speculatively, but wisely kept her distance. "Goddess, you really do smell good. I wonder if she did the same thing to Marcus." She lifted her chin and peered out the window toward the converted barn she shared with her boyfriend, her expression unreadable. "Maybe I should go see if he wants to have a late lunch."

"Oh, no." Clove wagged her finger as she looked Landon up and down, her eyes clouded. "You're going to the bakery with me. You're not going anywhere with Marcus, because I won't see you for the rest of the afternoon and I don't want to be by myself."

Landon's hand was busy rubbing my back. "Clove and Thistle have plans to eat all day," he noted. "Let's go back to your office and do something else, huh?"

"I just told you she already took a nap," Thistle pointed out. "Apparently Mrs. Little woke her up. She had something important on her mind when she first got here, but she never told us what that something was. We got distracted when we realized Clove was making us gain weight — and now she can't stop sniffing you."

"I like that part." Landon wrapped his arms around me and I could feel his lips curve against my forehead. "I'll let you put sprinkles all over me if we can go back to your office right now," he offered.

I was just about to agree when I felt a sharp tug on my hair. Thistle had gotten up without me realizing and was now pulling me away from the best thing I'd ever smelled.

"You need to focus," she insisted, dragging me back to reality. "If you fall for this doughnut thing it'll reinforce what happens when we smell like bacon. It's just a scent. You have to keep your wits about you."

That was easy for her to say. "You're right," I sighed. "I just ... he smells so good." I tried to break free from Thistle and return to Landon, but she kept a firm hold on my hair.

"Don't embarrass me," Thistle warned. "You're a grown woman. Keep your urges under control. If you're not careful, you'll jump him in public and we'll never hear the end of it from Mrs. Little."

I knew she was right. That didn't mean the doughnut smell wasn't divine. "I just can't seem to think straight now that he's here. I can't explain it."

"You know what would be fun," Landon mused. "Aunt Tillie should make you smell like bacon and then we can mix the bacon and doughnut smells." He didn't seem bothered by the turn of events. "If she did that, we wouldn't ever leave our bed again. That sounds like a perfect existence."

"I think you would be bored in a few days," Thistle countered. "Besides, we need to focus on the reality of our situation and not how badly we all want to rush to the bakery and lick every doughnut on the premises."

"I want a custard-filled one," Clove said morosely.

"Doughnuts don't have custard," I said, completely distracted by Landon's intense musk. "That's an éclair, or a roll, or a long john. Doughnuts are something else entirely ... and I want one."

Amusement lit Landon's features. "This is kind of fun."

"You're just feeling powerful," Thistle shot back. "We felt the same way the first time she made us smell like bacon. The feeling didn't last because every creeper in the free world tried to feel us up that afternoon. It'll happen to you with aggressive women."

"I think I can fight off a handful of women."

"I hope so, because Bay will draw the brunt of the town's taunting if you don't. People will give her pitying looks, and you'll get tired of denying that you're cheating on her. It will cause emotional upheaval even though, in her heart, Bay knows you wouldn't cheat on her. It won't be nearly as much fun as you think."

"I ... ." Landon broke off and rubbed his chin. "I didn't think about any of that." He brushed the hair from my face. "How long do you think Aunt Tillie is going to play this game?"

That was a good question. "I have no idea."

"You guys have to be careful around one another," Thistle warned. "In fact, you'll have to be careful with dudes and chicks, Landon. It's not just women who like doughnuts."

Landon's face paled. "I did not think about that."

His response made me grin. "It's not so funny now that the curse is on the other foot, is it?"

"I ... we'll see." He refused to let go of his dream regarding me and the doughnut aroma. "I actually came here for a reason. Apparently some slimy real estate agent has already started making calls to find out who will inherit Heather's house. I wanted to know what you guys could tell me about him."

"Wayne." I crashed back to reality in a hurry. "I already talked to him today." I filled Landon in on my wake-up call from Mrs. Little and my visit with Wayne. When I finished, he seemed genuinely puzzled.

"What do you think is going on?" he asked. "There must be something about the land itself that's causing them to act this way."

"The only thing I can think of is the pirate story."

Landon made a face. "You mean the pirate of the Great Lakes?" He was dubious. "That story doesn't make a lick of sense. Why would Mrs. Little want that house so badly now? It's been around for years."

"Yeah, but it was owned by the Lakin family," Thistle volunteered. She'd pulled even farther away from Landon and refused to make eye contact. "They're really rich. Like ... Hollywood dynasty rich. They had a stake in Detroit's early automotive years if I remember correctly. They had that big house and came up about five times a year. It was a total waste. There were only two parcels on the lake, but Mrs. Little couldn't convince them to sell."

"And we took the bigger parcel when I bought the camp," Landon said. "Do you think this is a reaction to us buying that land?"

I shrugged. "I don't know. I plan to pull whatever information I can on the property this afternoon. Wayne was something of a jerk, so I threatened to send Aunt Tillie after him. I need to call her. She's not a fan, so she should have no problem terrorizing him. I also want to research Arlen Topper to see if I can come up with a reason people are so intrigued with that property in relation to his history."

"That seems like a safe afternoon." Landon grinned. "I wholeheartedly approve."

"They're also going to have a competition to see who's going to be godmother of my baby," Clove added, finally dragging herself away from the front window. There was a suspicious smear that made me wonder if she'd been licking the glass because of the doughnut smell. I decided to wait until after Landon left to ask her.

"We are?" Thistle's forehead creased. "I don't remember agreeing to that."

"Well, you guys dumped me for an adventure last night and I'm feeling left out," Clove argued. "I want a godmother competition to make up for it."

I hesitated. "I don't know that we have time for that right now," I said. "Can't it wait until we figure out what's going on with Valerie's ghost?"

"No." Clove stubbornly folded her arms over her chest. "It can't wait."

"And what if we don't want to play the game?" Thistle shot back. "What will you do then?"

"Watch old episodes of *Little House on the Prairie* and make you cry all day," Clove responded without hesitation.

Thistle and I sucked in twin breaths of horror.

"Fine," I said, resigned. "We'll play, but I need to do actual research, too."

Clove clapped her hands and beamed. "Yay!"

I was still grumbling when I walked Landon to the door. "What are you going to do?" I asked.

"Keep at it," he replied, grinning when I rubbed my nose against his neck. "Are you sure you don't want to take a nap with me?"

"Just stand there a minute. I need another hit to get me through the afternoon."

"As long as you need, sweetie. I'm here to make your life easier."

He said the words, but we both knew he was enjoying this way too much.

# SIXTEEN

"I'm not carrying that around." Thistle glared with overt hostility at the voodoo doll Clove had wrapped in a towel. "It's not going to happen."

Clove feigned patience. "You agreed to compete for godmother duties."

"That's not how I remember things." Thistle ducked her head and turned to avoid Clove's insistent hand. "I'm not carrying that thing around. You can't make me."

Clove cradled the rag doll against her chest. "Is that how you're going to treat my baby?"

"That's not your baby."

"It is for today's purposes."

"But it's not. You realize that's not really a baby?" Thistle turned her eyes to me. "Maybe we should lock her up until the kid is born. She's clearly losing it."

That elicited a scowl from Clove. "I'm well aware that it's not a real baby. I'm not an idiot."

Thistle didn't look convinced. "We should call our moms," she stage whispered.

"Oh, you suck." Clove threw herself in the chair, holding the rag doll against her chest as if it really did have feelings. "Don't listen to her, baby. She's going to love you ... eventually."

"Oh, good grief." Thistle fumed, but her glare was directed at me. "Stop laughing! This isn't remotely funny."

"Oh, it's funny." I rested my feet on the table. I'd been mixing godmother competition duties with research and had one of the private books from the back of the store open on my lap. "This says there are certain poltergeists that can't be controlled by a necromancer. It also says that they get more and more destructive, to the point they have to be destroyed."

"How do you destroy them?" Thistle was eager to disengage from the baby competition and focus on anything else. "Are we going to need a potion? A ritual maybe?"

"It doesn't say. I don't think it'll be easy, though. Floyd was a regular poltergeist and he took a bit of work."

"We weren't regularly practicing back then," Clove pointed out. "We were dabbling, which was a great disappointment to Aunt Tillie. We've been better lately."

She was right. "Yeah. I guess." I sighed. I still missed the heavenly doughnut smell. "You don't think women all over town are throwing themselves at Landon, do you?"

Thistle smirked as she settled on the couch. "Probably. I wouldn't worry about it too much. I'm pretty sure he's a one-witch man these days."

"He doesn't seem bothered by the prospect, though," I noted. "He could at least pretend to be upset."

"It's fun for him now, when you're the one rubbing up against him. When Mrs. Little starts doing it, then we'll hear some crying."

The thought hadn't occurred to me and I immediately brightened. "I bet he's going to have to talk to her, too, because of her visit to me. She tried to make me swear I wouldn't tell anyone about her interest in the property, but we all know I never intended to follow through."

"That's weird, right?" Clove shoved the doll at Thistle. "Hold her. *Love* her."

Thistle rolled her eyes but finally accepted the doll, resting it on her chest as if it weighed twenty pounds and she was having trouble breathing. "I don't want to hear another thing about this stupid doll. Do you understand?"

Clove ignored her. "Are we assuming that Heather killed Valerie and the ghost turned into a rage machine and killed Heather as part of some revenge plot?"

I shrugged. "That's one possibility. Another is that someone else killed Valerie and enlisted her ghost to turn against Heather because that property is important for some reason. There might still be a human killer out there."

Thistle snorted. "You do realize how stupid that sounds, right?"

"Welcome to our lives," I said dryly.

"What if it's a mixture of both?" Clove asked. "I mean, like, what if Heather and Eric conspired to kill Valerie and her ghost was enraged but someone else came along to enslave her to kill Heather?"

I opened my mouth to dispute the idea but then snapped it shut. It wasn't as out there as I initially believed. "I guess that's possible," I conceded. "It seems a bit of a stretch, but everything we're dealing with is kind of a stretch."

"You met Heather," Thistle prodded. "Do you think she was capable of murder?"

"She was ... a facade," I replied, turning to my memory of the incident. "She made a big show of welcoming us, but an underlying current of nerves permeated the house. The thing is, I can't decide if she was nervous because she actually did something or because she didn't want to be judged for having a relationship with a man already involved with someone else."

"I thought you said she denied knowing Eric and Valerie were a thing," Clove interjected.

"She did, but I don't believe her. She might not have known at the very start, but I think she knew before everything came to a head. Eric is a tool. He probably started putting the moves on her right away. If Valerie was working in the same office, how hard is it to pick up on those vibes?"

"Good point." Clove bobbed her head and tapped her bottom lip. "If Sam ever cheats on me and his girlfriend kills me, I'm totally coming back as a poltergeist to haunt both of them. Valerie has the right idea. Revenge should be terrible ... and apparently she's good at it."

Thistle and I exchanged amused glances. That was such a Clove thing to say.

"I don't think you have to worry about that," I reassured her. "Sam is completely in love with you."

"And, from what I can tell, he's thrilled at the prospect of becoming a father," Thistle added. "I think you're okay."

Clove straightened. "I'm just saying. I think some things are worth turning into a poltergeist for."

That was also a Clove thing to say. "If Landon ever cheats on me I'll send Aunt Tillie after him. I won't even have to dirty my hands. She comes in handy for certain things, which is why I sent her after Wayne."

"I don't know why you went to him at all," Thistle said. "Why not go to Eric? He completed the sale to Heather. He would know more about her family ties."

"Yes, but Wayne was representing Mrs. Little, and she's the one so excited that the property may be on the market again," I countered. "Wayne is all kinds of dirty. It's possible Eric is simply stupid."

"He cheated on Valerie," Clove spat. "That makes him evil."

"Or weak," Thistle argued. "It sounds to me as if Val was clingy and Eric stayed with her out of habit. When Heather came along, he decided he wanted something else but had a hard time breaking ties."

"Yes, but did he fall for Heather because he was genuinely attracted to her, or because she had money falling out of her butt?" I asked. "His motivations are murky either way, but one makes things so much worse."

"That's a fair point," Thistle acknowledged. "Maybe we should head over to Eric's office and question him. Clove can watch the store."

"No way." Clove immediately started shaking her head. "I won't be left out again. Not two days in a row."

"You know we didn't cut you out of what happened last night to be mean," I challenged. "We were doing what we thought was right for you."

"Yes, keeping me from s'mores." Clove jutted out her lower lip. "You guys are just using the baby as a reason to cut me out of things. That's how you are."

"That's not true," I protested, annoyed. "Dani is dangerous. You would make an easy mark if she wanted to terrorize us. The only thing keeping her in check is fear of Aunt Tillie. She might overlook that fear if she thought she could control us by threatening your baby."

"She's also afraid of you," Thistle argued, her gaze pointed when it landed on me. "She knows you took out her aunt. It's you she wants to pay back."

I swallowed hard. "I'm well aware."

"That means she could go after Landon," Thistle persisted. "I know you want to believe she's still capable of being saved, but I don't believe it. She's biding her time and will attack at the exact worst moment, like when we're trying to fight off a murderous ghost bent on revenge.

"As for you, Clove, we really are trying to protect you," she continued. "I'm pretty sure the baby shouldn't be around waves of negative energy. That's all that's flying around whenever Aunt Tillie and Dani get in close proximity to one another."

Clove wasn't quite ready to cede the point. "Yeah, but you guys made the decision to cut me out before you even knew Aunt Tillie was coming."

That was true. "We still don't want Dani to use you as a weapon," I insisted. "It's better for you not to be around her."

"So ... just you and Thistle are going to be in constant danger?" Clove looked perplexed. "I guess I can live with that." The smile she shot Thistle was mischievous. "By the way, you won the godmother competition."

Thistle was taken aback. "Me? Why did I win? Bay answered more of the questions correctly."

"Yes, but you purposely tried to get them wrong." Clove's tone was breezy. "Besides, we do it in a circle. If you're my baby's godmother then Bay has to be your baby's godmother. I'm pretty sure you're going to give birth to the antichrist when it's your turn."

I straightened in my seat. That hadn't occurred to me. I pictured Clove as the ultimate helicopter mom. That was essentially the worst possible scenario. I hadn't considered what sort of evil Thistle would birth. "Wait. I think we should start the competition over. I wasn't really trying the first time."

"Oh, no." Thistle looked a little too pleased with herself. "Things worked out exactly as they were supposed to. This way I have to deal with Sam instead of Landon for the Wiccaning. I'm liking how this turned out."

Ugh. I should've thought this through. "Well, great. I ... ." I trailed off when the chimes over the door signaled Aunt Tillie's entrance. She swept in with her cape trailing behind her — and she wasn't alone.

"Hey, Annie." Thistle perked up and dropped the voodoo doll on the couch, completely discarding it, much to Clove's chagrin. "How's it going?"

Annie Martin and Thistle were close. It was Thistle who first noticed the dazed young girl stumbling down the road in front of the inn. She'd been in an accident with her mother Belinda, and it was only through magic that we managed to save the older woman.

Annie and Belinda had lived in the attic room at the inn for several months. Belinda worked for our mothers, saving money so she could eventually get her own place. Even though she was given the option to continue living at the inn rent free until she put more money away, Belinda opted to rent another place closer to town. She had her reasons, and one of them was the fact that Annie was so infatuated with Aunt Tillie that she began to emulate her at times.

Aunt Tillie was put in charge of our care quite often when we were kids. She was something of a reluctant (and absent-minded) babysitter. She found trouble at least three times a week when she was supposed to be watching us. As grateful as Belinda was for everything we'd done for her, she recognized potential trouble and had opted to move out on her own. She didn't want to keep Annie from Aunt Tillie, but she did want to limit their time together. Aunt Tillie didn't realize how her actions affected young minds, and with a huge pot field behind the inn — something Annie believed was oregano — Belinda put her foot down.

I believed Aunt Tillie was still sore about it.

"Hi, Thistle." Annie immediately went to the couch and climbed up beside my dark and twisted cousin. They had an unshakeable bond, and as fond as Annie was of the rest of us, Thistle would always be her favorite. "What are you guys doing?"

"We just had a competition to see who's going to be godmother to Clove's baby," Thistle replied, her smile smug. "I won."

Aunt Tillie snorted at the news. "Oh, you didn't think that one out, did you, Bay?" She shook her head and made a tsking sound. "Now you'll have to be godmother to Thistle's baby."

"Are you having a baby?" Annie's eyes went wide.

"I'm not having a baby," Thistle reassured her. "I'm not even married yet."

"My mom says Clove wasn't married when she got pregnant."

Now it was my turn to smirk. "Yes, Clove was a bad girl." I earned a scathing look from my cousin. "Thistle won't be a bad girl like that."

"Yeah." Annie nodded, her expression thoughtful. "I haven't seen you guys in forever."

Guilt washed over me. In truth, spending time with Annie had been a priority when she was staying at the inn — mostly because we thought breaks from Aunt Tillie were a necessity — but things had spiraled for us in the months since she'd moved out and we hadn't seen her much.

"We're sorry," Thistle offered. "It's been a crazy time."

"Because Clove got pregnant before she got married?"

Thistle nodded without hesitation. "That's exactly why."

"I hate you," Clove hissed, her eyes narrowing. "You're just the worst."

Aunt Tillie smirked and moved to the other side of the couch, leaving Thistle sandwiched between her and Annie. "I ran into Annie downtown. Belinda was shopping and Annie was bored, so she gets to spend some time with me. And her mother gets a bit of a break. It's a win-win scenario."

"What were you doing when you ran into them?" I asked.

"Stalking Wayne Lawson." Aunt Tillie didn't bother denying the truth. It wasn't in her nature. "He's a piece of crap, by the way. You were right about him being in cahoots with Margaret. I saw him going into her shop. Of course, he saw me too. I thought he was going to crap himself."

The image made me smile. "Well, that's something, right? Why do you think she wants the property?"

"I have no idea, but I plan to find out. If she gets that house, she'll be happy. You know how I feel when she's happy."

"Yes, you're bereft of joy," I agreed. My mind drifted to Hazel. "Have you checked in at the campground today? We promised her regular breaks from Dani."

"No, but I plan to go out there once I drop Annie back with Belinda," Aunt Tillie replied. "I'm in the mood to terrorize someone and Dani makes as enticing a target as anyone."

"Is Dani the girl that used the birds?" Annie asked, her expression dark.

Surprised, I flicked my eyes to her. "How do you know about that?"

"I heard the birds whispering."

It wasn't the first time I'd suspected that Annie had a bit of magic in her. In fact, the more time went on the more I suspected Annie was going to be a powerful witch — with the proper training. Her mother was aware that we wanted to spend time with her, mold her, but Belinda had been reticent. The bird information was troubling.

"What did the birds say?" I asked.

"They said she was bad," Annie replied, rubbing her cheek. "They also said you knew she was bad and didn't do anything to stop her."

"Me personally?"

"All of you," Annie said. "I don't understand why you're spending time with her instead of me. I can do stuff too. Shouldn't you want to spend time with me?"

I caught Thistle's gaze and saw she was feeling the same level of guilt.

"We want to spend time with you," Thistle reassured her quickly. "In fact, we're going to carve out some special time for you. We just need to make sure nothing else bad happens with Dani first."

"Why can't I be with you when you're doing that?"

"Because ... um ... ."

"It's not safe." Aunt Tillie swooped in to save Thistle. "I already told you that. You need to let it go for now. We'll figure something out as soon as this crisis is behind us."

"That's what you always say." Annie was petulant. "I miss hanging out with you guys."

"We miss hanging out with you," I said. "I'm sorry we've been so distracted. With Clove getting pregnant ... and then married ... and then the thing with the birds, we've been sort of negligent. We'll fix that going forward, I promise."

"Okay." Annie offered up a shrug and then turned back to Aunt Tillie. "Mom said we only have an hour and you said I could ride your scooter."

Aunt Tillie bobbed her head. "Absolutely. Let's do that." Her gaze met mine over Annie's head as they moved toward the door. Her message was clear. We needed to do better. Finding more hours in a day was going to be difficult.

Annie was a young witch who could do great things without going down the wrong path. We had to somehow encourage her.

# SEVENTEEN

I was still agitated about the godmother situation when Landon met me in the inn library before dinner.

"Hello, love of my life," he teased, leaning over to give me a kiss before he plopped down on the sofa next to me. When I didn't respond, his expression fell. "Don't I smell like doughnuts any longer? I thought for sure you would be on me the minute I walked through the door."

"What?" I jerked up my head and met his gaze. "Did you say something?"

"Oh, just feel the love." He mock grabbed at his heart and studied my face. "What's wrong with you? I expected to be your favorite person tonight. I thought for sure we were going to have to take dinner to go because you wouldn't be able to hold out."

He looked genuinely disappointed. "Well, you don't smell like doughnuts any longer."

He made a face. "That figures. Aunt Tillie knew I was enjoying myself and ruined it for me."

"Maybe. The doughnut smell is definitely gone. You do smell like something." I leaned forward and gave him a long sniff before screwing up my face in repugnance. "Cherry pie."

"Hey! That's not the face I want to see." He jabbed his finger at me. "You're supposed to find me irresistible. That face doesn't say irresistible."

He wasn't wrong. "No," I agreed. "It says 'I don't like cherry pie.'"

He stilled. "I've seen you eat cherry pie."

"When?"

"I ... ." He trailed off, his mind clearly busy. "Huh. You don't like cherry pie, do you? Blueberry? Yes. Blackberry? Absolutely. Apple? Hand me the whipped cream. You don't just dislike cherry pie, you dislike cherries in general."

I was amused it took him that long to figure it out. "Sorry to disappoint you."

"No, it's my bad. I knew you didn't like cherries. I always found it weird because we live so close to the cherry capital. You avoid cherry-flavored everything."

"That's not entirely true," I hedged. "I will drink cherry-flavored Diet Seven-Up ... and grenadine."

"That doesn't make me feel better." He propped his feet on the table and gave me a sidelong look. "I wonder why I smell like cherry pie instead of doughnuts."

"Probably because Aunt Tillie is testing the curse. She wants to see what aromas appeal to whom and then use them as weapons later."

"I want to go back to doughnuts."

I smirked. "How many women threw themselves at you today?"

"Only three — that's not including you, because we didn't quite get that far. And the mailman was a little friendly."

I laughed, delighted. "How did you fight them off?"

"It wasn't as difficult as you might think. I just repeatedly told them I was dating you and they were terrified enough to back off."

I didn't believe that. "And?"

"And I might've told them that you would put Aunt Tillie on the job if they didn't give me space. It turns out fear of Aunt Tillie is stronger than love of doughnuts. Who knew?"

That sounded right. I probably would've gone the same route. "Did you learn anything important today?"

"I learned Eric Savage is a complete and total jerk."

"I kind of figured that out myself."

"He's already trying to ascertain who can lay claim to Heather's house," Landon said. "When I mentioned that Wayne Lawson was also poking around, along with Mrs. Little, he almost had a meltdown. He couldn't get us out of his office fast enough."

That wasn't what I wanted to hear. "What about Heather? Was he broken up about her?"

"Well, that's the thing ... ." Landon rubbed his chin, debating. "He put on a good show for the first five minutes or so, but toward the end it was clear all he cared about was the property. He wanted to know who would be able to claim it. When I said we hadn't gotten that far yet, he was angry."

"Huh."

"Yeah, I mean ... he basically kicked us out of his office."

"That's interesting. At least, I guess it is."

"It's definitely interesting," he agreed, linking his fingers with mine and leaning his head so our hair flowed together. "I don't know what to make of it."

That made two of us. "It keeps coming back to that property."

"It does. What can you tell me about it?"

"I know the basics. The original structure, at least according to property records, which only go back so far, was a log cabin. At some point a house was built, and then torn down, and then another house was built. The Lakins had property on a different lake before, so they were familiar with the area, but they were always looking to upgrade. That's how they ended up close to the campground.

"The Lakins bought the house and tore it down ... and when I say tore it down, I mean they bulldozed it in a single day. We were in high school at the time and it was a big deal. Everyone came out to the old camp to watch."

"You saw that house being torn down?"

"Yeah. Why is that important?"

"I don't know that it is, but I'm intrigued. I don't suppose you remember if you saw people searching the property when you were out there that day?"

I hesitated. "Not that I recall. Why?"

He shrugged. "I don't know. That Great Lakes pirate story has my mind going in a million different directions."

"You think that Arlen Topper's money was buried on that property, don't you?"

"I think someone believes that," he clarified. "Whether it's true or not is anybody's guess. I mean, it's possible that's just some local legend with no basis in fact. It's also possible that the money was discovered decades ago and the finder never said anything."

I hadn't considered that. "Do you think the potential of finding the money is enough to kill two people?"

"I can't say that I believe with absolute certainty that Valerie and Heather were killed by the same person. It's possible that Heather killed Valerie and the ghost killed her in retribution."

"It's possible," I agreed. "It's also possible that Heather killed Valerie and someone took advantage of Valerie's ghost to kill Heather and steal the house."

"So many possibilities," he sighed. "That doesn't make our job easier."

He brought my hand up and pressed a kiss to my palm, grinning when I shook my head.

"You're feeling romantic."

He shrugged. "I was feeling much more romantic when I thought you'd rip my clothes off to see if all of me smelled like doughnuts. I'm still a little bitter about that. But I don't need the possibility of having my wardrobe shredded to rev things up."

"I'm shocked." I laughed when he kissed my cheek. "Don't you want to hear about my day?"

His expression reflected doubt when he pulled back. "I don't know. Last time I saw you was at Hypnotic, and your cousin was going to make you participate in a competition to determine the godmother of her unborn baby."

"I lost, by the way."

"Really? Are you sad?"

"I wasn't until I realized that Thistle winning will set in motion a chain of events that will reverberate through the rest of our lives."

He snorted. "That was Aunt Tillie-level dramatic."

He had a point, which I found grating. "If Thistle is godmother to Clove's baby, that means Clove will be our baby's godmother and I'll be godmother to Thistle's baby."

It was a convoluted chain, but Landon caught on right away. "Oh, man. That means we'll be godparents to Satan's urchin."

I laughed so hard I almost choked. "And you say I'm dramatic." I wiped the tears from my eyes. "Clove set the whole thing up to avoid being godmother to Thistle's kid."

"Of course she did." He pursed his lips. "You know," he said after a beat, "Marcus will be the father of any kid Thistle pops out. There's a chance it could be the best-behaved kid in the world. We're casting aspersions on a child that hasn't even been conceived."

"That's a very rational response. Just out of curiosity, who do you think will win in a battle of genes? Here's a hint: The Winchesters never lose."

His smile widened. "I guess that means there's a little blond mischief-maker in our future."

He'd been open lately to talking about children. He said he was in no hurry, but we'd visited Aunt Tillie's version of the future in a curse and he'd fallen in love with one of the daughters she showed us. He wasn't exactly fond of the other two, but he became quite attached to the one. I worried that he would be disappointed if he didn't get that exact child.

"We saw Annie today, too," I said, changing the subject. "Her nose is out of joint because we haven't been spending time with her."

"We haven't," he acknowledged. "I feel a little bad now that you mention it. I hadn't even considered it before."

"I tried explaining that we were busy with Clove's wedding. She overheard someone say that Clove got pregnant before being married and she won't stop mentioning it."

"We can make time for her," he said. "Come up with an outing and we'll take her somewhere. What about that weird museum with all the dead animals we went to a few months ago? She might like that."

"She might," I agreed. "The thing is, she brought up Dani. She wants to know why we're spending time with someone who was bad when she has magic too. She thinks we should be focused on her."

"We don't know that she has magic," Landon countered. "We assume — and we think she can see ghosts. She might be a normal little girl who sees the occasional spirit."

That was wishful thinking on his part, and I understood why he wanted to believe that. "You know that it's likely any kids we have will be witches, right?"

"I know." He squeezed my hand tighter. "I'm fine with that. It'll suck when we have a five-year-old who thinks it's funny to mess with me because I don't have magic, but we'll teach her respect and it will be fine. Annie is different."

"Why?"

"Because Belinda isn't a witch as far as I can tell. She doesn't know what signs to look for. She doesn't know how to help. You guys do, but you're not her mother."

I understood. "She won't stop at seeing ghosts. She told us she heard the birds talking.

"Mom and the aunts tried sitting Belinda down and talking to her after she first saw a ghost, but I get the feeling it didn't go that well," I continued. "Belinda didn't come out and call them crazy, but I think she wanted to."

"I don't," Landon countered. "I think fear made her want to shut them down because she couldn't fathom the sort of life her daughter would be forced to live if some of the horrific images she pictured came to fruition. She didn't think your mothers were crazy. She just wanted them to be crazy."

Oddly, that made sense. "If Annie heard the birds talking, her powers are growing pretty fast."

"What did she hear the birds say?"

"It wasn't words. She heard the birds cackling and knew they were communicating. On some level, she might've even sensed their fear. She doesn't realize what she heard. She's still too young for that. But it will come. It's not far off."

"Well, then we'll deal with it. Annie is a part of this family, whether Belinda wants to shield her from the craziness or not. We'll come up with a way to approach Belinda and explain what's happening. It just has to wait until after we deal with the crazy ghost ... and Dani ... and whatever other mayhem pops up between now and then. We'll figure it out."

"You sound so sure."

"I have faith that we can do anything as long as we're together." He leaned forward and pressed a kiss to the corner of my mouth. "That includes eating our weight in whatever fattening dinner your mother and aunts have conjured up this evening."

I laughed. "As long as there's no cherry pie for dessert."

He frowned. "Aunt Tillie and I are going to have a talk. This is not how this curse was supposed to go."

"I'm sure she'll jump at the chance to rectify it."

"No, she won't, but we're still going to have a talk."


**"IT'S ONLY TWO MILLION DOLLARS,"** Aunt Tillie whined as we made our way into the dining room. She sat at her usual spot at the head of the table, using her outdoor voice as she implored my mother. "I'll pay you back."

Mom was incredulous. "Where are you going to get two million dollars?" she challenged. "Where do you think we're going to get two million dollars?"

"Put the inn up as collateral," Aunt Tillie suggested.

"Absolutely not." Mom locked her jaw as we took our usual chairs. "It's about time," she barked, causing my shoulders to hop.

"And a happy how-do-you-do to you," Landon drawled.

Mom extended a finger in his direction. "Don't push me. I'm not in a very good mood."

"So we noticed," Thistle offered from the other end of the table. She sat next to Clove, who was enthusiastically pointing out items in a catalog of baby necessities (and not-so-necessities). Thistle looked as if she would've preferred being anywhere else, including back in fairy tale land, which was saying something.

"This is the Rolls Royce of baby changing tables," Clove explained. "It has a safety lip so the baby won't roll off and break her head."

"It's lovely," Thistle said. "I mean ... it's clearly the changing table to end all changing tables." Her eyes sought — and found — me. "I'll totally trade you godmother duties. We can stick Clove with my kid. I'll teach it terrible spells in the womb."

"We've already decided you're the baby's godmother," Clove argued, her tone clipped. "There's no getting out of it."

Watching Clove with the catalog made me wonder if I hadn't ended up with the better end of the deal after all. Thistle's kid was likely to have the worst mouth imaginable, but there were worse things.

"Why does Aunt Tillie want two million dollars?" Landon asked, grabbing a roll from the basket at the center of the table. "She's not trying to buy a homestead on the moon again, is she?"

"Don't be ridiculous," Aunt Tillie snapped. "I didn't want a homestead on the moon. I wanted one on Mars. When the apocalypse comes, you'll be glad I thought ahead. Now, stuff your mouth full of bread and shut up."

She turned a set of imploring eyes to me. "Tell your mother I'm good for the two million dollars."

That had to be one of the top ten oddest things I'd ever heard come out of Aunt Tillie's mouth. "What do you want the money for?" I asked, accepting half a roll from Landon. I was a firm believer if he ripped apart the roll and buttered it, the calories didn't land on my thighs. What? That's totally feasible.

"Don't worry about why I want the money," Aunt Tillie growled, grabbing a carrot stick from the appetizer tray and handing it to Peg under the table. The pig looked more interested in the cake, but she accepted the carrot, making a face as she chewed.

"She wants to buy that house across from the campground," Marnie volunteered. "The one where that woman died last night. She wants to buy it because Margaret Little wants it. She's determined to steal it out from under her."

Oh, well, I should've seen that coming. "I don't think we have the money to put a down payment on that place," I said. "As much as I enjoy torturing Mrs. Little, I think this one is out of our reach."

"Oh, don't be ridiculous," Aunt Tillie snapped. "Buying the house is simply the easiest way to annoy Margaret. It's not the only way. I have a whole list of actions that will drive her insane. If your mother won't help me with the first, I'll move on to the second."

"Which is what?" Landon asked.

"Which is going out there and finding the pirate treasure before she can."

"Great." Landon grabbed another roll. "Sounds like tons of fun."

"I'm glad you approve." Aunt Tillie's snarky side was on full display. "I plan to borrow your girlfriend and Thistle to help me."

"Hey! You're not leaving me out again," Clove snapped. "There's no danger in looking for pirate treasure."

"There is when we're looking on land a rampaging poltergeist haunts," Aunt Tillie pointed out.

I could practically see the gears in Clove's mind working as she reconsidered. "Hmm. Good point. I guess you can take Bay and Thistle. I want my cut of the booty if you find it, though. That only seems fair since I'm being cut out of the action."

"No problem." Aunt Tillie rolled her eyes until they landed on me. "What do you say? Do you want to look for pirate treasure with me?"

"Of course not," Landon answered for me, his mouth full of food. "There's no treasure out there."

"I wasn't asking you." Aunt Tillie made a face. "I'm serious, Bay. If Margaret is this hot to trot to get her hands on that property, there must be a reason. We can figure out why and beat her at her own game."

I had to admit the notion had a certain appeal. "Well, maybe." I cast a sidelong look at Landon, who appeared surprised. "I'm only going to make sure Aunt Tillie doesn't get in trouble. I'll act as a chaperone."

He didn't look convinced. "You're an adult. You make your own decisions. I have no say in this."

That seemed too easy. "You won't try to stop us from looking for pirate treasure on the property of the murdered woman?"

"Nope. I figure if you're out there with a group you'll be safe from the crazy poltergeist." He swallowed his mouthful. "I also think Aunt Tillie will reward me by bringing the doughnut smell back because I'm being agreeable."

I knew there had to be a catch.

"What? You don't like the rotating smells?" Aunt Tillie queried.

"Bay doesn't like cherries."

"Is that what that smell is?" Twila, who was walking behind Landon, leaned closer and sniffed his hair. "I love cherries."

The look on Landon's face was priceless. "I want to go back to doughnuts ... and I want Bay to be the only one to smell it."

"That's a tall order," Aunt Tillie said. "If I do that, I need you to promise me three passes from the law."

He frowned. "Do you have some big heist planned?"

"Don't worry about it."

I expected him to outright turn her down. Instead, he took me by surprise. "Make it so only Bay can smell it and you have a deal."

I was dumbfounded. "I can't believe you're letting her shake you down."

He shook his head. "Please. At most she's going to terrorize Margaret Little with more scooter shenanigans or possibly transport her wine across state lines. I can pretend to look the other way on both."

"What if she does something else?"

"We'll deal with it if it happens."

Aunt Tillie grinned. "I'm starting to like you more and more, even if you are 'The Man.'"

Landon returned her smile. "Right back at you."

"We're two peas in a pod," Aunt Tillie enthused. "And not the mushy ones."

That right there was a frightening thought.

# EIGHTEEN

It was still early enough in the season that the night air was crisp as we walked back to the guesthouse. In another two or three weeks, the nights would turn steamy. Landon said he preferred those nights because it meant we could roll around on the ground without freezing. I liked them because there was always magic in the air — especially on the bluff — that was hard to put a name to. I figured he felt the same thing, even if he didn't know how to put a name to it.

"What are you thinking?" Landon asked as he linked his fingers with mine and started swinging our joined hands.

I smiled at the playful interaction. "I don't know. Just thinking."

"No, you're chewing on something," he countered, releasing my hand and moving quickly enough to get a running start before landing on a large boulder. He stood several feet taller than me now and looked down, like a king surveying his kingdom. "I want to know what you're thinking."

I held out my hands and shrugged as I watched him move around the surface. "I can't wrap my head around everything that has happened," I admitted. "There are too many possibilities. I think I prefer having a definite direction to look in rather than trying to wade through eight threads, all of which overlap."

He blinked several times and then shook his head. "That's what you're thinking? I thought for sure I smelled like doughnuts again and you were trying to resist your urges."

That made me laugh. In fact, I laughed so hard I had to bend at the waist to catch my breath. "Oh, geez. I don't think I realized when we first met that you were such a comedian."

He hopped down and wrapped his arms around me, pulling me tight. "The doughnut smell is coming. I have faith that Aunt Tillie will uphold her end of the bargain."

"Yeah, I can't believe you agreed to that bargain. What happens if she gets in trouble digging up Heather's yard?"

Landon shrugged, noncommittal. "Then she becomes that shirt-tail relative of my girlfriend, a woman I barely know."

I chuckled, my fingers going to his cheek. "Funny and handsome."

"And in twenty minutes I'm going to smell like every dirty dream you've ever had of me." He leaned into my hand as it cupped his cheek. "Tell me what you're thinking, Bay. I know you've got more than just potential Great Lakes pirate booty on your mind. Talk."

He could read me well. I wasn't sure when it happened. Somewhere along the way, he'd become the person who knew me best. Given the fact that I'd grown up with Clove and Thistle, it should've been impossible.

And yet here we were.

"I need you to stay away from the campground," I said.

Whatever he was expecting, that wasn't it. His eyes went wide. "Why? I like it out there. I thought we would spend the summer having private bonfires and campouts."

"We can't do that with a teenager on the premises."

"And how long do you plan to keep her there?"

"I ... don't ... know. Until I'm certain she's not a danger to anyone. I don't think that's going to happen overnight."

"Bay, it's not going to happen at all." Landon let out a frustrated sigh and released me. I immediately missed his warmth but held my ground. "I love you more than anything in this world, Bay, but you have certain blind spots. Dani is one of those blind spots."

"She's a kid."

"Kids her age can be tried as adults."

"She can't be tried," I argued. "There's no evidence against her. You're in law enforcement. You must see that."

"Actually, I don't see that, Bay." Landon leaned against the boulder and pushed his hair from his eyes. "I was there when everything went down. You took them on alone — and I'm still annoyed about that — but I heard what was said. She was part of it. She wasn't some innocent kid being used without her knowledge. She was fine being used."

That was true, and I didn't like being reminded of it. "Landon, I don't want to argue about this." The argument kept circling and circling and neither one of us could give it up. It had grown tiresome. Fear fueled both of us. We couldn't simply ignore the potential argument when our entire future was riding on the outcome.

I turned my back to him and stared at the thick trees surrounding the property. "I know you don't understand why I can't cut her loose, but if she hurts someone else I feel as if that will be on me. I don't want that."

He blew out a sigh. "I don't want it either, sweetie." He moved in behind me and draped himself over my back, kissing my neck as he rubbed his cheek against mine. "I'm afraid, Bay." His voice was barely a whisper. "She's not a little girl. She could do a lot of damage on her way down ... and I'm afraid she's going to do that damage to you.

"You are brave ... and strong ... and you have the absolute best heart," he continued. "You make me laugh, too." His lips caused my skin to break out in goose pimples as he kissed the back of my neck. "But sometimes you're an easy mark because you want to believe in others so fervently that you don't see what's right in front of you."

"I'm not naive, Landon," I insisted. "I know she's not going to change overnight."

"You have to want to change to make it happen, Bay. She doesn't want to change. She's going to bide her time until she thinks you're not looking and then run. I think there's a legitimate chance she will try to wreak as much havoc as possible right up until the point she disappears. I don't want you to be caught unaware when that happens."

I pursed my lips. "What do you want me to do?" I asked finally.

"Stay safe."

"At what cost? We can't turn her loose out into the world knowing that she could kill again. We can't lock her up because she's powerful enough to hurt people should they try to cut her off from the outside world. That only leaves ... killing her." I swallowed hard. "Can you live with that?"

"What answer will make you feel better?" He was unnaturally calm. His body was warm pressed against mine, and I felt settled despite the potential tempest approaching. "I want you safe more than anything else in this world. I get that you see her as a child, but she's more than that. She's an adult ... and potentially deadly if we're not careful.

"You don't want me at the campground because you think she'll hurt me," he continued. "I'm not magical. You're tiptoeing around the topic even though we've discussed it before. You didn't get the response you really wanted, so here we are again.

"You believe I won't be able to defend myself," he continued. "You don't want to come out and say it because you're convinced it will damage my ego, but it's written all over your face."

I protested. "No. I know you're strong. You're brave, too. It's just ... you won't sense the attack if it comes. You can't, because you're not a witch. That's not meant to be an insult."

"I'm not insulted, but I am curious. Will you be able to sense when an attack is coming? If so, that will make me feel better ... even if I am worried about what sort of fight you might find yourself mired in."

"I'll sense it." I was almost positive that was true. I turned in his arms to face him. "It's going to be okay. We'll figure this out."

"How? You need to take the time to come up with real solutions if we want to get ahead on this, and I don't think you're there yet. You're too focused on Valerie Lennox and her crazy ghost, which I agree is a problem. You can't split your focus. I don't want you to, because it makes you vulnerable.

"Eventually, though, we'll have to deal with this," he continued. "I don't know what's going to happen. I don't want to be cut out of the decision. I want you to promise me we can work together and make sure that we get the best possible outcome for all those concerned when it's finally time."

I stared into the fathomless depths of his eyes and nodded. He needed to be part of the team, and I was terrified of making the wrong decision. This was definitely something we would have to do together.

"Just as soon as we get through the poltergeist problem — or whatever it is we're dealing with — we'll sit down and discuss it."

"Thank you." He rested his forehead against mine and gave me a soft kiss. "I love you, Bay."

A lump formed in my throat. He was so earnest. "I love you too."

He was quiet for a few moments, swaying back and forth as he held me tight. Then he whispered again and it caused my heart to fill with love.

"Do I smell like a warm doughnut with sprinkles yet?"

"I'm sure it will be soon."

**LANDON'S CURSE HADN'T KICKED IN** by the time we got back to the guesthouse, which was a great disappointment to him. After taking a bath, I decided to track down the bacon-scented perfume he'd purchased as a gift for Valentine's Day so we could have a little fun.

I couldn't find it.

"What are you doing?" Landon looked genuinely alarmed when he walked into the bedroom and found me going through his sock drawer.

"Nothing." I tried to act innocent, but I was bad at it. "Um ... nothing important."

His eyebrows migrated higher on his forehead as he moved closer to me. "Do you need something? Are your feet cold?"

"No. I just ... um ... ." I shouldn't have felt guilty. We lived together, for crying out loud. His expression made me feel like a kid caught doing something terrible. "I was just looking for the perfume." I lowered my eyes.

"What perfume?" His voice was even but his body remained coiled.

"The bacon perfume." I sucked in a breath. "I thought I might wear it to make you feel better about the doughnut thing."

"Oh." He almost looked relieved, which seemed ridiculous under the circumstances. "That's up here." He nudged me away from the dresser and closed the sock drawer with his foot, opening the top drawer instead. He handed the perfume to me and smiled. "I know people say that two spritzes are enough, but you can never wear too much bacon perfume."

"Okay." I felt suddenly out of touch with him. "I didn't mean to go through your stuff. I didn't think it was a big deal."

"It's fine," he said, waving off my half-hearted apology. "I just thought you needed something specific. Don't worry about it."

He said the right things, but I still felt off kilter. "Okay, well ... I guess I'll put this on. Do you want to watch a movie or something?"

"Absolutely." He leaned in and gave me a kiss that felt stiff even though it was a normal exchange. "Let's watch something that gets you in a romantic mood."

"So ... *Practical Magic?*"

He smirked. "You read my mind."


**THE FOLLOWING MORNING I** was still bothered by the exchange at the dresser. Landon was up before me and had already showered when I crawled out of bed. His eyes moved from his reflection in the mirror to me as I dragged a hand through my hair.

"You're running late this morning." He looked a little too smug. "You need to get moving if we're going to make breakfast at the inn."

"Okay." I was slow getting out of bed. "I'll hop in the shower."

"Did I tire you out?"

I knew what he wanted to hear. "You're a god amongst men."

"I already knew that." He leaned in to give me a kiss and I caught a distinctive scent.

"Oh, you smell like doughnuts again."

He pumped his fist. "You had better be the only one to notice. If she screwed me two days in a row I'll wrestle her down and dump pickled okra on her."

"She hates pickled okra."

"I'm willing to fight dirty to get what I want this go-around."

"I'll get in the shower. I'm kind of hungry."

"That's because I tired you out." He sent me a wink and then moved toward the door. "I'll make some coffee. You look as if you could use some caffeine."

He wasn't wrong. "Yeah. I just need to grab some clothes and a quick shower. I should be ready in twenty minutes."

"Sounds good."

I watched him go, this time without the warm sensation that usually permeated my body when I was close to him. His reaction to me looking in the sock drawer still bothered me a great deal.

I knew it was wrong even as I was doing it, and yet I couldn't stop myself. Within seconds of him leaving the bedroom, I was on my knees and his sock drawer was open. I rummaged through the contents quickly — the last thing I wanted was to get caught again — but came up empty. Frustration roiled as I searched again, but there was absolutely nothing there.

Had he moved whatever he was trying to hide? I was convinced there was something in the drawer he didn't want me to see. Was I imagining everything because I was losing my mind? It was possible Clove was influencing my emotions again, but that didn't feel right. This was more personal.

I searched one more time and then heaved out a sigh before closing the drawer. Why was I acting like this? I had zero reason not to trust him, and yet I was positive he'd almost exploded when he found me in the drawer the previous evening.

Was he hiding something, or was I overreacting? One outcome seemed much more likely, but I remained unsettled.

What was happening?

. . .

**AUNT TILLIE WAS DRESSED IN COLORFUL** leggings and her combat helmet at the dining room table when we joined the usual crew for breakfast. Thistle and Clove weren't present — they came for dinner more than any other meal — but everyone else was already eating as we sat down.

"There had better be bacon left," Landon grumbled, shooting me a look.

"You're late," Mom noted, sipping her coffee. "Perhaps you don't deserve bacon if you're going to be late."

"Don't threaten me," Landon warned in a teasing tone. He seemed to be in a good mood, though I was mired in doubt.

"There's plenty of bacon," Chief Terry said, gesturing toward the huge platter. His eyes went to me as I got comfortable. I saw worry there. "What's wrong with you?"

I wasn't exactly surprised by the question. He'd always been in tune with my moods. As a kid, I gravitated toward him. He'd always gone out of his way to cater to Clove, Thistle, and me. Our bond was especially tight, though, and that was on full display.

"Nothing," I reassured him quickly. "I'm ... perfectly okay."

He didn't look convinced. "You look tired."

"That's because we broke out the bacon perfume last night," Landon supplied.

Chief Terry pinned him with a glare. "You know, there are times I have an overwhelming urge to thump you. Don't say things like that to me. It makes me feel icky."

I smiled at his mild outrage. "I just didn't sleep very well," I explained. "I have a lot on my mind."

"Because of Dani?" Chief Terry's lips curved into a sneer. "I think I've made my feelings on the situation clear."

"You have, and I don't want to talk about it."

"Bay and I had a long conversation about Dani last night," Landon interjected. "She's aware of our concerns."

"I didn't realize you guys had been talking about it and you were presenting united concerns," I grumbled, making a face when Landon piled seven slices of bacon on my plate. He always thought food was the answer to every problem.

"Don't get grumpy because we love you," Landon chided. "You agreed that as soon as we figure out this thing with the ghost and untangle who killed who we're going to have a very serious conversation about Dani. You can't back out now."

"I have no intention of backing out." It took everything I had not to snap at him.

"Someone is crabby," Chief Terry intoned, widening his eyes.

"I just need caffeine," I countered.

"You'd better suck down a lot of it then," Aunt Tillie said. "You're going to need your energy for what I have planned today."

That was the sort of statement that caused shivers to run down my spine. "And what are we doing?"

"Looking for buried treasure. Thistle will meet us at the campground in an hour. We're taking the canoe across again. I'm going to find whatever it is that Margaret thinks she's going to put her grubby hands on."

"That's trespassing," Chief Terry noted.

"Does anyone here care about that?" she asked pointedly.

"I don't." Landon reached for the bowl of eggs. "In fact, I think it's a good idea."

"You do?" Chief Terry couldn't contain his surprise. "Why do you think that?"

"If they can find something out there, it might give us a clear motive. Right now we're flailing, and that's a feeling I hate."

Chief Terry rubbed his chin and focused on Aunt Tillie. "Just one thing ... wait, look who I'm talking to." He switched his attention to me. "Don't get caught out there," he admonished. "Try to fly under the radar. If we get a call and have to check it out, we'll have to explain things that we don't want to explain. Got it?"

I nodded, feigning solemnness. "Got it. You have nothing to worry about."

"Oh, please. If I had a nickel for every time you or your great-aunt told me that and it blew up in my face I'd be a rich man."

"Yes, but your life would be boring without us."

He grinned. "That's true. I guess you're better than the money."

"That's my philosophy," Landon agreed, stuffing his face. "Text us if you find anything good. Otherwise, be careful. And try to stay away from Dani. She shouldn't be involved in this."

On that, we wholeheartedly agreed.

# NINETEEN

Trips with Thistle and Aunt Tillie were never quiet. Today, the arguing started the second we reached the campground. Thistle was already in a foul mood because Dani was giving her grief. Aunt Tillie's presence only served to exacerbate things.

"I don't see why I can't go with you," Dani argued, following me around the campground as we readied to leave. "You have enough room in the canoe for four people."

"That's true." I handed Thistle a backpack. "It's not safe for you to go over there."

"Why not?"

"Because two women have been murdered over there."

"Yeah, but they had ties to each other, right?" Dani showed no sign of backing down. "I don't have ties to them or anything they were doing, so I'll be fine."

It was a rational argument. That didn't change the fact that I couldn't very well watch my back should Dani attack if I was already looking for Valerie's ghost. "It's not safe." I hated that I had to use the old standby. I sounded like my mother. I was one step short of telling her it was a school night.

"This isn't fair." Dani stomped her foot and turned toward Aunt Tillie. "I want to go with you."

"Well, we can't always have what we want," Aunt Tillie noted. "The world doesn't work that way. You have to get used to disappointment."

Dani narrowed her eyes. "I'm serious."

"I never would've guessed." Aunt Tillie's gaze was shrewd as she looked around. "Where is that green bag I brought?"

"This one?" Thistle lifted the bag in question from the canoe.

"That's it." Aunt Tillie's lips curved. "Make sure that's in a spot where it won't get wet."

I was instantly suspicious. "What do you have in there?"

"Don't worry about it." Aunt Tillie handed Thistle another bag. "I think that's it."

"I will worry about it," I argued. "I want to know what you have in that bag. Is it something bad? Why can't it get wet?"

"Because I don't want to blow up." Aunt Tillie climbed into the canoe without another backward glance. "Get us in the water," she demanded.

I worked my jaw, debating how far I should push things. Thistle decided to tackle the matter before I could make a decision, but she focused on something else. "Are those seashells on your leggings?"

Aunt Tillie nodded. "Why?"

"Because they look like wrinkled, old man ... things." She twirled her finger in the air, as if that was supposed to explain something.

Aunt Tillie snorted. "Oh, please. These look nothing like wrinkled, old man things. You need to watch some porn or something if you think these shells look phallic."

"I'm confused why you went for shells," I said, pushing the canoe. "That seems a little tame for you."

"No." Aunt Tillie let out a huff and stood, shifting so I could see the front of the leggings as she lifted her shirt. "This is why I bought them." When she gestured toward the crotch of the leggings I almost fell over. Not only was there a huge shell there, but it had what looked to be some sort of weird sea creature poking out its head.

"Holy ... ."

Thistle laughed so hard I thought she might fall out of the canoe. "Is that why you're wearing such a long shirt? I wondered."

"I don't want Winnie confiscating another pair of leggings," Aunt Tillie explained as she sat in her seat. "You have no idea what a pain she is."

"I have some idea," I countered. "She's my mother."

"Yes, well, she thinks she's the queen of the universe. I've had it with her. I'm thinking of cursing her until she leaves my leggings alone."

"Just don't make her smell like a cheeseburger," I suggested, grunting as I shoved the canoe as hard as I could.

Puzzlement creased Aunt Tillie's forehead. "Why?"

"That's Chief Terry's favorite meal."

Wickedness started rolling off my great-aunt in waves. "Hey, thanks for the tip."

"That was not a tip."

"It was in my head."


**AUNT TILLIE USED HER MAGIC TO POWER** the canoe. It took only a few minutes to reach the other side of the lake. I suggested paddling further down the shoreline so we could hide our things in the shade of a weeping willow. Only someone who was truly looking would be able to find what we'd left behind.

"What's really in this?" Thistle asked as she handed Aunt Tillie the green bag.

"I already told you. It's dynamite."

I rolled my eyes. "Oh, it is not. You only said it was explosive to mess with Dani. What's really in there?" Speaking of Dani, I flicked my eyes back to the shore we'd been on only minutes before and found her standing exactly where we'd left her. I couldn't see her face over such a great distance, but I could feel her rage washing against the beach with each wave.

Aunt Tillie stared at me blankly when I turned back to her.

"I'm serious," I prodded.

"It's dynamite," she insisted.

"Right."

"It's probably another pair of pornographic leggings," Thistle said. "She's got a thing for them. I'm not sure where she finds them, but I keep waiting for her to come up with a pair of *Star Wars* leggings so she has lightsabers poking out of her hoo-ha."

The visual made me laugh. "There's your next pair, Aunt Tillie."

"Laugh all you want, but I would totally wear the crap out of those," Aunt Tillie said, starting up the steep incline. She was in her eighties and generally pretty spry, but she struggled with the hill. Wordlessly, Thistle and I each grabbed an arm to help her the rest of the way.

"I totally could've done that myself," Aunt Tillie groused as soon as we were at the top of the hill.

"We know," Thistle and I said in unison, our eyes already busy scanning the trees.

"Which way do you want to go?" I asked. "I'm assuming you want to stick close to the house."

"Not really." Aunt Tillie looked in the opposite direction. "I want to go that way."

"Into the woods?" I asked dubiously. "If I remember correctly, it's pretty hilly there."

"Which is exactly why a pirate would want to hide his booty there," Aunt Tillie insisted. "Think about it. If you were trying to hide something of great value, would you put it in the flat spot where anybody could find it, or in there?"

She had a point. Still, though ... . "I don't think I would hide money out here regardless. That seems like a bad idea. That's just me, though."

"My adventurous spirit totally skipped you." Aunt Tillie made a clucking sound as she shook her head and started walking. "You wouldn't believe how many jars I have buried around our property. That was the thing to do back in the day."

I was taken aback. "Um ... wait. Are you saying you have jars of money buried on the Overlook property?"

"No, I have jars of money and magic buried on my property. Don't forget, girls, I own most of that land. I let your mothers pretend they're in charge because I don't like doing menial labor ... like paying bills."

"I see." I glanced over her head at Thistle, who looked dubious.

"Why would you bury money in jars when you're so old and could die at any moment?" Thistle queried. "I mean ... all that money is going to go to waste if you croak tomorrow. That's pretty stupid."

"I'm middle-aged," Aunt Tillie fired back. "I'm not dying anytime soon."

"Of course you're not," I soothed, scuffing my feet against the ground as we continued through the trees. I had no idea what we were looking for, but I kept my eyes trained on the ground for signs of disturbance. "Can I ask you guys something?"

"Sure," Thistle answered automatically.

"No," Aunt Tillie responded.

"Don't you at least want to hear the question before you shut me down?" I challenged.

"Um ... no." Aunt Tillie shook her head and suddenly veered to the right. "This way."

I slowed my pace. "How do you even know where to look?"

"I have what you might call mental magic." She tapped the side of her head for emphasis without slowing. "I'm so smart my brain can't be housed entirely

155

inside my head, so there's excess floating around. Sometimes it picks up on little things that nobody else notices."

That sounded unlikely. "Well ... neat."

"Oh, you're so full of crap you should double as a Porta-Potty," Thistle shot back. "You're just wandering without any sense of purpose. We're not going to find buried treasure if we go about it like this."

"Do you really think we're going to find buried treasure regardless?"

"Of course we are," Thistle replied, not missing a beat. "Think about it. Mrs. Little wants this property so much she's salivating. There must be a reason."

I'd been thinking about that. "What if she just wants to live on a lake?"

"She's allergic to water," Aunt Tillie countered. "She doesn't care about the lake."

"She's not allergic to water," I scoffed.

"Then why does she smell that way?"

"I ... you're just saying that to be persnickety." I opted to change course. "I'm just saying that it's possible Mrs. Little doesn't have ulterior motives. Maybe she always dreamed about living on this lake and thought she had a golden opportunity when the campground came up for sale. It's entirely possible that she was broken-hearted when she realized Landon and Aunt Tillie snaked it out from under her."

Thistle and Aunt Tillie shot me twin looks of disgust.

"Grow up," Aunt Tillie said, adjusting our trek to the right yet again. "You must be slipping in your old age or something, because that's definitely not what's going on here. Margaret is an evil person. What do evil people want, Thistle?"

"To carry out evil deeds," Thistle replied perfunctorily.

"That's right." Aunt Tillie beamed at her as if she were Peg and had just done a trick. "Margaret is evil. If she wants this place, it's because she has evil deeds on her mind."

"If you say so." A nearby tree caught my attention. The leaves on the ground at its base had been disturbed. I made my way to it. They'd ignored my earlier question, so I decided to ask it again. "Can I ask you guys something?"

"I would really rather you not," Aunt Tillie replied. "We're here for a specific reason, not to listen to you ask questions that you think are witty and insightful but are really boring and tedious."

I pretended I didn't hear her response as I ran my fingers over the ground. It looked as if someone had walked through this area recently, but there was nothing more than a few light tread patterns to lead me to that conclusion. "Do you ever think Landon is weird?"

Neither Thistle nor Aunt Tillie immediately responded, causing me to slowly raise my eyes and seek them out. "What?" I asked self-consciously when I found them both staring at me.

"You just asked if we thought a man who would rather dress you up as a slice of bacon than watch you slink around in lingerie is weird," Thistle noted. "And, oddly enough, it's the second time this week you've asked that question."

Aunt Tillie snorted and put out her fist in an effort to get Thistle to bump it. She'd been desperately trying to get us to play that game after watching an NBA matchup two weeks ago and deciding it was the "hip" new thing. "Good one."

Thistle gave her a "not in this lifetime" look and moved to a fallen tree. "Why are you asking if we think Landon is weird?"

"Well ... ." I could've kept it to myself. Part of me knew it was the right decision. The other part, though, was feeling antsy. I needed a second opinion.

I told them. I explained about the drawer and how he acted. I made sure they knew he went back to acting normal immediately after. When I finished, Aunt Tillie was the first to roll her eyes.

"You're such a whiny baby sometimes," she complained.

I made a face and focused on Thistle. "It's not weird that I'm worried, is it?"

Unlike our great-aunt, Thistle took a more measured approach — at least for her. "I don't know that I would use the word 'weird,'" she started, clearly choosing her words carefully. "The thing is ... Landon loves you."

"I know Landon loves me." Suddenly, I was feeling defensive. "It's not that I don't think that he loves me."

"Then what is it?"

"Well ... what if he has something freaky in his sock drawer?"

"Aunt Tillie once kept a poisonous snake in her sock drawer and we still hang out with her," Thistle pointed out.

"That snake wasn't poisonous," Aunt Tillie argued. "He just had a bad attitude."

Thistle planted her hands on her hips. "I looked that snake up online. It was definitely poisonous."

"Ugh. You're such a kvetch. Now that Clove is married, are you going to take over as the resident kvetch? I should've seen that coming."

Thistle ignored her and kept her eyes on me. "Have you considered that he might've had something he simply didn't want you to see?"

My eyebrows practically flew off my forehead. "Um, yeah! Why do you think I'm so worked up? I mean ... what if he had photos of another woman in there? What if he had a second cell phone because he's been working undercover as a spy? What if there were diamonds or something that he stole from a crime scene hidden in his socks?"

"Oh, well, I was wrong," Aunt Tillie deadpanned. "You're clearly the new kvetch."

Thistle flicked her ear to silence her. "Or he had a dirty magazine in there. Maybe he had some weird sexy bacon massage oil he wanted to surprise you with. Maybe he had a gift in there for you and he's holding onto it for a special occasion."

That hadn't occurred to me. "The bacon oil sounds most likely."

"It does," she agreed. "Why are you jumping to the worst possible conclusion?"

That was a good question. "Because I'm agitated," I replied. I didn't need introspection to come up with an answer. I already knew. "Landon is making noise about Dani. He's right. She's a danger to him ... and Chief Terry ... and Clove. I shouldn't be helping her because she's already crossed the line. And yet I can't help myself."

"You can't help yourself because she's still a kid," Aunt Tillie volunteered. "It's the age screwing you up. If she was an adult, you would be over it already. You would be preparing to do what needs to be done."

"And what is that?" I was almost afraid to hear her answer.

"We either have to kill her or bind her powers," Aunt Tillie replied. "Those are pretty much our only options."

A whoosh of air escaped my lungs and my eyes practically popped out of my head. "Bind?" Why hadn't I thought of that? Was I so far gone I'd missed the obvious answer? "That's right. We can bind her powers." I was talking to myself, but that didn't stop the others from responding.

"We can," Aunt Tillie agreed. "I've already got Thistle ordering special herbs for us. They should be here in a few days. I think we all agree the kid isn't going to get any better. The safest thing we can do is strip her of her magic."

"And you're certain we can do that?" Thistle challenged. "I mean ... that's not something we can screw up if we want people to remain safe."

Aunt Tillie rolled her eyes. "I'm not a novice. I know how to bind someone's powers. The spell is powerful, but we have more than enough witches to carry it out, even if Clove's powers are malfunctioning because she's a walking hormone."

"You're all heart," Thistle said, poking Aunt Tillie's side and grinning.

"I forgot all about binding her powers," I admitted, some of the weight I'd been carrying for the past few weeks lifting. "I thought the only choice was killing her."

"Well, that's a dark thought," Aunt Tillie drawled. "We're not assassins, Bay. But there will be another matter to deal with if we strip her powers. She'll be out for vengeance. She'll come gunning for us when she realizes."

"Yeah, but if we strip her powers, then we can let Landon have his way and lock her up," I noted. "That might be the best of both worlds."

Aunt Tillie's expression was unreadable. "She's a powerful witch. She won't let us bind her willingly. We'll have to trick her when it's time."

"Hey, compared to what I was picturing, I'll take it. I think with your devious mind we should have no problem getting exactly what we want."

"That's good." Aunt Tillie beamed. "Now, can we go back to looking for buried treasure and forget about Landon being weird and the evil witch across the lake? We're focusing on me and my needs now, and I need to beat Margaret."

"Fine." I managed a smile as I went back to looking at the prints. "Someone has been here, but I don't know that they found anything."

"Over here, too." Thistle gestured toward a patch of earth that looked to have been dug up — and re-covered — recently. "I don't know if anything was in this hole, but Aunt Tillie is right, although I'm loath to admit it. People were definitely out here looking for something."

"So, what do we do?" I asked. "Do we dig up the holes?"

"Of course not," Aunt Tillie replied. "Do you know how much work that would be?" She grabbed her green bag and started rummaging inside, coming back with what looked like a stick of dynamite. "I told you I came prepared. Now, back up. I've got this completely under control."

I leaped for her before she could find her lighter. "Holy ... !"

# TWENTY

We found at least twenty spots that showed signs of recent digging. Despite Aunt Tillie's insistence that we allow her to throw a stick of dynamite into the center of the nearest sites, we were no closer to figuring out what our killer (or killers) thought was buried in the earth. We decided to leave and come back later.

"You're going back?" Landon didn't look happy when I announced our intentions to him and Chief Terry over lunch at the diner.

"Do you see a better option?" I asked. "Whoever is digging out there is more likely to come back after dark. We might be able to catch them in the act."

"You also might run into an ornery poltergeist."

"True, but we didn't run into Valerie today. In fact, I didn't even sense her — and I don't think Heather stayed behind."

"I don't know if that's good or bad." His fingers were gentle as they brushed against my face. When he pulled them back, he had a small twig pinched between them. "Were you guys wandering around the woods?"

"As a matter of fact, we were." I took back the twig. "Aunt Tillie had a feeling, and she turned out to be right."

"Those words send chills down my spine," Chief Terry intoned, kicking back in his chair to sip his iced tea and eye me from across the table. "Since when does Tillie having a feeling constitute anything good?"

"Since she's the one who found the holes." I saw no sense holding back on this one. "She also came up with another idea — for Dani." On impulse, I gripped Landon's hand tightly, causing his eyebrows to hop. "It's a really good idea."

"Please tell me there's such a thing as witch reform school," he said. "I'll have the Explorer packed and ready to take her in ten minutes flat."

"No, but ... we can bind her powers." I whispered the last part, keeping my voice low so the others in the restaurant wouldn't overhear.

Landon didn't react.

"Didn't you hear me?" I challenged. "We can bind her powers. That means she can't use them against anyone."

"Okay." He nodded and shot me an encouraging smile. "I'm not sure how that works."

"I forget you're such a witch novice." Impulsively, I leaned over and kissed the corner of his mouth. I was feeling so much better now that Aunt Tillie had given me a viable path that I couldn't remember half the fear that had been twisting me in knots only six hours earlier. "In a nutshell, we would perform a ritual that strips her magic. She wouldn't be able to curse anyone or call to her powers."

"Really?" Landon was clearly intrigued. "How dangerous is that for you?"

"Well, she won't go down without a fight," I acknowledged, sobering. "We'll all have to work together. I'm not saying there won't be any danger, but it's a path that doesn't make me want to cry."

He cupped my cheek. He knew as well as I did that we'd both been circling the same argument for close to two weeks. Fear of and about Dani ripped through both of us regularly. We needed to express that fear, and it manifested in the form of deep conversations and heavy arguments. "Then we'll figure out what needs to be done."

"We have to keep quiet and not mention it to her until we're ready. Thistle ordered some herbs. We need to put together a few things — hex bags and maybe a potion or two — before we can start."

"I won't say anything." He leaned forward and pressed a kiss to my forehead. "I'm glad you're excited about this."

His tone told me he was still worried. "Landon ... ."

"Shh." He kissed my forehead again. "What do you smell?"

That's when I realized what he was truly doing and started to laugh. "You're ridiculous." My shoulders shook with mirth when I pulled back. "I still smell you. You're good."

"You didn't comment."

"I'm sorry." I twined my arms around his neck and whispered. "You smell so good I want to take you right back home and spend the day in bed."

"Now we're talking." He wrapped his arms around me for a long hug. When he pulled back, he was serious. "I really am glad you think this is a workable plan. I'd be lying if I said I wasn't worried about what happens after you strip her powers."

"Yeah, I've been thinking about that too," I admitted. "She seems the type to hide in the woods with a gun and try to pick us off one by one once she realizes what we've done. That's where you come in."

"Oh, good." He feigned a pleasant smile. "I was wondering if you were going to include me."

"Once she's non-magical, she can be put in a hospital or a detention center. She won't be able to magically hurt anybody, and the staff can be trained in how to take care of her mental needs, which are the real concern once you move beyond the damage she can do with her magic."

"Oh." Realization dawned on his handsome features as he brushed his hand over his hair. "I kind of like this idea. We'll have to come up with a few handy lies to explain where Dani has been."

"You also might want to figure out a way to shut her trap if she starts talking about witches," Chief Terry interjected.

"No." I shook my head. "That will make the doctors think she's nuttier than she really is. If she starts spouting off about having powers and how a group of witches took them away from her, what will people think?"

He tilted his head to the side, considering. "You know what, Bay? I'm starting to like this idea too. If you're capable of this binding thing, why didn't you think of it sooner?"

"I'm not sure. Aunt Tillie brought it up as if it was the most normal thing while we were wandering around the woods. I could've kicked myself. It was right there all the time. I don't know what's wrong with me."

Landon swooped in to respond. "I know. You're overwhelmed. You need a whole week of nothing but me ... and you ... and bed. Some bacon wouldn't hurt."

Chief Terry extended a quelling finger in Landon's direction. "Why would you say something like that in front of me?"

"I like to get your heart rate going." Landon grinned, never moving his eyes from me. "It's fun ... and it keeps you in shape."

"I've decided I'm going to ignore you for the rest of the day," Chief Terry huffed, staring through the front window. "You're dead to me."

I couldn't contain the smile spreading across my face. "Oh, you really are one of us now."

His brow furrowed. "Don't make me stop listening to you too, Bay."

"Never." I smiled long enough that he had no choice but to return it — even though it was a bit huffy — and then turned back to Landon. "I just stopped in to tell you that I'll be running around the countryside tonight with Thistle and Aunt Tillie. Oh, and I wanted you to know that I have an actual plan for Dani, so you have nothing to worry about."

"You can't tell me that you're running around with Aunt Tillie and then add there's nothing to worry about and expect me to agree." He winked. "As for Dani, I'll continue to worry until I'm certain she's completely under control. I am hopeful but ... reticent. That's a word, right?" He looked to Chief Terry for confirmation.

"I'm not a thesaurus."

"It's a word," I reassured him. "I'm not telling you this because I believe everything is completely solved. I just want you to know that I have a plan. You don't have to keep having deep conversations with my mother because you're worried."

He opened his mouth to speak but halted. For a moment, I couldn't help but wonder if he'd been talking to my mother about something else. He didn't come right out and say it, but he seemed surprised by my knowledge that they'd been talking behind my back.

"Like I said, I'm going to worry about you until Dani is out of our lives and no longer a threat to anybody," he said. "I do feel better, though, if that relieves some of the stress you've been carrying."

"Some," I promised, although my stomach was doing that uncomfortable dancing again. "You're not going to try to talk us out of stalking people at Heather's property, are you?"

"Nope."

"No?" I was understandably dubious. If history had taught me anything, it was that Landon didn't like when we snuck around in the middle of the night muddling his investigations.

"I've decided that you are who you are," he explained. "You like to wander around in the dark with Thistle and your great-aunt and find mischief. I knew that from the beginning. You remember the whole cornfield incident.?"

I scowled. How could I ever forget? It was right after we'd met. He was undercover and I was in trouble. He got shot trying to protect me. That's where it all started. "You're not still bitter about that?"

He smirked. "No. I consider myself lucky."

"Lucky? How?"

"I got you out of the deal. Sure, I also got crazy women wearing matching tracksuits who like to dance naked under the full moon. I also got your nutty great-aunt, who carries a shotgun and wears a combat helmet, but you were definitely worth it."

I went warm all over. "Thanks. You were worth it too."

"Of course I was. As for running around at night, what can I do?" He held out his hands and shrugged. "I'm trying to be a better man."

"You're already a great man."

"Yes, but I'm a man who sometimes struggles with the fact that you don't need me."

"I ... you ... I need you." I meant it. "Why would you think I don't?"

"Perhaps that came out wrong," he said quickly. "I didn't mean you don't need me overall. In a fight, though, more often than not, I'm a detriment. That became very clear when you were taking on Diane. You were a badass and I was the guy trying to figure out how to make the situation better without risking making it worse.

"You changed my life, Bay," he continued, beaming at me. "You're a pain in the butt sometimes, but you're my pain in the butt. I've reconciled myself to the fact that you're going to do what you're going to do. Guess what? I'm okay with it."

They were the words I'd always wanted to hear. I smacked a loud kiss against his lips. "We're definitely going to put that doughnut aroma to good use when I get back tonight."

"Oh, geez." Chief Terry slapped his hand over his eyes. "Now you've got her doing it. You've corrupted my little sweetheart."

My grin only widened. "We'll be careful. I promise. If I get coverage, I'll even text so you know when to expect me."

"That would be great." Landon turned back to his lunch. "Try to keep Aunt Tillie in line. I worry about her the most."

"Oh, don't worry. We confiscated the dynamite. She'll be fine."

He nodded. "Good. I ... wait." He broke off, a fry halfway to his mouth. "What dynamite?"

Uh-oh. "Did I mention you changed my life too? I can't thank you enough. Gotta go."

**I SPENT THE AFTERNOON AT THE CAMPGROUND,** giving Hazel a much-needed break. She took off to town, leaving me with Dani, who proceeded to pout her way from one end of the campground to the other while emitting dramatic sighs and wrinkling her nose.

I pretended I didn't hear her. It was a tried-and-true tactic I'd learned from my mother when I was a teenager. I used to act just like Dani — er, well, without being a murderer, that is — and my mother punished me by not acknowledging my teenage angst. She was trying to get me to go to her — and it worked like a charm.

"Aren't you going to ask me what's wrong?" Dani asked finally, on what had to be her twentieth circle. She plopped down on the picnic table bench across from where I was working on my computer and fixed me with a petulant glare.

"I already know what's wrong," I countered, amused. "You're angry that we didn't take you with us earlier and you want us to bring you on whatever adventure we've got going tonight."

Her eyes lit with excitement. "You're going on another adventure tonight?"

Oh, well, crap. She'd had no idea. Sometimes I'm nowhere near as smart as I like to think I am. "We're heading back across the lake once it gets dark," I replied, refusing to lie. She had to get used to not getting her way. Her life would likely take a swerve in the upcoming days and she was going to have to learn to adjust.

"Can I go?"

I was expecting the question. "No. It might be dangerous."

The scowl that took over her face was ugly. "Why do you always say things like that? I know about danger. I can handle myself."

"You're still young."

"And yet I'm stronger than you," she muttered. Whether or not she meant me to hear her was difficult to determine. The one thing I knew with absolute clarity, though, was that she was slipping further from the ideal we were trying to set for her. We were almost out of time.

"I'm sorry. This is a ... difficult ... situation. We're trying to see if we can catch people doing stuff over there. It's not someplace we can comfortably take you while guaranteeing your safety." That sounded reasonable, right?

Instead of pushing further, Dani wrinkled her nose. "What sorts of things are you trying to catch people doing? Oh, wait. Are you trying to catch people doing the dirty? I bet it's your boyfriend. He's always struck me as the cheating type."

That got my full attention. "Landon isn't a cheater."

"Oh, please. He's got Hollywood hair. Everybody knows that guys with

Hollywood hair can't stop themselves from cheating. It's a biological fact. I even saw it on television or something."

"Uh-huh." I pressed the heel of my hand to my forehead. She was giving me a headache and it wasn't even dark yet. "Did you see that on one of those Kardashian shows?"

"Hey, those chicks know what they're talking about. They've had problems, and men were at the center of all of them."

"Yes, that's obviously the case."

"I don't see why I can't go with you," Dani persisted. "I'd be good if you're trying to scope him out and figure out who he's cheating with."

"He's not cheating with anybody." I was certain of that, despite my earlier freak-out. "That's not in his nature."

"Yeah? I thought the same thing about my dad."

"This is different."

"Because it's you?"

"Because ... it just is."

"If you say so." Dani was dejected as she got to her feet and turned toward the cabin. "How do you expect me to win your trust if you won't let me do anything?" she called over her shoulder as she trudged away.

It was a fair point. "This is too dangerous. I'm sorry."

"Whatever."

I was still focused on her retreating back when I heard footsteps behind me. When I turned, I found Hazel watching with sympathetic eyes.

"How's it going?" she asked in her relaxed, amiable tone.

"She's upset."

"So I gathered. Don't take it personally. She gets upset over everything." Hazel sat at the table across from me. She looked rested and relaxed. The break had been good for her, even if it left me feeling antsy.

"She found out we're going back across the lake tonight. She's angry we won't take her with us. I tried explaining it's too dangerous, but she doesn't see it that way."

"Why are you going back?" Hazel asked.

"Someone has been digging holes over there, and I have to believe they're looking for something specific. If we knew what that something was, we could narrow down our suspect list.

"I think they're digging after dark," I continued. "We want to be there tonight if anybody shows up. If we can figure out who we're dealing with, we might be able to solve these murders."

"And then focus on Dani," Hazel surmised.

I hesitated. "Yeah. We've actually come up with a potential idea on that front."

"Really? And what's that?"

"It's too complex to get into, especially out here with prying ears." I pointedly inclined my head toward the cabin. "Suffice it to say that if everything goes as planned, we might have this entire situation 'fixed' in a few days." I used the appropriate air quotes for emphasis.

"Don't keep me in suspense. I'm dying to know the plan."

"Later." I waved off the question. I had no doubt Dani would either drag the information out of Hazel or figure out a way to eavesdrop if the conversation continued. "It's a good idea, I promise you that. We'll get into details in a few days — after we deal with all of this."

"Okay. I guess I can survive a few more days."

I hoped she was right.

# TWENTY-ONE

We waited until cover of darkness to set out in the canoe. We were halfway across the lake — Aunt Tillie opted for a more leisurely pace this time because we were trying to avoid discovery — when my phone dinged.

"Hey!" Aunt Tillie twisted from her spot in the bow of the canoe. I could make out her features thanks to the moon — it wasn't joy she was emitting. "You need to turn off your phone on an op. Everybody knows that." She turned to Thistle for confirmation. "Tell her. Your phone is off, isn't it?"

"It is," Thistle nodded solemnly.

I made a face when Aunt Tillie turned back to me. "I forgot. Give me a break." Landon's number was on the screen when I pulled out the phone. I had to avert my eyes from Aunt Tillie before I could answer. That didn't stop me from noticing Thistle had her phone out and was only now silencing it. Typical.

"Hi." I whispered the greeting as I hunched in my seat and tried to pretend Aunt Tillie wasn't glaring at me."

"How's my favorite witch?" he asked.

"Well, right now Aunt Tillie is glaring at me because I forgot to shut off my phone, so I guess it depends on which of us is your favorite."

"That's not even a contest. I'm picking up takeout so you'll have something to eat when you get back to the guesthouse tonight. Do you want a hot beef sandwich or spaghetti? It looks like they have that sauce you like."

"I'll have the spaghetti." Aunt Tillie growled, which made me shrink even further. "I don't know that I can talk on the phone right now. We're heading across the lake."

"Okay. I just want to remind you that it would be best for everybody if you didn't get caught."

The admonishment made me smile. "We won't get caught. I promise."

"I also want to remind you that I smell like doughnuts and I will have your favorite spaghetti waiting for you. I might even be naked."

That only made me grin wider. "I'll keep that in mind. Hopefully we won't be out here too long."

"That would be nice," he agreed.

"Hang up that phone before I throw it in the lake," Aunt Tillie warned.

"I have to go," I said ruefully. "Aunt Tillie is going to start melting down."

"Okay. Just ... keep looking over your shoulder, Bay. Follow your instincts."

"I will." This was hard for him. Before, he might've tried to come with us. He realized this was something we needed to do on our own ... and for more reasons than one. "I won't be too late."

"Okay."

"I love you, Landon."

I could hear the smile in his voice. "I love you, Bay."

Aunt Tillie was still scowling when I disconnected. "You guys are officially disgusting," she lamented, shaking her head as she turned back to the approaching shore. "I mean officially disgusting."

"They're totally disgusting," Thistle agreed, shooting me a knowing look. "I think Bay should be punished for having her cell phone on when we left for a spying mission. Instead of doughnuts, you should make Landon smell like liver and onions."

I glared at her. "Don't even ... ."

"Liver and onions, eh?" Aunt Tillie turned haughty. "Maybe that's what I'll make Marcus smell like because you lied about having your phone off earlier. That might be justice."

Thistle's mouth dropped open. "How did you know?"

"I have invisible eyes in my head."

"I think you mean eyes in the back of your head," I countered.

"I have invisible eyes everywhere," Aunt Tillie said. "Now, shut your holes. We need to be quiet. We'll never catch evil people if you two don't stop yammering."

I wasn't convinced we were going to catch evil people at all. She had a point, though, so I snapped my mouth shut.

. . .

**WE LEFT THE CANOE UNDER THE WILLOW** again. The drooping branches provided natural cover, and it was a safe place to climb in and out of the canoe without tipping. If we needed to escape in a hurry, we would be able to do so unseen from here.

Once on land, Aunt Tillie took the lead. She conjured magical sentries — balls of enthusiastic light — to illuminate our way. I wasn't surprised when she led us right back to the spot where she'd wanted to throw the dynamite.

"We'll wait here," she announced.

"Great." Thistle exchanged a quick look with me and then frowned at the ground. "I guess we'll be sitting on the ground. We should've brought over some of those canvas chairs so we'd be comfortable."

"Shush!" Aunt Tillie pressed her finger to her lips.

One look at her determined face told me it was going to be a long night.

We got comfortable, Aunt Tillie positioned between us. It was still early, but I told myself that anyone coming out here to dig wouldn't want to be out all night. If someone was going to risk coming out tonight, they'd probably do so fairly early.

We sat in relative silence for the first hour. Aunt Tillie was intent on listening to every sound the forest had to offer. Thistle was busy filing her fingernails. I had nothing to do but stare at the moon. I was about to suggest we walk around — my backside was killing me because the ground was so hard — when I heard a sound.

At first, I thought I'd imagined it. There was a slight breeze and the water was on the other side of us. It could've been the waves lapping the shore ... or even an animal.

I heard it again.

I glanced to Thistle to see if she was picking it up, and her eyes were keen.

"Evil has arrived," Aunt Tillie whispered, immediately hunkering lower to the ground and rolling to her stomach. She reminded me of a ninja, ready to do her business. She was dressed all in black — the inappropriate seashell leggings nothing but a distant memory — and she was intent on the direction of the noise.

Because it was expected of us, Thistle and I followed suit. I'd tucked my blond hair up in a knit cap to hide it. Thistle's hair was dark enough that it didn't stand out in the limited light. I tensed, cocking my head, and then held my breath when I heard a voice.

"We've already checked this area," a female voice snapped, impatience practically flooding the crisp night air. "Why would we come back here?"

"Mrs. Little," Thistle mouthed when I risked a glance at her.

I nodded. It was definitely Mrs. Little. It seemed Aunt Tillie had been right. Evil was most definitely here ... and Mrs. Little was at the center of all of this. We were never going to hear the end of it.

"We're out here because I've read the map," a male voice shot back. "You've read it too. I know you have. Arlen Topper buried his treasure out here."

I stilled, surprised. Were they really looking for pirate treasure? Sure, I'd said as much to Landon, but I'd always thought it had to be a joke. I figured there was something simpler at the heart of this. Apparently I'd been mistaken.

"No, I don't know that," Mrs. Little huffed, planting her hands on her hips as she stopped in the middle of the small clearing. She obviously thought they were alone, because she didn't as much as glance around to see if anybody was watching. Of course, what were the odds anyone would sneak out to the property and hide in the bushes just to catch people trying to dig holes on a murder victim's land? Yeah, I don't want to do the math either.

"How can you not know that?" The male voice was familiar, but I was having trouble making out his features given the way he positioned himself with his back to the moon. "I came to you when I found that map in the first place. You agreed the map indicated there was money to be found here."

"Out here, yes. Out here." Mrs. Little used her "you're being a moron" voice and gestured toward the expansive property. "It's not as if they had tools to make this an exact science back then. If you ask me, the X on that map could be just about anywhere."

"That shows what you know." The man sounded frustrated, and the sarcasm he displayed was familiar. "I've studied that map over and over. I'm certain that the treasure is here."

Mrs. Little's tone was withering. "Well, if you're certain it must be true. You're a man, so you can't possibly be wrong."

"Oh, don't give me that. I'm just saying that I spent all this time studying the map."

"You also suggested I buy the campground so we'd have an easier time searching," Mrs. Little fired back. "Look how that turned out."

"How was I supposed to know that an FBI agent was going to swoop in at the last second — with the help of an outside real estate agent for that matter — and buy the place out from under us? I would have to be a mind reader to know that."

"It seems we should've known." Mrs. Little sounded bitter. "Tillie has made it her life's mission to make me miserable. She knew I wanted that campground. Bay knew it too. I bet she used some sexual magic or something to get Landon to buy it for her. That seems right up her alley."

I frowned. I didn't have sexual magic. Also, suggesting Landon could be duped by something like that was ... well, insulting was too kind a word. Of course, if I really did dress in a bacon costume and roll around in bacon grease for an hour he would most likely do whatever I asked. Scratch that. He could be duped.

"Hey, I saw that chick up close and personal when she was in my office asking questions yesterday. I would let her manipulate me with sex."

Wayne. That's why his voice sounded familiar. It now made sense that he was conspiring with Mrs. Little. They were essentially the same person, just wrapped in different costumes. Mrs. Little employed Wayne the first go-around when she wanted to buy the property, so it made sense that she would use him this time to finally complete the deal. They had another chance to get their grubby hands on the land — but why go through with the purchase if they could find what they were looking for and walk away without emptying their bank accounts?

"Don't be crass," Mrs. Little admonished.

"You just said you didn't like her," Wayne protested.

"That doesn't matter. You're still crass."

"You also said she used her feminine wiles to convince that FBI agent to buy the campground for her."

"I'm sure she did. That doesn't mean you can badmouth her. I don't like it."

Mrs. Little had an interesting set of morals. The fact that she was standing up for my virtue now — well, kind of — fit her persnickety personality. The woman was often a mystery, one I rarely cared to unravel.

I opened my mouth to whisper a suggestion to Aunt Tillie when another noise, this one from the west, drew my attention. I couldn't be sure, but I was almost positive another figure was emerging from the darkness. My heart seized. I was convinced it was Valerie's ghost coming to kill the trespassers. Instead, it was another familiar face — and he didn't sound happy.

"I knew you were out here. There's no point in trying to hide."

It was only then that I realized Mrs. Little was trying to obscure herself behind a large tree. Her hips were too wide for it to be effective.

"Nobody is trying to hide," Mrs. Little snapped, stepping to the forefront and planting her hands on her hips. "What are you doing here?"

"I'm doing the same thing you are. I'm looking for the treasure. Don't be an idiot. I knew you would be out here — especially now that Heather is dead and you think you can steal this property. I have no intention of allowing you to make the discovery."

I shook my head. How could this be happening?

"What makes you think we would possibly include you in this little outing, Eric?" Mrs. Little challenged, using a sickeningly sweet voice that turned my stomach. "After you screwed us, I told you it was the last time. We're not working with you."

Eric Savage. This just kept getting weirder. Were they all working together?

"Hey, it's not my fault that the FBI agent used an outside representative to buy the campground," he snapped. "We all thought that we were going to luck out when that property came on the market. He swooped in out of nowhere and stole it from us."

I smirked. The news that Landon had screwed up their plans made me happy, even as I tried to wrap my head around what sort of devil's bargain this oddball trio had struck.

"I'm not talking about the campground," Mrs. Little fired back. "I'm talking about the Lakin house." She gestured toward the dark house in the distance. "You knew we wanted it, but you sold it to an outsider."

"Hey, I'm a real estate agent," Eric argued. "I didn't seek her out. She came here looking for that specific house. It's not as if I can just turn up my nose at a commission that big. I tried to fix things."

"Yes, by dating her," Wayne noted. "That was so smart ... for you. The rest of us, however, didn't have easy access to the property."

"I was going to figure out a way to get you guys out here," Eric argued. I could tell he was lying. He wasn't very good at it. "I didn't have enough time. Things happened so fast. First Valerie ... and then Heather. It's a mess."

That was a nice way of putting it.

"Yes, speaking of Valerie and Heather, why did you kill them?" Mrs. Little challenged, causing me to tense. "Don't you think it would've been smarter to cut ties without murder?"

Eric balked. "I didn't murder them. How could you think that?"

"Look, both of the women you were dating died within the last week. You make the most sense as a suspect."

"Except I have no motive," Eric fired back. "I was having no problem sneaking out of the house and searching the property after Heather passed out every night. She had a drinking problem, for crying out loud. She had three bottles of wine and Ambien with dinner every night. I didn't need to kill her."

"Then why is she dead?" Mrs. Little demanded, her frustration obvious. "It seems impossible that both of them wound up dead like that unless you had something to do with it."

"I didn't." Eric's voice squeaked. "I can't believe you think I'm a murderer. I want the treasure, but I wouldn't murder to get it."

Even though I didn't trust him — he had a certain smarmy quality that turned my stomach — I believed him. Killing Valerie and Heather worked against him, so it made no sense that he killed them unless he was a sociopath. He was a user, no doubt, but he wasn't killing for the thrill of it.

"We need to stop this," Wayne ordered, taking control. "We're trespassing on land where a murder occurred two nights ago. We don't have time to stand here and argue. We need to work together, even if we don't like each other."

"Or trust each other," Mrs. Little grumbled, crossing her arms over her chest. "Fine. We'll work together. How do you want to do it?"

"Well, for starters, I think we should head in this direction." He gestured directly toward our hiding spot, which made my heart skip. "We haven't spent much time over there yet."

I shifted a bit, prepared to grab Aunt Tillie's arm and draw her away, when a faint keening filled the night. I stilled, the hair on the back of my neck standing on end, and when I looked to the north I could just make out an ethereal figure flitting between the trees — barreling directly toward us.

"Oh, crap." I blurted out the words as I scrambled to my feet.

Mrs. Little, Eric, and Wayne were so surprised at the sight of me climbing out of the ditch they let loose gasps.

"What are you doing out here?" Mrs. Little screeched.

"We're hunting evil," Aunt Tillie replied, appearing at my side. "It looks like we found some."

"You're trespassing," Eric hissed.

"That's ballsy," Thistle shot back, joining the fray. "You're trespassing."

The argument would've been entertaining under different circumstances. "We have to run," I insisted, grabbing Mrs. Little's arm and giving her a vicious push. "We have to get out of here."

"What are you talking about?" Mrs. Little argued, fury lining her face. "We're not leaving. We just got here. If you think you're stealing the treasure from us, you have another thing coming."

"I don't care about the treasure." I looked to the sky and cringed as the screeching became more pronounced. Other than Aunt Tillie, I was the only one who could hear it. "We have to run right now."

"Why?" Wayne asked dubiously.

"Because the ghost is about to hit the fan," Aunt Tillie replied. Unlike me, she was braced for battle. She'd already come to the realization that running was out of the question. "Things are about to get real."

Valerie's ghost was upon us.

# TWENTY-TWO

My instincts kicked in and I moved directly into Valerie's path.

"No," I ordered, my voice booming.

"What is going on?" Mrs. Little demanded as the leaves began to flap, a wicked wind whistling through the small clearing. "What is ... this?" Her eyes widened as she looked at the nearest tree. It began bending, as if giving way to an unseen force. She didn't understand that Valerie's ghost was that force — and she was ticked.

"Go!" I roared, focusing my full attention on Valerie. Her eyes glowed red again, hot embers of hate.

"You don't belong here," the ghost intoned. "This isn't your place. This is my place." There was something odd about her cadence, as if she wasn't choosing the words. There was almost an overlap to the statement, as if two people were speaking.

"Valerie ... ." I hesitated, unsure what to say.

"Valerie?" Mrs. Little's voice was a shriek now, so she could be heard over the wind. "Valerie is dead."

Here's the thing about Mrs. Little: She knows. Deep down, somewhere inside, she's well aware of what we are. She's been present for far too many weird occurrences to believe otherwise. Between enchanted wishing wells, Floyd's poltergeist, magical opponents who defied explanation, she knows ... and yet she refuses to acknowledge it. The realization is too much for her.

"Don't be a moron, Margaret," Aunt Tillie snapped. "There's more than one sort of evil haunting this place. How can you be such an idiot?"

Mrs. Little's eyes flashed with rage, the furious wind forgotten. "Who are you calling an idiot?" She reached out, as if to wrap her hands around Aunt Tillie's neck, but Thistle was too fast for her.

"Stop this!" Thistle demanded. "Unless you want to die, you have to run."

"You'd like that, wouldn't you?" Mrs. Little planted her hands on her hips and bobbed her head, reminding me of a chicken. "You've concocted a plan to frighten us off the land because you want the treasure. I'm not falling for it."

"How are they controlling the weather?" Wayne shouted over the wind. He'd edged closer to the trees on the far side of the clearing and it was obvious, to him at least, that running seemed like the better option.

"Yes, Margaret, how are we controlling the weather?" Aunt Tillie drawled.

"Probably through mass hypnosis," Mrs. Little replied. "I've long thought that's how you do just about everything. I saw a documentary on con artists, and that's how they do it. I bet you went to Vegas and learned from one of those magicians ... or maybe one of those tarot readers in New Orleans."

"It's not mass hypnosis. It's ... Eric!" I realized what was going to happen too late to stop it. Valerie hadn't immediately seen her ex-boyfriend, but when she finally caught sight of him her rage grew. Up until that point, I'd thought I'd seen the limits of her fury.

I was wrong.

The ghost zeroed in on Eric and turned her immense energy in his direction. The wind picked up, and it felt as if we were trapped in a tunnel with a tornado pressing down.

"What's going on?" Eric's voice trembled as he edged backward. "I don't understand. I ... is Valerie really here?"

He'd obviously heard me call her by name despite the nonstop chatter from everyone.

"She is and she's pissed." I moved with the intention of shoving him until he started running, but the shift jolted him.

Fear overtook his features. His face twisted into a mask of horror. In his haste to move away from me, he missed the fallen log we'd been hiding behind only minutes before. I could see the moment he realized he was going to fall, and the sympathy I felt for him was almost as great as the fear. He arced backward, his arms flailing wildly for balance. Valerie, now an apex predator, recognized the moment of weakness and swooped in his direction.

"No!" I wanted to help. There had to be something I could do. And yet, even as Valerie completely superimposed her ethereal form over Eric's flailing figure, I knew it was too late.

"What's happening?" Mrs. Little screamed, her eyes the size of saucers. She couldn't see the ghost. She could only feel the wind ... and hear Eric's death gasps as he fought what had once been his girlfriend.

There was no commanding her. There was no controlling her. There was no stopping her. There was nothing I could do, and the helplessness that washed over me was like a tsunami.

"Bay, we can't stay here," Thistle warned. She had Mrs. Little's arm firmly in her grip and was dragging the older woman toward the water's edge. "We have to go."

I snapped my attention to Aunt Tillie, who looked grim. "We have to do something."

"It's too late," she said at the same moment Eric's ragged gasps ceased. The lines in her face deepened as she briefly pressed her eyes shut, displaying grief before she shuttered and focused on the realities of survival. "I'm sorry." She grabbed Mrs. Little's other arm and started pulling. "Let's go, Margaret. Unless you want to be eaten as a ghost's dinner, you're done here."

When I checked the spot where Wayne had been standing, I found it empty. Common sense had finally overcome his irrational fear and he'd fled into the night. I had no idea in what direction, although I figured he was probably fine as long as he didn't stop or look back. And why would he? As far as he was concerned, only death remained in these woods. Nobody went hunting for death.

Valerie floated over Eric's body. There was determination in her voice, and glee curved her lips. "You don't belong here. This is my domain now."

"You're the one who needs to go," I insisted, refusing to back down. "You've done more than enough."

"That's for me to say."

My stomach curdled as her lips spread into a defiant sneer. "You need to go." Before I even realized what I was doing, I called out to the other ghosts in the area. It was the only thing I could think to do. Within seconds, ethereal figures, including Viola, appeared behind me.

"I was watching the Kardashians," Viola complained. "Why would you interrupt my show like that?"

"Get rid of her," I ordered in my most authoritative voice. I didn't recognize the other ghosts, but they snapped to attention and focused on Valerie.

"Fine," Viola sniffed, "but you owe me a favor." Her face contorted as she shifted into attack mode. "Let's get this beyotch! Khloe is about to lose yet another man. She has bleeding tragic taste, but I can't miss her being crushed again."

The ghosts needed little prodding. They moved as a unit and descended on Valerie. For a moment, she looked as if she was going to put up a fight. The change in the atmosphere must've been too much for her, though, because she started floating backward.

"This isn't over," she warned, defiant. "This is my land."

"So you've said, but it's mine for now. Go."

Valerie fled and the ghosts gave chase. That left Thistle, Aunt Tillie, Mrs. Little, and me to deal with the aftermath.

"WHAT HAPPENED?"

Landon was apoplectic by the time he found us in the woods. I'd called him right away, knowing we needed help with Eric's body, but it took him a long time to find us, even with his GPS linked to my phone.

I didn't immediately answer. I was too tired. He had his arms around me before anyone else could respond on my behalf.

"Why can't you have a normal night of mayhem like everybody else?" he whispered into my ear, combing his fingers through my hair.

"I knew this was a bad idea," Chief Terry announced, his eyes immediately going to Eric's body. "Landon said, 'Oh, they're fine. They're adults. They can trespass without any problems.' Guess what? You can't trespass without any problems. Ugh." He slapped his hand to his face and looked to the stars, as if silently asking, "Why me," while lamenting his lot in life.

"It wasn't our fault," Thistle insisted. She sat on a fallen log next to Aunt Tillie. Other than her hair being out of place thanks to the wind, she seemed fine. "It just ... happened."

"What was he doing out here?" Landon asked, his eyes searching my face as he pulled back. He looked worried.

"Looking for buried treasure," Aunt Tillie replied.

"Buried treasure?" Chief Terry was incredulous. "Are we back to that? I can't even ... . The Great Lakes pirate didn't have any money. That's an old wives' tale, for crying out loud."

"Well, Mrs. Little, Wayne Lawson, and poor Eric thought otherwise," Thistle replied. I was glad she didn't seem to be having trouble finding words to explain what had happened because I was at a genuine loss. "Apparently they've been searching this property for a long time."

"But why?" Chief Terry's frustration was palpable.

"They found a map," I volunteered finally, forcing a wan smile at the relieved look on Landon's face. Apparently he thought I was in shock or something, and the fact that I could speak meant I was slowly shaking myself out of my unfortunate state. "I don't know where they found it. We didn't have time to ask. By the time they really started getting into it, Valerie was already heading this way."

"What happened?" Landon asked in a softer voice, his fingers gentle against my cheek.

I told them in halting terms, backtracking a few times to get the timeline correct. Aunt Tillie continuously corrected me when I got something wrong — which was her way — and at a certain point Landon threatened her with a jail cell if she didn't stop interrupting.

"Good luck with that," Aunt Tillie muttered, although she stopped throwing in her two cents all the same.

When I finished, Landon turned his attention to Chief Terry. "How are we going to cover this up?"

"You can't cover up Eric's death," I insisted. "He must have someone who cares about him. We need to get his body back to town so his family can bury him properly."

This time the amusement that flitted through Landon's eyes was legitimate. "I didn't mean that we should cover up the death, Bay. I meant your involvement. We can't very well include in our report the fact that you guys were out here to surprise someone looking for buried treasure."

"Oh." That made sense. I rubbed my cheek, considering. "Wayne and Mrs. Little saw everything. You have to take that into account. Mrs. Little took off the second our backs were turned. We didn't even realize she was gone until it was too late. She's probably already preparing her story."

"Define 'everything,'" Chief Terry prodded.

"Everything." I held out my hands, helpless, as he viciously swore under his breath. "Mrs. Little accused us of causing the wind. She said it was mass hypnosis."

"And Wayne?" Landon asked.

"He took off. I'm not sure when. He might not have seen what happened to Eric — it was really fast, and he couldn't see Valerie — but he knows something terrible happened."

"We'll have to rein them in," Chief Terry said, shaking his head. "This is just ... the worst. How do we fix this?"

I felt bad. Really bad. "I'm sorry."

"Don't," Landon admonished, pulling me against him. "This isn't your fault. There's no way you could've known what would happen."

"That's right." Aunt Tillie was full of bravado now that she realized Landon and Chief Terry were willing to go to the mat for us. She easily skirted Thistle, who was trying to corral her, and moved closer to Eric's body. "I bet the medical examiner will find he had a stroke or an embolism. There are no marks on his body."

"Which is different from Heather," I noted. "She had a broken neck."

"Which she might've done herself when she realized there was an entity in her house," Aunt Tillie supplied. "Think about how freaked you would be if you sensed a malevolent presence in your house in the middle of the night. She might've tripped and fallen while trying to get away."

"The medical examiner is labeling her death suspicious but not necessarily criminal, though that's not a real determination," Landon offered. "He said it could go either way. Eric was our prime suspect, so I'm not sure what's going to happen. My understanding is that Heather's mother has contacted the ME's office to claim the body, but it hasn't gone further than that."

I nodded. "Does that mean Heather's mother is likely to inherit the house and property?"

"I don't know," Landon said. "We haven't gotten that far yet. It's on our list for tomorrow.

"Someone is controlling Valerie's ghost." I was more convinced of that than ever. "I very much doubt it's Mrs. Little. That seems to indicate that someone else has heard this buried treasure story. Whoever we're dealing with is smarter and more powerful than our other suspects."

Landon's hand went to the back of my neck and rubbed at the tension there. "Who else knows about the pirate legend?"

The question was directed at Chief Terry, who shook his head. "Everybody knows the legend. It's even included in one of the summer festivals."

"Yes, the kissing booth turns into an 'Argh, I want to kiss your booty' event," I volunteered.

Despite the serious nature of the conversation, Landon's eyes brightened. "How did we miss that?"

"I think that was the week we were moving in together. We didn't hang out at the festival that week."

"Well, we're not missing it next year. I definitely want to kiss your booty."

I smiled and rested my head on his shoulder, taking a moment to absorb his warmth. "Chief Terry is right. It could be anyone. The list of people who haven't heard that story is short. Like, really, really short."

"It's not." Landon was firm. "We're dealing with someone who knows the story and has the ability to control a ghost. That can't be a very long list."

"No, but we could be dealing with someone who has managed to hide her abilities for a very long time," I said. "We must be dealing with a witch. That's the only explanation that makes sense."

"I agree, but I think you're overlooking the obvious answer."

I was confused. "And what's that?"

Landon inclined his head toward the lake. "There's a witch right over there, on the other side of the lake. And she's probably heard the stories her entire life. She's near the property, and her babysitter has been taking long walks to get away from her."

My heart sank. I hadn't wanted to consider the possibility, but I'd done it all the same. Each and every time, I ruthlessly shoved the notion out of my mind. But now it made sense.

"Dani." I exhaled heavily and looked to Aunt Tillie.

"It's possible," Aunt Tillie said after a moment's contemplation. "She grew up in this town. All the kids are aware of the pirate story. They all make fun of it, but Dani is a kid in crisis. She wants to run, but she doesn't have any money. This would solve that problem."

"So, what do we do?" I asked.

"We have to go back to the campground anyway," Thistle said. "We have to question her. She'll deny it, but if we're lucky we might be able to catch her in a lie."

Dani was a good liar. She could easily snow us if she put solid effort into it. Still, it felt like our only option. "Let's do it."

**HAZEL WAS A PACING MESS WHEN WE BEACHED** on the other side of the lake. Chief Terry and Landon stayed behind to deal with the medical examiner. They'd decided to go the anonymous call route. We couldn't be present if they planned to sell that narrative. That meant escaping across the lake before they started calling.

"Thank the Goddess," Hazel gasped when she saw us, scurrying in our direction. "I've been trying to call but you didn't pick up."

She was white as Valerie's ghost. "Our cell service is spotty over there."

"And we had an incident," Thistle added. "We weren't paying attention to our phones."

"What's wrong?" Aunt Tillie demanded, her interest keen.

Hazel wrung her hands. When she didn't immediately speak, I prodded her. "Well?"

"It's Dani. She melted down after you left."

"Melted down how?" I asked, suspicious energy pooling in my chest.

"She kept going on and on about how you would never trust her and she was sick of being treated like a child," Hazel explained. "I tried to talk her down, but ... she wouldn't listen. She was enraged. I tried to make her go to the cabin, but she refused. She ... um ... lashed out with her magic." She held out her arm, showing a red splotch on her shirt. It looked like blood.

"How is that possible?" Thistle asked. "I thought we warded the property."

"We did," Aunt Tillie argued. "It's impossible."

"Well, she did it." Hazel looked resigned. "After she attacked me, she took off on foot. She's gone. I didn't think she could leave the property, but she did."

I was dumbfounded. "What are we going to do?"

"Pray," Aunt Tillie replied grimly. "We have to hope she doesn't hurt someone before we track her down. Landon was right — and you have no idea how much I hate admitting that. Dani's doing this. She's the only one powerful enough."

I felt sick. "I'll call Landon." I pulled my phone from my pocket. "He'll want to know about this."

"There's nothing he can do," Thistle pointed out.

"He'll still want to know. This is ... bad."

Aunt Tillie nodded. "It's definitely bad. The kid is dangerous and now she's out there wreaking havoc. We have to find her — and fast."

# TWENTY-THREE

I waited up for Landon.
The bedroom was dark when he made his way into the room and I could hear him as he dropped his clothes. His body was warm when he climbed in next to me and I immediately turned and let him draw me in.

"Bay." His voice was barely a whisper as he inhaled deeply and pressed me tight.

He smelled like doughnuts, which would've been romantic under different circumstances. "The medical examiner?" I asked.

"He didn't question us. Don't worry. It's going to be okay."

"But Mrs. Little."

"Don't worry," he repeated. "Go to sleep. Morning will be here soon enough. We'll talk about it then."

"Okay." I pressed my face to his chest and listened to the beat of his heart. "I really am sorry. I didn't think it would turn out like this."

That elicited a low chuckle. "Nobody thought it would turn out like this. It really is okay. Now go to sleep."

"Okay." I pressed my eyes shut and willed sleep to claim me. After a few minutes, I couldn't stop myself from asking another question. "Do you think Mrs. Little will tell people what happened?"

He snorted. "Do I think Mrs. Little is going to tell people that you guys killed a man she was trespassing with? No."

"We didn't kill him."

"No, but it might look like that from her perspective. My guess is that she'll keep her mouth shut while waiting to see how things shake out. That will benefit us — at least over the short haul."

"That's good, right?"

"It is ... if I can ever get some sleep to recharge to deal with it."

"Sorry." I closed my eyes again but I simply couldn't settle. "What if she doesn't do what we think she will?"

"That does it." Landon took me by surprise when he rolled me over and landed on top of me. I could see the wicked gleam in his eyes thanks to the moon shining through the window as he stared me down. "You won't shut up until I make you, will you?"

We'd had a horrible night. Everything that could go wrong had. Love welled up for him despite all that, and I managed a smile. "What do you have in mind?"

"Well, I do smell like doughnuts. It would be a shame to waste that."

"It would."

"And you need to be tired out if you're ever going to shut off that busy brain of yours."

"I do need to be tired out."

"I have an idea."

"I'm putty in your hands."

"That's exactly what I'm counting on."

**WE WERE BOTH MORE SETTLED WHEN WE** let ourselves into the inn through the back door the next morning.

Aunt Tillie sat in her usual spot on the couch, Peg at her side, and yelled at the television. "It's not going to rain today. Stop saying it's going to rain." She shook her fist at the weather forecaster, a perky blonde with boobs that spilled out over the top of her shirt.

"Is that Misty Showers?" Landon asked, his gaze fixed on the television.

I narrowed my eyes. "How do you know the forecaster's name?"

He masked his excitement quickly. "I have to watch the news for work."

"And you need to know what the weather is going to be like when you're chasing bad guys," Aunt Tillie added helpfully.

"That too." Landon nodded. "It's perfectly innocent."

"Uh-huh." I didn't quite believe him, but I didn't have the energy to call him on a mild deceit. We had bigger things to worry about. "Did they say anything about Eric's death?"

Aunt Tillie shook her head. "That's why I was watching. I got distracted by the stupid weather girl — seriously, that's the only job in the world where you can be wrong seventy-five percent of the time and not get fired — but they never mentioned Eric."

"As far as I know, word hasn't spread yet," Landon noted. "I don't think it will be long. I'm sure the rumor mill will begin grinding."

"Especially since Margaret was out there," Aunt Tillie said. "She's probably been putting her spin on the story since before sunup. We're going to have our hands full on that front."

"Landon doesn't think so," I countered. "He thinks she'll keep her mouth shut because it's in her best interest to make sure nobody knows she was out there."

Aunt Tillie let loose a disdainful snort. "Are you new?" She pinned Landon with a dubious look. "That's not how Margaret operates. She'll spread a false narrative so we spend more time covering our behinds than watching where she's sticking her nose. It's a classic distraction technique."

"And how do you know that?" Landon challenged.

"I know things."

"She has invisible eyes in her head," I teased.

"Laugh all you want, but that's true." Aunt Tillie used the remote to turn off the television and stood. "Margaret will be an issue. If you want to stop her, you'll go on the offensive and keep her off that land."

"Keep her off the land?" Landon's hand moved up and down my back as he pinned my great-aunt with a look of suspicion. "Are you certain you're not suggesting I stop her from going out there so you can take over the search?"

"Don't be ridiculous. I'm not evil. I just think it would be wise to limit Margaret's movements."

"I'll consider it." Landon prodded me toward the kitchen door, the scent of fresh bacon drawing us both in that direction. "You're overestimating Mrs. Little. She's probably terrified that you guys will send some invisible wind hunter after her to ensure she doesn't talk."

"Really?" Aunt Tillie snapped her fingers to get Peg to fall into step with her. "Do you really think, after all the time and effort Margaret has put into this endeavor, that she'll let it go just because something happened that she can't explain? She lives in Hemlock Cove. Do you have any idea how many unexplained happenings she's managed to explain away?"

Landon opened his mouth to answer, but I cut him off.

"She's right," I said. I didn't want to pile additional worry on him, but I couldn't shake the feeling that things were going to get worse before they got better. "Mrs. Little can't be corralled unless you go directly at her. She won't do the right thing simply because it's the smart move. That's not who she is."

"I'll talk to Terry," Landon said, prodding me toward the door. "We'll figure it out. Breakfast first."

The kitchen was empty but it looked like everyone was just getting settled around the dining room table when we slid through the door. Thankfully the weekend guests weren't due to arrive until the afternoon, so we were free to talk things over.

"I don't understand why family breakfast was mandatory this morning," Clove complained, her eyes lighting up when she saw the platter of fresh doughnuts. "On the other hand, family time is very important. I'm always open to spending more time with my family."

Amused, Sam grabbed the platter and held it up for her. "Pick what you want."

"This isn't for me," Clove said. "It's for the baby. She likes ... this one." Clove snagged a cake doughnut with sprinkles even though she knew it was my favorite.

Landon, perhaps reading my mind, snagged the doughnut's twin before anyone else could claim it and dropped it on my plate.

I beamed at him. "I really love you sometimes."

He returned the smile. "Right back at you." He smacked a loud kiss against my lips, earning a dirty look from Chief Terry, and then glanced at the others around the table. "So, as most everybody knows, we had a bit of an incident last night."

"We heard at least some of it," Mom confirmed. "Aunt Tillie went straight to her room when she got back, but Terry filled me in when he came to bed."

Now it was my turn to be grossed out. For my entire childhood — at least after I'd given up on the idea of my parents getting back together — I'd gravitated toward Chief Terry as my father figure. Even now that my father was back in town, more often than not I went to the chief to make me feel better. I'd always wanted him with my mother. The reality was hard to swallow, though. I'd seen them in bed together weeks ago. I was still trying to scrub the image from my brain.

Still, that was something to grouse about when we didn't have a murderous ghost to deal with.

I laid everything out for them in a clinical manner. Now that I was separated from what happened a bit, my emotions weren't as raw. When I finished, everyone started talking at once.

"How did he die?" Marnie asked.

"Who is going to sell real estate in town now?" Twila chimed in.

"Do you really think Dani's behind this?" Mom looked positively nauseated at the thought. "She's just a girl."

"She's a girl with an interesting skill set," I countered. "She's powerful. Apparently more powerful than we realized."

"Landon figured it out," Thistle volunteered as she slathered her toast with strawberry preserves. "He suggested that we had a likely suspect across the lake. We hadn't truly considered Dani."

"I did kind of wonder about it," I hedged. "It was one of those things that I thought and then immediately dismissed. I didn't believe it could be her ... and now that we know it's most likely her, I feel oddly detached."

"And she attacked Hazel?" Twila made a tsking sound. "That's horrible. We should invite her here to spend the day. We can fix that injury and allow her to rest."

"That's a good idea," I acknowledged. "She was pretty down on herself last night. She blamed herself for what happened."

"It's not her fault," Mom argued.

"I don't know that she feels the same way. She's spent the most time with Dani since this started. She'd warned us before that Dani was showing signs of ... unfortunate behavior. It's just not good."

"We can figure it out," Mom said. "We need to break things down. Where would Dani go?"

"The obvious answer is the house she grew up in, but Lorna and Nick are gone," Thistle volunteered. "After Lorna found out what Dani had done to her own father, she wanted to protect her son. I think she figured the daughter was a lost cause but there was still a chance for the son."

"Do we know where they went?" Marnie asked.

I hesitated and glanced at Chief Terry. "I don't, but I'm sure there's a way to find them."

"I'm sure there is," Chief Terry acknowledged, "but do we want to risk involving them in this now that they've made a clean getaway?"

"What if Dani is already on her way to them to take her revenge?" Mom challenged.

"And what if Dani is somehow monitoring to see who we make contact with?" Chief Terry fired back. "I'm not sure I'm comfortable being the chink in the armor that leads to them being taken down."

"That's fair," I said hurriedly, holding up my hands in capitulation. The last thing I wanted to bear witness to was a fight between Chief Terry and Mom. That might be more horrifying than the sex I kept picturing. "Odds are she's still here. Why she chose to act last night is beyond me, but she's clearly controlling Valerie's ghost.

"Chief Terry brought up a good point," I continued. "He said every kid in the area knows the Arlen Topper legend. It's possible Dani heard talk of buried treasure on the property and decided to find it so she could make her getaway. She could've been going over there two or three times a day for all we know. Apparently the wards weren't working correctly, so she was always free to come and go."

"I didn't think about it, but you're right," Mom said. "I don't understand any of this. If she could leave, and was so unhappy, why did she stay?"

"She didn't have anywhere else to go," Aunt Tillie added. "She was always feeling us out, trying to push boundaries. Hazel told me that the kid was trying to get in her dreams and give her nightmares."

That was the first I'd heard of that. "What?"

Aunt Tillie nodded gravely. "Hazel said the kid was pushing horrible pictures into her head, like bloody scenes from horror movies and the things she wanted to do to her mother. At least she thought it was Lorna. She never saw a face, just heard screams."

"Why didn't you say something?" I was dumbfounded. "If she was doing that, I should've known."

"And then what?" Aunt Tillie's gaze was plaintive when it landed on me. "Bay, you're a strong girl. You're smart, too, although I reserve the right to take that back the next time you or your boyfriend tick me off. You also have a soft heart, which is why you've never fully embraced the things that you can do."

Landon stirred. "I happen to like her soft heart."

"Of course you do," Aunt Tillie shot back. "You're trapped in the center of her heart and you benefit from all the lovey-dovey things she says to you. You get a moony look on your face sometimes when your gazes meet across the room. You speak without words ... and it's gross."

"I agree," Chief Terry intoned, although he winked at me. "They're totally gross. I'm going to start carrying a squirt gun so I can spray them when they get annoying at meals."

I rolled my eyes. "That's not really what we should be talking about. That honor belongs to Dani. If she was terrorizing Hazel ... ."

"I'm trying to explain why nothing was said to you," Aunt Tillie supplied. "It's that soft heart of yours. You didn't want to think of anything bad happening to Dani, so you made excuses for her behavior. You kept dragging Landon into the same conversations because you were terrified of dealing with her harshly. You didn't want to accept that Hazel was struggling with the girl, so you didn't see it.

"Now we have no choice but to deal with it," she continued. "Dani could very well go on a rampage now that she's free. She's got a poltergeist on the payroll, and from what I saw last night, Valerie is getting more and more deranged."

I'd been thinking about that too. "We have to break the hold Dani has over Valerie."

"How do you suggest we do that?" Landon asked.

"I'm not sure." I was at a loss. "I'm guessing Dani has something of Valerie's and that's how she's controlling her ghost."

"How did she get it, though?" Clove asked, her mouth full of doughnut. She was so engrossed in her meal she didn't notice she had chocolate smeared on her cheek. Or it's possible she simply didn't care. It could've gone either way given the way she was mowing through that doughnut.

"She's been leaving the campground from the start," I said. "She could've run into Valerie on the other side of the lake. Maybe she was going over there to get some time to herself and stumbled upon Valerie when she was spying on Heather and Eric."

Landon stroked his chin and nodded. "That makes sense. If Dani ran into Valerie, maybe Dani killed her to shut her up. Then Dani realized she could control the ghost and make her do her bidding. Whatever she picked up from Valerie that day is what she's using to control the ghost."

"So we have to find Dani, strip her of all her belongings, and sever the tie with Valerie's ghost," Thistle added. "Then Bay can send the ghost on her way and Dani will have to deal with us on her own."

I nodded. "Did those herbs come in? The ones we need to strip her powers?"

"They're due today."

"I can work on that," Aunt Tillie offered. "It will take a few hours. We have to find the girl before we can use it. I'm not sure our standard locator spells will be effective. If she figured out how to enslave a ghost, she probably knows how to shroud herself. We might be facing an uphill battle just in finding her."

"And yet I don't think she's ready to leave," I said. "I think we're the only true tie she has now that her mother and brother are gone. She can't leave without money ... or besting us. She could come to us out here."

"There's no way she's getting through the wards." Aunt Tillie was firm. "I'm not sure how she managed to break the wards at the campground, but these were drawn with blood and tears. I strengthened them until there was zero give left after Diane's incursion. They won't fail to a teenage hellion."

"That's a pleasant image," Landon muttered, shuddering at mention of blood and tears.

Aunt Tillie ignored him. "This house is safe."

"Then this is where Clove has to stay," I said, cringing when my cousin glared at me. "I'm sorry." I held up my hands to ward off what I was sure would be a righteous fit. "You have a baby on board. You can't be wandering around with a demented witch on the hunt for us."

"I agree with Bay," Sam said. "It's best if you stay here."

"But I want to help," Clove whined, the splotch of frosting on her cheek even bigger than before. "I'm sick of being cut out of things."

"You can help with the research," I suggested. "We need to read up on the pirate and whatever spells Dani may be using to control Valerie. Information is critical."

"We'll keep Clove here," Mom agreed. "She'll be safe. What are you going to do?"

That was a very good question. "Find Dani." There was nothing else to do. "She's out there somewhere — and I think she's close. After that, we'll put together a plan and take her down. We no longer have a choice. She can't stay here. She's too dangerous."

# TWENTY-FOUR

I wasn't surprised when Landon suggested I join his search team upon leaving the inn an hour later.

"I'm not trying to stifle you," he promised. "That's the last thing I want. It's just ... it seems that it would be smart for us to stick together. That way nobody will be caught unaware."

He had a point, but it was coming from an irrational place. "You're afraid she's going to seek me out and kill me."

A visible shudder went through him. "You make the most sense as a likely target, Bay." He was using his most pragmatic voice, so I knew he meant business. "She saw you take out her aunt. You gave her another chance, but that memory is seared into her brain. She wants to hurt you."

I regarded him for a long moment. "We've never really talked about it. Do you think I did the wrong thing that day?"

"Absolutely not." He swept closer, his eyes turbulent like a storm, and grabbed my hands. "It was kill or be killed that day. She wanted to take you out. Heck, she wanted to take all of you out. You were the one standing in her way, though, and you would've been first if she'd had the strength to carry out her plan."

What he said made sense and yet ... . "I keep wondering if I could've found a way to spare Diane, if Dani wouldn't have completely fallen over the edge of sanity. I know you'll say I'm crazy, but ... it's here." I tapped the side of my head. "It's right at the forefront of my brain."

"Then you need to shut off your brain. You know I like my women slow and smelling like bacon." He was going for levity, even offered up a sloppy smile, but then he sobered. "Bay, you did what you had to do. Dani crossed the line to crazy town long before you took out Diane. She was involved in the murder of her own father. She was willing to take out her mother. You didn't create that problem, or exacerbate it. In fact, you went out of your way to save her when nobody else would have."

"I guess." I rubbed my forehead. "We have to find her, Landon." My voice turned plaintive. "If she kills someone else ... ."

"We'll find her." He rubbed his hands up and down my arms. "I promise. We just need a little ... help. We also need to stick together." He was firm.

"Just out of curiosity — and I'm not asking to delay my answer — but if you felt Aunt Tillie was the key player in this, would you insist she go to work with you?"

"Absolutely," he answered without hesitation. "I protect all the residents of Hemlock Cove equally."

I waited, dubious, and he smirked. "Or maybe you're the most important thing in the world to me and I refuse to risk you," he acknowledged. "That doesn't change the fact that I'm right. We need to give Aunt Tillie and Thistle time to make that potion. They need a few hours. We can't give Dani an opening at you until our plan is in place."

Everything he said made sense. "I still have to go after her at some point," I reminded him. "You said it yourself. I make the most sense as bait. Have you wrapped your head around that yet?"

He hesitated and then nodded. "I know you have to be in the thick of things. For now, though, it's better if you're with me."

"Okay." He was right, and I didn't want to start the day with an argument. "We have to stop at the newspaper office first. I need to find Viola."

He furrowed his brow. "Why?"

"I have to apologize for what happened last night — and then I need to ask her for a favor."

His face was blank. "I don't understand."

He wouldn't, couldn't really. "I used her and other ghosts in the area — people I've never met — to fight off Valerie. I didn't give them a choice."

Realization dawned on his handsome features. "And, in typical fashion, you think that makes you some sort of villain. Bay, you're not a bad woman. You did what you had to do to protect everyone present."

"I'm well aware. I still don't like commanding the ghosts without giving them a choice. But I told you before that I'm open to doing it when certain situations arise. That doesn't mean I can't apologize."

"Fine." Landon threw up his hands. "Apologize to Viola. Then you can come with me to shake down Mrs. Little."

Oddly enough, I was looking forward to that portion of the day's festivities. "Thank you."

He linked his fingers with mine as we returned to our walk. "Just out of curiosity, what favor are you going to ask of her?"

"To find Dani."

He slowed his pace but didn't release my hand. "Can she do that?"

"In theory. Dani is smart. She knows what I'm capable of. If she wants to block against ghosts, there's every possibility she'll do it."

"But what if she wants to use the ghosts to draw you into a trap?"

I flashed a smile. "Now I see why you're such a highly regarded investigator."

He frowned. "Ugh. I should've seen this coming. You think she'll set a trap through the ghosts."

"I'm counting on it. I need Viola to find her. Dani won't show herself until she's ready. At least we'll know where she is when the time comes — if this plays out the way I think it will."

"Okay. Viola first." He leaned in and gave me a kiss. "Bay, when it's time to approach Dani, I want to talk about the plan before we enact it. That's only fair."

"I know. I'm probably going to have to be the one to challenge her, and I might be alone when that happens. You realize that, right?"

He worked his jaw and then nodded. "We'll tackle that when it's time. For now, I want you close to me. We'll cover every contingency when it's time to take on Dani. I want your word that we'll do it together if at all possible.

"I know that you might get separated and if she goes after you alone you'll have no choice," he continued. "I want you to protect yourself no matter what. If there's a choice, I want to be involved."

I should've seen that coming. Of course he would want to be involved. "We'll figure it out."

"Good." He wrapped his arms around me and held tight. "I love you ... but sometimes I think you're going to give me an ulcer."

That made me laugh. "If it's any consolation, you still smell like doughnuts."

"I know. Aunt Tillie fixed it so I can smell it too. There are times I almost want to molest myself."

I laughed so hard tears formed in my eyes. "I love you too."

"I know." He swiped at the tears. "We're in this together, Bay. Don't forget that when things get hairy."

"I won't. You have my word."

**UNLIKE THE PREVIOUS GHOST AT** The Whistler — Edith, a woman I still had mixed feelings about — Viola was volatile. She was also easier to deal with than the previous resident. When I offered her my heartfelt apology, she rolled her eyes.

"I like a good fight," she said. "It was fine, but what was up with that ghost?"

"She's being controlled."

"Who's doing the controlling?"

I told her about Dani, showed her a photo, and then asked for my favor. She perked right up. "I'll find her," she promised. "You have my word." She saluted and then disappeared.

From the couch in my office where he'd planted himself so I could do my thing, Landon arched an eyebrow. "Mission accomplished?"

I nodded. "She doesn't even seem upset."

"So in other words, you felt bad for nothing. I'm sensing a pattern here, Bay."

I offered up a half smile. "Maybe I have a problem."

"You do. You're harder on yourself than you have any cause to be, especially because I happen to believe you're pretty much perfect."

I shook my head. He was always my biggest cheerleader, and I appreciated it. "I think you might look at me differently than most people."

"I certainly hope so." He extended his hand as he stood. "Are you ready to shake down Mrs. Little?"

Now that was something I'd been looking forward to. "Do you think we'll make her cry?"

"That's something Aunt Tillie would ask."

"Maybe I'm turning into her."

He mock shuddered. "Now that is a frightening thought. Oddly, though, I'm okay with it. I understand why that woman gets Aunt Tillie's dander up. She's a horrible excuse for a human being ... and we're nailing her today."

He sounded sure of himself. I'd been around Mrs. Little enough to know that she wouldn't go down without a fight, and I was spoiling for one. "Let's do it."

. . .

**CHIEF TERRY MET US IN FRONT OF** Mrs. Little's store. He had a folded piece of paper in his hand and a grim look on his face.

"Did you get it?" Landon asked.

"Get what?" I asked.

"I got it." Chief Terry looked ready for battle. "It was easier than I thought. When I explained to the judge who I was going after and why, he only asked for basic evidence — delivered verbally nonetheless — and then signed it. He seemed almost gleeful."

I was still lagging behind the conversation. "What is that?"

Chief Terry sent me a mischievous smile. "I think you should find out when Margaret does. It might be more fun."

As a Winchester, there was little I hated more than being left out of the loop. "Tell me now."

"That would be unprofessional." He winked at me. "I'm nothing if not a diligent public servant."

"Fine." I pouted as I followed them into the store. "This is pure torture."

"You'll live." Chief Terry cleared his throat once we were inside, and when I peered around his broad shoulders, I found Mrs. Little dutifully dusting a shelf. "Margaret."

Mrs. Little's shoulders stiffened as she turned. Her gaze bounced from face to face, finally landing on mine. She didn't look happy. "If you're here to arrest me for what happened last night, you should be aware that I've already talked to my attorney and he's taken my statement on the record. He knows that Bay killed Eric Savage."

My mouth dropped open. "Excuse me?" My voice was shrill. I couldn't believe her audacity.

Landon shot me a quelling look and I immediately snapped my mouth shut. I was supposed to be an observer, a witness if called upon. I wasn't an active interrogation participant by design. This was on the law enforcement contingent of our group, and I'd agreed to that stipulation before being included. I couldn't go back on my word now.

"We have witnesses to the events of last night, and that story won't fly," Chief Terry said gravely.

"Well, given your relationship with the woman in question, I'm guessing I can get both of you booted from this case and an independent investigator will see things differently."

It was a brazen threat, I had to give her that. Landon and Chief Terry were prepared for it, though.

"That's certainly your prerogative," Landon said. "You should know that I contacted the Michigan State Police last night. I anticipated this reaction. I forwarded everything we had on the case.

"When I got to the part about you and Wayne Lawson fleeing the scene after being there illegally, they were quite interested," he continued. "I explained how Bay, Thistle, and Tillie Winchester were at the campground when they heard noise and went to check it out. Given the tragedies that have occurred on that property the last few days, it's only natural they gave in to their curiosity."

I pressed my lips together and stared at him in wonder. He'd done much more during the time that we were separated last night than I realized. He'd essentially built a wall that Mrs. Little had no hope of scaling, and he was unveiling it now. I was floored. I was also kind of hot for him, and it wasn't just the doughnut smell this time. That would have to wait for later, though.

"Excuse me?" Mrs. Little was a master manipulator. She understood that going on the offensive was her best bet, and that was on full display now. I had no doubt that she'd been rehearsing her response to Chief Terry and Landon's interrogation since she'd departed the lakefront property when our backs were turned. "If your precious girlfriend and her family were so worried about what was happening on that property, why didn't they call you?"

"They tried," Landon replied smoothly. "Unfortunately, cell reception is spotty out there. They couldn't reach us. Rather than risk another dead body showing up, they decided to offer their help. When they arrived at the location, they found you, Wayne Lawson, and Eric Savage conspiring to dig up the land on property you don't own and steal something you believe is buried there."

Mrs. Little looked like a guppy as her lips moved but no sound came out. I had to turn away to keep from laughing. This was going better than I could've possibly hoped.

"We want to know what it is that you're searching for," Chief Terry demanded.

Rather than immediately answer, Mrs. Little narrowed her eyes at me. "You set me up."

I shook my head. "I'm pretty sure you did this to yourself," I argued. "You thought you were going to find a hidden stash of pirate treasure. I mean ... pirate treasure? Really?"

She exploded. I expected it, but not this fast. "Arlen Topper was real. He lived on that property. He died without leaving his estate to anyone. That money didn't just disappear. It's out there."

"Even if it is, it doesn't belong to you," Landon said.

"If I find it and there are no living heirs, it does belong to me," Mrs. Little snapped. "I've researched the situation. I know."

Landon remained calm, his training kicking in. "And the property owners have nothing to do with it?"

"There are no property owners. Heather Castle is dead. The house and the land are in limbo."

"Her estate owns the property, and the legalities of that are being sorted out as we speak," Landon said. "You have no claim to anything you find out there. In addition to that, if you're committing a crime during the initial discovery, all monetary gains are forfeit."

Mrs. Little glowered. "You can't keep me from that treasure. We've been looking for months. We're narrowing down the location. We've put far too much work into this to simply give up because you say we can't look."

"We're not the only ones who say that," Chief Terry said. "A circuit judge has signed off on it." He produced the sheet of paper and shoved it in her direction. "Margaret Little, you are formally prohibited from visiting the property located at 1356 Looking Glass Lane. If you trespass, we have immediate grounds to arrest and incarcerate you. Do you understand?"

I was loving the moment. I found myself drifting closer to Landon. It felt as if an explosion was about to level the room and I wanted to protect him should Mrs. Little turn into a small hurricane and start clawing his eyes out.

"You can't do this." Tears formed in Mrs. Little's eyes. "I haven't done anything wrong."

"You're the only one who believes that," Chief Terry challenged. "And I hate to break it to you, but I think you know deep down that what you've been doing *is* wrong. I don't know why you've chosen to go this route. I really don't care. If you're caught out there again, I will take great pleasure in hauling you to jail."

"As for an independent investigator, one should arrive this afternoon," Landon added. "He'll have questions for you."

Vitriol practically dripped from Mrs. Little's curled lips. "And what happens when I tell him that three witches killed a man last night?"

"I don't know." Landon didn't look bothered by the question. "I suggest you float that idea and we'll find out."

I couldn't hide my surprise at his response. "Landon ... ." I kept my voice low, but he gave me a short, almost imperceptible shake of his head.

"This isn't over," Mrs. Little warned as she crumpled the paper in her hand. "You won't keep me from what I've earned. You stole that campground from me, and Eric stole the house from me, but I'm nowhere near done."

"That sounds like a healthy attitude," Chief Terry noted. "I meant what I said. If you show up on that property again, it will be my great pleasure to arrest you. I'll even do a public perp walk and take you into the police department through the front door."

"I think I know a few people who would be happy to film that," Landon volunteered. "One of them drives a scooter while wearing a cape."

"I won't let you beat me," Mrs. Little gritted out. "I just ... won't. We're not done."

"Oh, we're done," Landon shot back. "The fact that you're the only one who doesn't realize it is on you."

# TWENTY-FIVE

I could barely contain my excitement until we exited the store. "That was so fun!"

"Shh." Landon slapped his hand over my mouth and moved me until we were away from the window. His smile was sloppy when he met my gaze. "Who's your favorite person in the world?"

"Betty White."

He frowned.

"You're a close second." I threw my arms around his neck and hugged him tight. "It's like Christmas. I've never seen her react like that. She was so angry."

"She was," Chief Terry agreed as he looked up and down the street. He seemed nervous. Mrs. Little was angry, but she had no power to change things — at least not this soon.

"What's wrong?" I asked as Landon kept close, his top shirt button open. I had a feeling it was so I had no choice but to inhale the intoxicating scent of doughnuts and potentially lose my head. He would be perfectly fine if I forgot that we had a dangerous witch to deal with and dragged him across the road to my office.

"Did I say anything was wrong?" He was the picture of innocence as he returned his focus to me. "I'm just ... reveling in my win."

That was a lie — and Chief Terry never lied to me. "No, you're afraid." I didn't need Clove's heightened powers to read him. When we were kids, he was capable of hiding things from us when he told himself it was for our own good. As we grew more accustomed to his mannerisms, he slowly lost that ability. Now he was nearly incapable of telling an untruth and getting us to buy it. "No, something is wrong." I turned my eyes to Landon. "Tell me what's wrong."

"I don't know." Landon kept one arm around me as he turned his head to Chief Terry. "Bay's right. You're a terrible liar. What gives?"

I balked. "I didn't say he was a liar."

"Thank you, Bay," Chief Terry said, glaring at Landon. "At least one of you isn't a pain today."

"I was thinking it, but I didn't say it," I clarified. "You're all worked up all of a sudden. That makes me antsy. I don't like being antsy."

"I don't like it either," Landon noted. "I smell like doughnuts, for crying out loud. She's supposed to be falling under my spell so I can distract her from getting into a witch fight this afternoon. That can't happen if you keep acting like that."

Chief Terry heaved out a sigh. "There might be one problem."

"With Mrs. Little?" I felt as if I was dragging. "I don't understand."

"Not Margaret. I thought of it as the conversation was winding down with her, though. It's something we should've discussed over breakfast, but it slipped through the cracks and now I feel it's my responsibility to deal with it."

I waited but he didn't volunteer the information.

"Don't keep us in suspense," Landon snapped. "If we've forgotten something, you need to tell us what it is. Is Bay in danger?"

"Not Bay," Chief Terry responded. "Dani isn't going to attack in the middle of the street."

Landon tentatively lowered his arms. "So ... what did we miss?"

Chief Terry's eyes landed on me and he swallowed hard. "We locked Clove up at the inn because she makes an obvious target. She's with your mother and aunts. Tillie is with Thistle. Someone would have to be stupid to go after them. You're with us. Landon and I aren't magical, but we can hold our own if it becomes necessary."

"Yeah," I said. "I agree with all of that."

"There is one other way to draw your attention."

I couldn't fathom what he was having such a hard time saying. "You're going to need to spell it out for us because I'm not catching on to what you're so terrified to say."

"And we don't have time for nonsense," Landon noted. "Just tell us."

"Fine." Chief Terry threw up his hands in frustration, as if we'd somehow managed to force him into an uncomfortable situation despite the fact that he'd done it to himself. "Here it is: You have three other family members in town. You don't often pay them the attention you should, but they make likely targets because everybody knows they're related to you."

My heart sank. "Dad."

"And Warren and Teddy," Chief Terry confirmed. "If someone wanted to hurt your family without immediately getting caught, what better place to go? Dani could take over the Dragonfly."

I hadn't even thought of my father. How bad of a person did that make me? My eyes were plaintive when I turned to Landon. "We have to go out there."

"We do," he agreed, immediately prodding me forward. "I didn't think of them either. The chief is right. They make excellent targets."

I shuffled my feet as I worked to keep up with him. "It makes me a bad daughter that I didn't even think of him, doesn't it?"

"No, it doesn't." He was firm. "You're a good daughter ... who had an absentee father for much of your life. Of course you thought about the family you spend the most time with first. That's only natural."

He said the right words, but I couldn't help believing he was making excuses for me. "I should bake him cookies or something when I have time."

"That sounds lovely." Landon opened the door to Chief Terry's vehicle so I could hop in. "Make it a double batch. You know how I feel about cookies."

"The same way I feel about doughnuts."

He grinned, sympathy lighting his eyes. "It's going to be okay. It's not too late and we remembered. We'll make sure they're safe and then go from there."

"We didn't remember. Chief Terry did."

"Yes, well ... he's part of the team. It still counts as a win for us."

I was glad he could say it with a straight face, because I wasn't sure I could.

**MY FATHER AND UNCLES HAD OPENED** the Dragonfly Bed & Breakfast a year ago. They claimed they didn't return to Hemlock Cove to engage in a competition with our mothers, but sometimes it felt like that. Either way, they wanted to make amends for disappearing on us when we were kids and became regular visitors in our lives.

The relationships were a work in progress. Clove was having the best luck because she refused to admit she was still bitter about the way her father took off when she was a kid. Thistle and I didn't have that problem, which meant

# TO LOVE A WITCH

we were often shuffling through minefields when interacting with our fathers.

"This is a nice surprise." Warren greeted us at the door, his gaze momentarily landing on Chief Terry before settling on me. "Just you today? I was hoping you brought Thistle and Clove."

"I'm sorry." My mouth was suddenly dry as I fumbled for the right words. "This was an impromptu visit."

"Oh?" Warren, much like Clove, had a bad poker face. It was obvious he was wary. Aunt Marnie, on the other hand, could lie with the best of them. That was one thing Clove missed out on when it came to her mother's genes. They looked like twins, but Marnie was meaner and more deceitful ... and proud of it.

"Yeah," I confirmed, forcing a smile I didn't feel. "We were just sitting around downtown and your names came up, so we thought we'd stop in for a visit." I craned my neck to look over his shoulder. "Is my dad around?"

Warren nodded, his eyes thoughtful. "He is."

"And Uncle Teddy?"

"He's here, too." Warren folded his arms over his chest. "Is something wrong, Bay? You're acting odd."

I wanted to argue with the assumption, but he was right. I was definitely acting odd. "I'm fine." I flashed my most angelic smile. "I just want to see my dad."

"Okay. Come on in."

Landon pressed close to me as I eased through the door, his voice a whisper in my ear. "When you smile like that you look like the Joker."

I was horrified at the thought. "Jack Nicholson or Heath Ledger? Or, wait ... please tell me it's not Joaquin Phoenix."

"Try Jared Leto."

Oh, no. That was the worst. "I'm sorry." I rubbed my sweaty palms over my jeans. "I'm a nervous wreck. I don't know what's wrong with me."

"I know what's wrong with you. You're a terrible liar."

"You say that like it's a bad thing."

"In this particular case, it is. Let me do the talking with your father."

Given the fact that Landon and my father had a tempestuous relationship on the best of days — and that was putting it mildly — the notion seemed absurd. I was too nervous to argue, though. I simply nodded like an idiot.

Dad and Teddy were behind the counter chopping vegetables when we slid through the door. My father was the first to look up, and his face split into the widest grin I'd ever seen when he caught sight of me.

"There she is." He abandoned his project and hurried in my direction, wiping his hands on a towel as he closed the distance. "Well, let me see it. I've heard about it, but he wouldn't let me see it."

I was confused. "See what?"

My father grabbed my left hand and tugged it up, his eyes briefly going wide before he slid his gaze to Landon, who was shaking his head and making a series of exaggerated expressions straight out of a YouTube soap opera.

"What's going on?" I asked. That felt like the question of the day, but I simply couldn't keep up.

Dad dropped my hand and his face froze in one of those half smiles you see on people's faces when a major faux pas occurs at a family dinner. "Nothing is going on," Dad reassured me quickly. "I simply wanted to see your outfit." He beamed at me as he took in my capris and T-shirt. "It's lovely. That shirt is nice on you. It brings out the color of your eyes."

The shirt was black and featured a pair of rhinestone lips. "I don't understand." I glanced at Landon. "Am I missing something?"

"Of course not, sweetie. Your dad is right. Black is a good color on you."

That wasn't really an answer. I cocked my head, prepared to demand he own up to whatever was going on — I was convinced I was no longer imagining it — when Chief Terry stepped in and took over the conversation.

"I'm sorry we have to bother you like this," he started, cringing slightly as he held my father's gaze. Their relationship often bordered on ugly. Chief Terry believed my father was a weak man and had abandoned me at the time I needed him most. As a result, Chief Terry stepped in and did all the fatherly things Thistle, Clove, and I needed growing up. My father was bitter because he believed another man usurped his territory. It was a whole big thing that nobody had time for.

"I'm guessing something is wrong," Dad noted, his jaw clenching. "If you guys stopped by for a visit in the middle of the day, it only makes sense that something is terribly wrong. That's how it goes, right?"

I cringed. We'd promised to make more of an effort to spend time with them when it wasn't a witchy emergency. We'd been doing better ... kind of. That didn't mean we were perfect by any stretch.

"This isn't like the other times," I argued. "I mean ... not really. This time it's not our fault. Er, well, I guess it's kind of my fault because I insisted on trying to help Dani rather than kill her the day before the wedding. I thought I was doing the right thing."

Dad held back a sigh, but it looked as if it took monumental effort. "Okay, let's start from the beginning," he prodded.

That's what I did. Sure, I nut-shelled the problem — there was no way he could truly understand what we were up against — and when I breezed through everything that had happened at the lake, he made a clucking sound with his tongue and shook his head.

"Wow," he said, shifting his eyes to Teddy. "I just ... wow."

"The important thing is that they're all okay," Warren interjected. That was another thing he gave to Clove, blind optimism and an annoying dollop of naïveté. He couldn't seem to keep from looking on the bright side, just like his daughter. "Things could be worse."

Dad made an exaggerated face. "Oh, yeah? How could things be worse? No, Warren, I want an answer."

"Well ... there could be a knife-wielding maniac creeping up to our back door or something," Warren offered. "That would be worse."

"Actually, I think that would be better," Teddy countered. "A knife-wielding maniac would still be human. Right now we have a murderous teenage witch on the loose and she thinks Bay has somehow ruined her life. She's looking for revenge, and she has magic on her side when she decides to dole it out."

Apparently Teddy was better at nut-shelling than me.

"I'm really sorry," I offered. It was the lamest response I could offer, but it was true. "I don't know what to say."

"Also, it would be worse if Tillie was sneaking around again," Warren offered helpfully. "This is better than that."

Teddy nodded. All I could do was rub my forehead.

Dad shook his head. "Bay, you're not to blame for this. It sounds to me as if you let your big heart get ahead of your brain — as usual — and now it's backfiring. Nobody blames you."

"I kind of blame her," Teddy argued.

Ah, yes, speaking of things our fathers passed on to us. Mine gave me the ability to get over being angry in five minutes. Thistle's gave her the ability to be snarky even in the face of certain death. I thought Thistle's father-supplied superpower might be better.

"It's not her fault," Dad insisted. "She was trying to do the right thing. It backfired on her — which seems to be the Winchester way — but you can't fault her for what she was trying to do."

"The important thing is that you're here because you want us to do something," Warren noted. "We're willing to do whatever it takes, but ... I'm a little nervous it's going to hurt."

"We don't want you to do anything," Chief Terry countered. "It's more that

"... we need you to be vigilant. You haven't had anyone make a reservation out of the blue in the past three weeks or so, have you?"

Dad furrowed his brow and moved to the computer resting on the opposite counter. "I don't think so. Let me check."

"You're worried that she booked a room here," Teddy surmised. "You think she might try to hide in plain sight and then threaten us if Bay and the others go after her. You're going to take her down."

The remarks were directed to me so I nodded. "We can't let her wander around killing people. We're trying to find her. Even as we speak, Aunt Tillie and Thistle are putting together a potion to bind her powers. You shouldn't be in danger long ... but you are in danger until we can track her down."

"All the reservations for this weekend were booked at least three months out," Dad noted, straightening. "That's good, right?"

Landon nodded. "It is. You can't let anyone wander in and try to book a room."

"We obviously wouldn't rent to a teenager."

"She might not look like a teenager to you," I pointed out. "She could glamour herself, which means she could look like anyone. It's best to just deal with the people who made reservations and not allow anyone else on the premises."

"How are we supposed to stop her from coming on the property?" Warren challenged. "It's not as if we have a no-vacancy sign out there. We're a bed and breakfast, not a motel."

He had a point. "I don't know." I glanced at Landon. "What should we do?"

"I'll put one of my uniforms out here," Chief Terry replied, his tone no-nonsense. "He'll sit outside and call if anyone approaches on foot. Dani doesn't have a car."

"She could steal one," I said.

"She could, but I doubt she would want to risk that. We don't know that she would think to come out here. This is just a precaution. You've got Viola out looking for her. Once we have that potion and a location, all we have left is the fight — now that I say that out loud, it sounds absolutely ridiculous. We're trying to end this today. That's what I'm getting at."

Dad worked his jaw, his eyes linked with those of Chief Terry. For a moment, I sensed trouble, but the potential for explosion passed quickly.

"We'll be careful," Dad promised, his lips flattening into a tight smile for my benefit. "You don't have to worry about us. Just worry about yourselves."

I nodded in thanks. "As soon as things are clear again, we'll set up a dinner," I promised. "I desperately want to know what you and Landon aren't telling me regarding your greeting earlier. For now, I'll let it go because I'm a magnanimous person."

Landon shook his head and groaned. "And that right there you definitely got from Aunt Tillie."

Sometimes inherited traits came in handy. I happened to like the one that didn't allow me to be an easily-snowed idiot. "Thank you."

"It wasn't a compliment."

"It was to me."

# TWENTY-SIX

We checked in at Hypnotic next. The longer we went without seeing Viola, the more nervous I grew — to the point Landon decided to admonish me.

"Sit down, Bay," he instructed, gesturing toward the open spot on the couch next to him. Aunt Tillie and Thistle were finishing their potion, a cauldron bubbling in the open spot behind the couch. Landon seemed perfectly content watching them work, his feet propped on the table.

"I'm helping Aunt Tillie and Thistle," I argued, even though it was the furthest thing from the truth.

"No, you're not." He patted the couch again. "You're hovering because you're nervous. You keep checking every corner for Viola. She'll find you when she's managed to do as you asked. You can't make her arrive before she's ready."

"Actually, she can," Thistle countered. She had an eye dropper in her hand and was measuring out a liquid I didn't recognize. "She's a necromancer. She can make ghosts do whatever she wants just by wishing it."

Landon shot her a look. "You're not helping."

"Oh, sorry. I didn't know I was supposed to be helping." Thistle shot him a smile so saccharine it made my teeth hurt. "I'll try to do better, King Landon."

"You jest, but that's the perfect title for me." He patted the sofa again. "Bay, come on. You're making me tired ... and you're going to need your energy for when we do track Dani down."

I knew he was right. That didn't mean I was in the mood to be ordered around. "I'll sit," I said, scooting into one of the chairs instead of settling next to him on the couch. "But not where you want me to."

"Fine." He made a face. "I smell like doughnuts. If you sit next to me, then you can smell the doughnuts too."

"You just want me to sniff you."

"That's not true. I want you to rub yourself against me, too."

I didn't allow myself to laugh. If I did, he might skate on answering questions about the weird way my father had greeted me. "Tell me what you and Dad have going on and I'll sit next to you," I offered after a beat.

"Sit next to me and I'll tell you what your father and I have been talking about," he shot back.

"I like my way better."

"I think you need to be the giver today, Bay. I've given quite a bit over the past week and all I've gotten in return is threats from Mrs. Little and an unfortunate evening when I smelled like cherry pie and you didn't want to touch me."

His expression was so hangdog I almost gave in. Then I remembered he was acting weird. I didn't like people who acted weird ... except for Aunt Tillie ... and Thistle ... and Clove ... and sometimes my mother ... and almost always Twila. Wait, where was I going with this?

"Tell me," I insisted, my temper building. "I know something's going on. My father was expecting our visit, but for a different reason. I don't understand why he would think that unless you promised him something."

"Come here and I'll tell you."

I was suspicious, and rightly so. "Tell me and I'll come over there."

"Oh, geez." Aunt Tillie emitted a gagging sound as she tirelessly worked with Thistle. "You two are about to make me throw up my breakfast. Do you have to flirt in front of me like that? You know it gives me the trots."

I frowned. "How can listening to us have a conversation — it's not flirting, no matter what you think — give you the trots?"

"Because too much sugar gives me the trots and you two are seriously five seconds away from mounting one another." She paused what she was doing long enough to fix Landon with a pointed look. "You have a job to do. Do you want me to take away the doughnut smell? If you can't focus on your job, I'll have to remove the spell. Is that what you want?"

Landon looked pained. "You can't do that. I haven't even gotten to enjoy it yet. Not really, at least."

"Whose fault is that?"

"Yours!" He jabbed a finger at her. "You came up with the bright idea of dressing in black and hiding in the woods to find out who was digging holes."

"Um ... and it worked like a charm."

"Eric Savage is dead."

"Yes, well, that part leaves a little to be desired," Aunt Tillie acknowledged. "But now we know who's behind all of this. We wouldn't know if we hadn't gone. We're thirty-five minutes away from having the potion we need. Then all we have to do is find Dani, make her drink it, and have the little men in white coats drag her away. Easy-peasy."

Landon's glare was withering. "I'm going to make you sit down with a dictionary tonight and defend every single word you just used. As for what happened last night being a good thing, I'm pretty sure an argument could be made for the exact opposite."

Aunt Tillie blinked and stared at him. "Yup. The doughnut smell was too much. I think we're going to have to walk it back. Maybe we'll start with almonds or something. We'll have to ease you into having this much power."

"Don't even think about taking this smell away," he warned. "We had a deal ... and I went out of my way to mess with Margaret Little today. You owe me."

"Not to take his side, but he did mess with Mrs. Little very well today," I offered, studying my fingernails. With each passing moment, my agitation grew and it became harder to pretend I was okay with what was about to happen. "You would've been so proud."

"Fine." Aunt Tillie turned back to the cauldron. "You can keep your curse for the time being. You'd better start using it, though. You're going to be the boy who cried doughnut if you're not careful."

The visual made me smile ... and then I remembered I was annoyed with him. "Seriously, what's going on with you and my dad?"

"Oh, geez, Bay." Landon looked away. "It's not a big deal. They have that huge field behind the bed and breakfast and I asked them if I could set up a private picnic there. He thought I was bringing the basket for us today and I promised to let him approve the menu."

"Seriously?" I couldn't help being a little disappointed. "That's the big secret?"

"I'm trying to make inroads with him, Bay," he explained. "He doesn't like me. I plan to be in your life for a very long time. He wants to be involved in things that are generally controlled by your mother and aunts. I thought I would help both of us out with this picnic idea.

"The only problem is that we were supposed to have the picnic this week. Instead we've been dealing with murderous teenagers, dead bodies, and a ghost that can kill you," he continued. "Just once I'd like to be able to pull off a romantic afternoon without a single hiccup. Is that too much to ask?"

I stared at him blankly. He seemed wound up, which meant that the Dani situation was getting to him, too. "I'm sorry." I didn't know what else to say. "You're very romantic. I love the picnic idea. Having my dad help was a stroke of genius. I ... am so sorry."

"Oh, geez." Landon shook his head. "I'm still going to throw the picnic. There's no stopping me. As for the other stuff, that's not your fault. I didn't mean to yell like that. I'm just ... afraid."

"What are you afraid of?" I was truly curious.

"It's almost time, Bay. That potion will be finished in less than an hour. Viola will show up around the same time. Then that will be it. We'll walk into another fight and I'll be powerless to do anything to help you. It freaks me out sometimes."

He was open, emotionally naked, and altogether enticing. "It freaks me out sometimes too," I admitted, moving to the couch and sliding close. "It's going to be okay, though."

His smile was wry. "Isn't that supposed to be my line?"

"I think it's a line we can share." I pressed a kiss to the corner of his mouth and inhaled deeply. "As soon as we have Dani in custody and stripped of her powers, I'm going to sing the Dunkin' Donuts jingle and roll you really hard." I paused after the words escaped. "Huh. That sounded more romantic in my head."

He barked out a laugh and pulled me tight. "I can't wait." The kiss he graced me with was soft and sensual, and for a moment I forgot we were in the middle of a catastrophe. Then a splash of water hit me in the face and I was forced back to reality.

"What the ... ?" I wiped the water from my face and glared at Aunt Tillie. She had an open bottle of water and looked ready to murder someone.

"No!" She jabbed a finger in our direction. "I will totally remove the smell if you don't stop that."

"Don't threaten me," Landon warned. "We had a deal. In fact ... ."

I lost track of what he was saying when an ethereal whirlwind arrived in the store. Viola, her hair perfectly in place despite the entrance, looked almost gleeful when she came to a stop.

"Well?" I asked expectantly.

"I found her. It wasn't easy."

I smiled, but it was more of a grimace. It was time.

. . .

**THE FACT THAT WE ENDED UP BACK** at the house on the lake held a certain amount of synchronicity. It seemed there was a message in there somewhere, a lesson maybe, but I came up blank as we parked in the driveway.

"It's empty," Chief Terry noted from the front seat. Thistle sat in the passenger seat, leaving the back for Landon, Aunt Tillie, and me. Landon insisted we sit together so we could talk, but we'd made most of the drive in silence.

"She's in there." I was certain. I wanted to kick myself for not thinking of it sooner. "She was smart to do it this way. She didn't have far to walk. We were here, but looking in a different direction. She waltzed right into the house and set up shop."

"And she has a ghost to protect her," Thistle noted. "Maybe she's a genius and we didn't realize it."

"Maybe." I rubbed my forehead. "Everyone remembers what we're doing, right?"

"We remember." Thistle looked resigned. "This is going to work, Bay. I know it's a lot to deal with, but it's going to work."

"It is," I agreed, although I mostly said the words for Landon's benefit. I recognized that he more than anybody else needed to hear it. "You guys have to stay here.

Landon scowled. "I'm still not clear about why we have to stay here. We have rubber bullets. We could incapacitate Dani from a distance if need be."

I held on to my eye roll, but just barely. "She won't fall for that."

"You don't know." He sounded desperate. "Bay, let me go with you. Don't do this alone."

"I don't have a choice." Of that I was quite certain. "I know how to fight off Valerie this time. I still can't have you out there. You'll be a distraction."

"But you can have Thistle and Aunt Tillie?"

I felt helpless in the face of his angst. "They're witches. They have magic to protect themselves."

"Whatever." He threw his hands in the air and stared straight forward. We'd put him in the center so Thistle and I could use the doors without risking him having to step outside and make himself vulnerable.

"I'm not trying to hurt you," I insisted. "I just ... need you to be safe."

"I need that for you too." His voice was low.

"Landon ... ."

"Son, you have to pull it together," Chief Terry interjected, his voice tight. "I don't like it any better than you do, but if we're out there she'll make a mistake because she's desperate to protect us. A mistake in this situation could cost her life. You don't want that."

Landon screwed up his face. "Since when are you on her side in situations like this? You're supposed to be on my side."

"I'm on both your sides. She's doing the best she can. You have to let her go."

Landon muttered a few words under his breath that I couldn't quite make out and then focused on me. His eyes were bright, clear, and full of love. "Don't you leave me, Bay. Keep your mind on what you're doing. You're better than her. You're smarter than her."

"And you have me," Aunt Tillie added, pushing open her door. "Nobody is badder than me. Now come on. If I have to watch you two fall over each other a second longer I'll be sick to my stomach."

Under different circumstances I would've laughed. That seemed like the wrong reaction here. "I'll come back to you," I promised, pressing my hand to his cheek. "There's no getting rid of me. You're stuck with me ... forever."

"You'd better make sure that's true." He let loose a growl as he kissed me, long and deep. Then he squeezed my hand and nodded. "Kick her ass."

That finally nudged a smile out of me. "Consider it done."

**WE WERE BARELY OUT OF THE VEHICLE WHEN I** called to the ghosts. Viola was the first to appear. I'd told her it was coming and she seemed excited.

"I'm like your general, eh?" Her eyes sparkled.

Aunt Tillie snorted. "Good grief."

I ignored my great-aunt and nodded. "You are my general." I glanced around to count the ghosts I'd managed to call. Seven. It was a decent number, though with the amount of rage fueling Valerie I wasn't sure it would be enough. "You know what you have to do."

Viola nodded. "We need to keep the ghost busy until you can kill the witch."

"We're not going to kill her unless we have to," I clarified. "If we can break that spell, Valerie should return to some semblance of her former self. When that happens, she can cross over — or at least stop murdering people."

Viola smiled. "Maybe she'll want to stay and hang out. She's probably not so bad when she's not all Hulked out."

I had no idea if that were true. "Maybe."

"Cool." She shot me two thumbs-up. "We'll handle the ghost. You worry about the rest of it."

"That's the plan."

Viola moved to disappear but I stopped her. "The basement, right?"

She nodded. "That's where she is."

"Thanks. You've gone above and beyond."

"It's fun. I like it."

She had an odd sense of fun, but I let it go. Within seconds, Viola had gathered the rest of the ghosts and they moved toward the house. I had no idea where Valerie's traumatized spirit was, but I had to trust them to handle her. It was Dani I had to worry about.

"Let's go," I said, moving up the steps. "I want to put this behind us."

"You and me both," Thistle intoned.

I tested the doorknob and found it unlocked. I shouldn't have been surprised. Dani wanted us here. She wasn't going to make it difficult for us to find her. I sucked in a breath, pushed open the door, and reached out with my senses. A malevolent force waited inside, but there were no traps by the door.

Aunt Tillie and Thistle wordlessly followed as I slipped inside. I had to fight the urge to look over my shoulder, to glance at Landon one last time. I feared that if he saw the hesitation he would attempt to run to my rescue regardless. It took great courage to let me handle this. I couldn't test that further.

I wasn't familiar with the house, so it took us a few minutes to find the stairs that led to the basement. They weren't illuminated. Apparently Dani preferred some cat-and-mouse shenanigans to an outright immediate battle. Perhaps that would play to our advantage. At least that's what I told myself as Aunt Tillie ignited her locator fairies and the stairwell glowed brightly.

With each step, my heart pounded harder and my breath came in shorter gasps. By the time we hit the bottom of the stairs, I was an agitated mess.

There was only one door. I exchanged quick looks with Aunt Tillie and Thistle, got nods from both, and used my magic to blow open the door.

What I found inside was ... confusing.

Dani was there, as we expected, but her arms were bound behind her and she was gagged. Her skin was pale, her eyes wide and pleading, and an aura of terror emanated from her.

"What the ... ?" Aunt Tillie took a purposeful step forward.

"It has to be a trap," Thistle said. "It's the only thing that makes sense."

"It's definitely a trap," I agreed, things solidifying in my mind. "Just not the trap we thought."

# TWENTY-SEVEN

"Wait!"

Thistle had her hands on Dani's gag faster than I thought possible and I barely managed to keep my wits long enough to stop her from yanking it free.

"What?" Thistle froze, her eyes wide. "Don't we have to know what's happening here?"

In an ideal world that would be true. Given what was happening in Hemlock Cove recently, I couldn't say. I glanced at Aunt Tillie. "Can we trust her?"

Aunt Tillie held out her hands and shrugged. "Do we have a choice?"

I cast another look at Dani and then nodded at Thistle. "Fine. Remove her gag."

"Yes, your highness," Thistle muttered, dragging the handkerchief from the girl's face. "If you try chanting or casting a spell I'll shove it right back in your mouth," she warned, her eyes flashing.

Dani rolled her eyes and focused on me. "I can't believe you found me."

She looked sincere, but I knew better than to fall for her act. She clearly wasn't alone in this. That didn't mean she wasn't a part of it. "I had help."

I glanced around the room, frowning. It looked like a standard basement. In fact, other than the couch Dani was trussed up on, there wasn't any furniture. Apparently Heather hadn't had a chance to decorate the space before she was killed. "It's Hazel, isn't it?"

I wasn't sure how I knew. In the moment I saw Dani tied up on the couch, though, I flashed back to Hazel's reaction at the campground the previous night. Even though she hit all the right emotional notes, things felt slightly off ... and now I knew why.

Dani nodded, solemn. "I wasn't expecting it. She came into the cabin last night, right after you guys crossed the lake. She said she wanted to talk — we were talking nightly so I didn't think anything of it — and she gave me a cup of tea.

"I was in a bad mood because I thought you were being mean. She started pacing by the window and talking. She was saying weird things," she continued. "She insisted I drink the tea. I did because I was too tired to argue. After I drank about half of it, she started saying really weird stuff."

"Like what?" Aunt Tillie kept one eye on the door as she listened to Dani recount her tale. "She said that you guys shouldn't be over there, that you were making a mess of things. She didn't understand why you insisted on being involved in a police investigation. She was really ... like, jittery. It was hard to keep up with her.

"I started getting sleepy and I realized she'd put something in the tea. But it was too late to do anything about it. I fell asleep, and when I woke up, I was here."

"Do you know this place?" I asked.

She shook her head. "No. Can you undo the ropes? My arms are numb."

I hesitated as I regarded her. "Are you working with her?"

Dani narrowed her eyes. "You just found me tied up. Why would you think I was working with her?"

"Because we can't trust you," Aunt Tillie replied simply. "Your motivations aren't exactly clean here, Dani. You hate us and want to dole out retribution. We have a real problem here with Hazel and that ghost she created. We don't have time to deal with your nonsense, too."

"Then let me go." Dani kept her gaze on me. "Cut me loose and you'll never see me again. I won't attack you. I'll just ... leave."

"We can't allow that." I felt sick when I realized I'd allowed Hazel to oversee Dani's recovery after the previous incident. It was likely the older woman never had any intention of helping the teenager. Dani never had a chance ... but that didn't mean I was stupid enough to believe anything that came out of her mouth. "You're not meant to be a witch."

Dani's mouth dropped open. "Excuse me?"

"You're not meant to be a witch," I repeated. "This isn't the life you're supposed to lead. You're not even-tempered enough to wield magic."

"And she is?" Dani was incredulous as she nodded in Aunt Tillie's direction. "Are you kidding me? She's, like, the worst person imaginable. She does horrible things to her enemies. I've heard stories! I know she likes to torture that unicorn lady."

"She does," I agreed. Lying was out of the question given how far we'd come. "Her tortures are little, though. You killed your father. You tried to kill your mother. I have no doubt you would've killed your brother."

"I ... that was my aunt." Even as she said the words I recognized the moment reality finally set in. She was still a child in some respects, but the acceptance on her face reflected adulthood. "I ... just wanted to make my aunt happy."

"And your father died as a result," I said gently. "You're not meant for the magical world, Dani. Your impulses are ... unfortunate. We've tried to help you, but you wouldn't accept the help."

"I can't." Dani's eyes were clear. "Whenever I look at you I see the woman who killed my aunt. I can't just suddenly be your best friend."

"There's only one way we can let you go."

"And what's that?"

I nodded at Aunt Tillie, who produced the potion bottle from her pocket.

"What's that?" Dani asked, her expression twisted. "Are you going to kill me?"

"We're not executioners," I reassured her even though there was a time I worried we would have no choice but to kill Dani. "This potion will strip your powers. It will make you a normal human. If you willingly drink it, we'll cut you loose and send you on your way."

Dani balked. "How long does it last?"

"Forever. We could reverse it at some point, but I don't see that happening. If you want a life — a true life — then you need to drink the potion and put Hemlock Cove in your rearview mirror. You can't overcome what was done here."

Dani's eyes were wide and pleading as she glanced between faces. "And what if I don't want that?"

"You don't have a choice," Aunt Tillie replied, matter-of-fact. "We're going to give you this potion whether you want it or not. We can't untie you until it's done. You can have the peace of mind of knowing that you made this choice — the right choice — or you can have us force it on you. The outcome will essentially be the same."

"Not quite," I countered. "If you force us to pour the potion down your throat, we'll keep you tied up until Landon can get state hospital workers here to take you. You can't be trusted with the general populace. If you do this willingly, there's at least a chance for you."

I could see the gears of her mind working. "All I ever wanted was to be special."

I nodded in understanding. "I get it, but magic doesn't make you special. Deeds do. You can still be a special person. You just can't be a witch."

I expected to find desperation in her eyes when they locked with mine. Instead, I found resignation.

"Fine." She attempted to shrug despite her arms being tied behind her back. "Take my magic. Anything is better than staying in this town. I want to be free of this place ... and you people."

Aunt Tillie pulled the cork from the bottle and moved it to her lips. "You made the right choice."

"I didn't really have a choice," Dani countered. "I can't stand you people. I hate this place. I want to go somewhere else. There's only one way that will happen."

"There is," Aunt Tillie agreed. "Open up."

Dani swallowed hard, cast one more look in my direction, and then did as requested.

I watched as she gulped three times. The contents of the bottle were gone in an instant. Other than a shimmery haze that washed over her after the first swallow, she looked the same.

"How do you feel?" Thistle asked as she started untying the ropes.

"Like I hate you guys and want to be out of here," Dani replied. "How am I supposed to feel?"

Her response almost made me laugh. Almost. "You have to wait," I instructed once her hands were free and she started rubbing her wrists. "Hazel has a ghost — she's mutated it somehow — and it's murderous. You can't wander around until we handle that situation. When we're done, you're free to go."

"So ... you just want me to wait here?" Dani looked dubious. "There's not even a television."

"What's more important?" Thistle asked. "A television or your life?"

"I might need some time to think about it."

Okay, that was enough to garner a chuckle. "If we don't see you again, Dani, good luck."

She held my gaze for a moment and then nodded. "Same to you. By the way, I didn't know Hazel was evil. I knew there was something up with her —

she disappeared a lot — but I thought she was a drunk. I didn't know she was capable of this."

That made two of us.

**WE LEFT DANI IN THE BASEMENT AND RETURNED** to the main floor. The house was eerily quiet and I couldn't wrap my head around Hazel's end game.

"She's outside," Aunt Tillie said, taking me by surprise.

"She is?" My eyebrows hiked. "How do you know that?"

"I can hear Valerie screaming."

I stilled, confused. When I cocked my head to listen, I heard only the wind. Then I remembered there had been no breeze when we walked into the house — Valerie was bringing the wind.

"I don't ever want you to play the selective hearing game again," I hissed, bolting toward the door. "You hear just fine."

The world outside had changed drastically in the ten minutes since we'd escaped inside to face an enemy who turned out to be something else entirely. The trees bent from the force of the wind and Valerie was indeed screaming as she circled Chief Terry's vehicle. My heart dropped when I took in the scene. Landon and Chief Terry were still inside, their faces gone white. It was clear they registered the wind, but the screaming ghost was lost on them.

"We have to get them out of there," Thistle said, starting forward.

Aunt Tillie's hand shot out and grabbed her arm. "They're safer inside."

"Unless one of those trees falls on them," Thistle argued.

I hadn't considered that. My stomach twisted. "Where is she?"

"There." Thistle pointed toward a small hill about two hundred feet away. Hazel stood on it, clad in a black robe. Her hair whipped in the wind as she glared at the police vehicle. She didn't as much as look in our direction.

"She doesn't see us," Aunt Tillie noted. "We can sneak up on her."

As if hearing Aunt Tillie's voice over the wind, Hazel slowly turned her head, her eyes seeking — and finding — us.

"So much for that idea," Thistle said dryly. "I think we're going to have to take her head-on."

"Only because you jinxed us with your big mouth," Aunt Tillie hissed.

I ignored their bickering, chalking it up to nerves, and kept my gaze locked on Hazel as I stepped out from under the eaves of the house.

"Bay, this is a different situation than we initially envisioned," Aunt Tillie warned. "You can't just go over there and beat her with your fists and call it a day."

"I've got this," I reassured her, grim.

Landon reacted in the vehicle when he saw me and reached for the door handle. Chief Terry grabbed his shoulder to stop him and they began arguing. I ignored them and kept my focus on Hazel.

Even as the wind whipped my hair and drowned out everything around us, I talked in my regular voice as I advanced on Hazel. "Did you do this for buried treasure?"

She responded in the same even tone. "It's real. I saw the maps Margaret had. There really is treasure out here. I just have to find it before they do."

"How did you see the maps?"

"She showed them to me when she was enlisting me to spy on you before the solstice celebration." She looked haughty. "You didn't see that coming, did you?"

My anger grew. If I started screaming now, I might never stop ... not until she was dead. "You came to town with an agenda." I flicked my eyes to Aunt Tillie, who looked smug rather than afraid.

"I told you!" Aunt Tillie stomped her tiny foot for emphasis. "I freaking told you she couldn't be trusted! Did you believe me? No. You said I was overreacting. You said not everybody was an enemy. Well, who was right?"

I let out a pent-up breath. "You were right."

"And who deserves to be queen of the universe?"

"Don't push it," Thistle warned. "We just said you were right. There's no need to drag it out."

Aunt Tillie's glare was withering. "Bay said I was right. You've yet to utter the words."

"And don't hold your breath."

I forced myself to tune them out and kept my focus on Hazel. "What did Mrs. Little hope to gain by sending you in as a spy?"

"She wanted proof of what you are. She thought if I could film some of your rituals that she would be able to turn the town against you."

"That's preposterous," Thistle argued. "Hemlock Cove is built on witch mythology. That's how we make our money."

"Fake witches," Hazel countered. "Margaret is comfortable with humans pretending to be witches. She's not comfortable with real witches being witches."

"Why would you agree to that?" I challenged. "You're a witch."

# TO LOVE A WITCH

"A broke witch," Aunt Tillie answered for her. "She lost her house ... and her retirement ... and essentially lives out of her car."

"You knew?" I was furious. "Why didn't you say something?"

"It was none of my business," she sniffed, squaring her shoulders. "Being poor isn't a crime. I thought she was struggling. I didn't know she was working for Margaret. I assumed she was working against us, but that's just because she's a horrible person.

"When she volunteered to help with the Dani situation I thought there might be hope for her," she continued. "I see now that she took advantage of us because she wanted to get close, make us trust her. She couldn't get the information she needed because I've never found her trustworthy. She needed to get past my walls."

"Yes," Hazel said dryly. "That's what I needed. You didn't give it to me, though. Even when I selflessly volunteered to take care of Dani ... ."

"Which wasn't all that selfless because it gave you a place to stay rent-free," Thistle pointed out.

Hazel pretended she didn't hear the dig. "Tillie is a hard nut to crack. She always has been. Still, if she'd been the only holdout I would've gotten what I needed right away. But you younger three ... ." She shook her head in disgust. "You're all so wrapped up in each other that you don't consider the feelings of others. It's entitled ... and frustrating ... and I'm not even a little sorry about what I've done. Trying to reason with me won't work."

"We're not interested in reasoning with you," I shot back. "We're trying to understand. Mrs. Little offered you money for proof that we're witches ... and you filmed us."

"I tried to film you the night of Clove's wedding, but I was being watched too closely by her." She jerked her head in Aunt Tillie's direction. "After that, you guys were around often, but you never put your magic on display. All you did was snark at one another. Oh, and occasionally you and your boyfriend would talk about bacon and start giggling like middle-schoolers. Do you have any idea how obnoxious that is?"

"She's not wrong," Aunt Tillie offered. "I'm the one who said you guys were gross first. I want credit."

I wanted to throttle her, but Hazel was our concern. "Was it during one of these clandestine meetings with Mrs. Little that you learned about the purported treasure?"

Hazel nodded. "Sometimes Margaret talks to hear herself talk. She doesn't realize how stupid that is. When I first heard what she was saying I thought she was nuts. She's deranged where you guys are concerned. Seriously deranged. She's convinced that Tillie has ruined her life on purpose."

"She's not wrong," Aunt Tillie offered.

Hazel barreled forward as if Aunt Tillie hadn't interjected. "The more I listened, the more I thought she might be on to something. The history books were very clear about where this pirate lived. Out here — and he had a lot of money.

"Still, I thought it was a wasted effort ... until the map showed up," she continued. "That map clearly indicated the treasure was on this side of the lake. All I have to do is find it. But I can't do that as long as Margaret and her little friends are sticking their noses in. I also can't do it when heartsick girls are running around the property spying on people and constantly crying about being dumped."

And that was the final piece I needed confirmed. "You killed Valerie."

"She caught me out here. I couldn't be certain she wouldn't tell someone. Then you guys would've realized I wasn't watching Dani like I said I would. And that's it." She craned her neck. "Speaking of Dani, where is she? I thought for sure you would bring her with you. I figured she'd make an appealing additional target."

"Dani is no longer your concern," I replied. "In fact, she's no longer anyone's concern."

"Did you kill her?" Hazel looked intrigued at the prospect. "I didn't think you had it in you, but I'm impressed. You're growing into the sort of witch I always knew you could be. With Tillie's influence, I figured you were a lost cause. Maybe not."

"She's not dead. She's simply no longer a concern," I countered. "Why did you enslave Valerie's ghost after you killed her? Why not just let her go?"

"Hey, she stayed behind on her own. She was a whiny little thing and wouldn't shut up. Kept talking about her boyfriend cheating on her. When it first started, I was just trying to keep her quiet. Then I realized that the control I managed to exert over her could be used for other reasons ... and I took advantage.

"I need to be able to cover the property without fear of being discovered," she continued. "Once Valerie's death became known, that wasn't really an option because you guys were traipsing all over the place. So were the cops. When you add Margaret and her merry band of mischief-makers, well, the place was just getting too crowded. I had to scare people away."

"So you killed Heather?" That was the part that made no sense. "All that did was bring more attention to your doorstep."

"I didn't mean to kill her." Hazel almost looked contrite. "I was trying to scare her. She refused to acknowledge there was another presence in the house. No matter what Valerie did to frighten her, she ignored it. She refused to see ... until it was too late.

"I didn't take into account the level of Valerie's rage," she continued. "She couldn't be fully controlled, and she somehow warped into something else. She killed Heather on her own. Believe me, that's not what I wanted."

"And yet you still control her," I pointed out. "Why not cut her loose if she's so volatile?"

"She's the best weapon in my arsenal against you," Hazel replied, her eyes darkening. "You're strong, Bay. Being able to command the ghosts makes you stronger. I need a level playing field and Valerie provides that."

I had news for her: I wasn't going to allow that to happen. "How do you think this is going to end?"

"I kill all of you and Margaret gets the blame," Hazel replied without hesitation. "Everyone in town knows she's enraged. She's at her breaking point. It won't be a stretch for people to believe she snapped and killed the three of you."

"And them?" I gestured toward Landon and Chief Terry.

"They happened upon the mass murder and were caught off guard. She managed to get the jump on them."

I was incensed. "She's eighty. She can't get the jump on three witches and two cops."

"She's also nutty," Hazel pointed out. "She's unpredictable. It will be a true tragedy, but when the dust settles, I'll have a clear shot at this property — and the treasure."

We stood silent. I had no idea what to say. Aunt Tillie, of course, never had that problem.

"Except there is no treasure," she volunteered.

When I risked a glance in her direction, I found smugness.

"Of course there's treasure," Hazel shot back. "There's a map."

"I made the map." Aunt Tillie's lips curved. "I knew Margaret wanted the campground so badly that there had to be a reason. I poked into the minds of her friends and found her treasure idea. I decided to play with her ... and actually found a guy in Traverse City who is great at drawing up maps that look like antiques. All he wanted in return was a case of my special wine."

And that's when the final piece fell into place. "You put all of this into motion."

"I didn't know it would turn into this," Aunt Tillie countered quickly. "I wouldn't have taken it that far. I ... didn't know."

I believed her. "It doesn't matter now." I pursed my lips and regarded Hazel. "Now what are you going to do? The treasure is fake and you're a murderer. Your ghostly creation has killed two people and you've killed one. You've also kidnapped a teenage girl and threatened us. You have nowhere left to go."

"I can still kill you," Hazel hissed. "Now I have even more of a reason to want you dead."

Aunt Tillie had been right all along, loath as I was to admit it. Hazel was never the witch we thought she was. It was too late to correct things. We had to stop her here.

"You can try," I acknowledged, "but you won't win."

"And why is that?"

"We're better than you," Aunt Tillie replied, her eyes flashing. "Just watch." She threw her hands in the air and started throwing out Latin words. *"Ignis. Exitium. Sella."*

Thistle frowned. "Fire. Destruction. Chair. What the heck are you going to do with a chair?"

She probably shouldn't have asked, because the magic Aunt Tillie ignited was a spectacle. A shower of fire arced from her fingertips and flew directly at Hazel, who managed to throw up a rather impressive shield spell. The destruction part of the curse came in the form of twirling branches that descended on the woman from every direction, a twister of tree-branch terror. As for the chair, the stone bench parked near Heather's pretty garden lifted with a great groan and started barreling directly toward Hazel.

It was an impressive display.

"You'll have to do better than that," Hazel screeched, launching her own magical assault. The bulk of it was directed toward Aunt Tillie, but a hard lash of magic struck my cheek and caused me to duck low.

"They're going to kill each other," Thistle warned from my right. "We can't just sit here and let them throw magic at each other like that. As soon as Hazel feels she's losing, she'll go after Landon and Chief Terry."

I was well aware — and I had a plan.

I closed my eyes and summoned the ghosts. I had no idea where they'd been hiding during the run-up to the battle, but they came in force when I called to them.

"Oh, you found her," Viola said, smiling easily when she caught sight of

Valerie, who looked lost and confused because Hazel wasn't issuing orders. "What do you want us to do?"

"Hold her back," I instructed. "I'm going for Hazel."

"We've got it." Viola took off in that direction, like a blue streak of energy. In Chief Terry's vehicle, I saw Landon sit up straighter, as if he'd seen the movement. It was obvious he was aware something was happening. From his perspective, it probably looked like we were caught in a windstorm.

"Let's finish this," I said grimly, nodding at Thistle. "Help Aunt Tillie. Keep Hazel's attention on you."

Thistle didn't look thrilled at the prospect. "What if you need help?"

"I won't." I thought of everything Landon had said. "I've got this. I know what to do."

Thistle didn't question me further. She nodded and then rolled in the other direction, landing on her feet and raising her hands above her head. "*Arbor*," she screeched, aiming her magic at the tree on Hazel's left.

The double assault was sufficient to have Hazel grappling. Her back was to me when I moved from my hiding spot. I broke into a run.

It was as if time stood still for a brief moment. Hazel focused her magic on trying to keep the tree from striking her. Aunt Tillie doubled her assault. Valerie, under siege by the other ghosts, snapped her head in my direction.

I didn't have much time, so I did the only thing I could. "*Glacio.*" I put as much effort into the magic as I could, and for one triumphant moment I thought it had worked. Hazel was smarter than I gave her credit for, though. There was a sneer on her face when she turned and reflected the magic back in my direction. She'd been expecting the subterfuge.

Unfortunately for her, I had anticipated the possibility. I dropped to my knees and skidded to a stop, my jeans ripping against the hard earth as my skin tore underneath, but I dodged the returned spell.

"*Moriri!*"

I had never cast a death curse. I never thought I would have to. The people I loved most in the world were in this field, though, and we would all die if we didn't take out Hazel. It wasn't like with Dani. I was still on the fence if there was something redeemable in her. I did not have that dilemma with Hazel.

The magic ripped out of me with enough force that it grabbed the ghosts, who abandoned their fight with Valerie and turned on Hazel.

At that moment, realization dawned on Hazel's face. She saw the anticipation of the ghosts as they moved in her direction. She was strong, but not fast. She couldn't dodge the spell. At the moment the magic hit her, the ghosts descended — and began ripping her soul apart.

I closed my eyes, blocking out the pain and destruction, and sucked in a breath.

Hazel didn't scream. She was gone almost before it began. Nobody cheered. Nobody looked. It was too terrible to watch.

I waited for the sounds to die down. They'd been gone a long time before I registered it, and then I felt Landon's arms come around me from behind.

"You did so good," he whispered, drawing me close. "You ... are amazing."

With that, I allowed myself to lean back.

It was over, though the ramifications would reverberate for a very long time.

# TWENTY-EIGHT

Dani was gone by the time we got back to the house. I wasn't surprised. Landon looked as if he wanted to press the issue when he was told what had happened, but his concern for me overwhelmed him. He simply nodded and said Dani was on her own.

He didn't want me alone, but he and Chief Terry had things that needed to be done on the property. I wasn't sure how they were going to explain it — I really didn't want to know — and I was more than happy to leave with Thistle and Aunt Tillie when they gave us the go-ahead.

"Put her to bed at the inn," Landon instructed in a low voice. "I do not want her anyplace alone. I'll be there as soon as I can."

Thistle hesitated and then nodded. "She'll be okay."

"She will be," he agreed, forcing a smile for my benefit as he slid over and pressed a kiss to my forehead. "I love you, Bay. You did everything exactly right."

In my head, I knew that. The results were still jarring. "I'm just tired. I'll be fine tomorrow."

He didn't look convinced, but he nodded. "I'll be there as soon as I can."

I didn't think I would sleep, but I dropped off the second my head hit the pillow. I didn't even hear him enter the room, but I sensed the moment he climbed into the bed ... and my dreams shifted from dark to warm. There were even doughnuts.

AMANDA M. LEE

When I opened my eyes the next morning I felt refreshed, but shaking the memories of the night before wasn't easy.

"I have to check on Valerie," I murmured when I felt Landon's arms tighten around me. He'd spooned up behind me in sleep without moving the entire night, as if standing guard for whatever might come and comforting me at the same time. He was good like that.

"You don't have to do that today."

"I do. We have no idea if she's still dangerous."

He hesitated and then sighed. "I'm not certain what I saw, Bay, but I'm pretty sure Valerie's ghost is already gone."

"What do you mean?"

"I saw her. I'm not sure how, but I saw her. And I saw Viola. When Hazel fell, the other ghosts ... ripped her apart."

I swallowed hard, a lump suddenly forming in my throat. "How did you see them?"

"I don't know. It's not the first time I've seen ghosts."

That was true. Once, the ghost of a little girl from a long-forgotten era appeared and told him I was in trouble so he could arrive in time to help hold off a murderous threat.

"I'm sorry for her," I said after a few seconds. "I was hoping to save her."

"Bay, you can't save everyone."

"I didn't save anyone this time."

"That's not true." He shifted me in his arms so I had no choice but to look at his face. "You saved Chief Terry ... and Thistle ... and Aunt Tillie. You gave Dani a fighting chance. She might still screw up, but it's not on you if she does. You save me every day of our lives."

Tears burned the back of my eyes. "That was kind of sweet."

He chuckled at my reaction before leaning in to give me a soft kiss. "I'm a sweet guy."

"That's why you smell like doughnuts."

His grin widened. "Does this mean you're finally going to give me some love for that? I've been waiting."

I hesitated before answering. It felt wrong to enjoy myself given the fact that I'd killed a woman the night before, but what was the point of being in this world if we didn't live our lives to the fullest?

"Yes," I said finally. "But not here. I want to go home and spend the entire day holed up with you. I don't want anyone to bother us. I just want to watch movies, hang with you, and enjoy the aroma of doughnuts."

He nodded solemnly. "It sounds like a tough job, but I think I'm up for it.

We need breakfast first. Your mother won't let us go without giving you a good once-over."

I hadn't considered that. I'd barely seen them the night before. I hadn't wanted to answer a lot of questions, so Aunt Tillie sent me upstairs. I was grateful for the reprieve. That would end this morning. I found, oddly enough, I was okay with it.

"Breakfast and then a hermit day." I brushed my fingers over his stubbled cheek. "And you can't shave. I like when you look like a male model."

He smirked, his eyes flashing. "Whatever you want today, you get."

"I might want pizza delivered later."

"Just for the record, Bay, you never have to worry about me wanting pizza."

"Okay." I burrowed close. "Just give me five minutes and we'll go down."

He held me as tightly as humanly possible without crushing me, his lips brushing my forehead. "However long you want. I'll be right here."

**ONE WEEK LATER**

Life returned to normal — well, normal for the Winchester family — and memories of Hazel's death faded faster than I would've thought possible.

I went back to work, published the paper with a special memorial section for Heather, Eric, and Valerie, and resumed sparring with Thistle and Clove, the latter demanding we participate in another competition to see who would be the baby's favorite aunt. So far, we were resisting, but that would probably change.

Breakfasts continued at the inn, as did dinners. In fact, it was a dinner I was leaving tonight, the warm summer air a comfortable blanket as I exited through the back door. Landon had already headed back to the guesthouse — he'd received a work text during dinner and realized he'd forgotten to send a file — so I was on my own. I was happy for a few minutes to myself to ponder how things had fallen into place so quickly.

Hazel's death was ruled a heart attack. At least that's what the medical examiner put in his report. Part of me would always wonder if Landon exerted pressure for a ruling that included natural causes to protect me. He would never admit to it, but I felt it ... and I was okay with it. Hazel wasn't worth my tears, or guilt, so I refused to engage in either. She'd gotten what was coming to her. My part in her downfall might always be a cause for concern, but I tried not to dwell on it.

Aunt Tillie always said dwelling on the past was a great way to waste a future. For once, I took the words to heart.

I was halfway back to the guesthouse when I noticed twinkling lights on the bluff where we held our solstice rituals (and occasionally danced naked under the full moon). I was certain my mother and aunts were still at the inn, though I didn't recall seeing them when I left. I decided to investigate. It was likely Aunt Tillie doing ... well, Aunt Tillie things, but I wanted to be certain.

The minute I stepped into the clearing I found myself transported to a magical land.

Above me, thousands of multicolored lights twinkled. They floated free, unattached to electrical cords.

Around me, white butterflies flapped their wings as they flitted through the open area, leaving trails of glowing dust as the entire clearing lit up with magical intent.

There were candles. Thousands of them. Someone had not only lit them, they'd enchanted them to float.

And there, in the center of everything, was Landon. He wore a tuxedo and a smile.

"What is ... ?" I trailed off when I saw the velvet box in his hand, my heart skipping as the scene began to coalesce.

He waited. It was as if he knew I needed a moment to collect my breath. In the back of my mind I knew this would eventually happen ... and yet I didn't picture it like this. I figured he would sit next to me on the couch one day, toss a ring in my lap, and say something like, 'How about it?' while laughing like a loon. This was beyond all of my wildest dreams.

"How ... ?" My eyes drifted to one of the butterflies. It wasn't real. It was an imagining out of some romantic's fevered dream. It was beautiful, and it stole my breath.

"You didn't think I was going to go small, did you?" He looked pleased with himself.

"I ... um ... ." My mouth was dry and I couldn't seem to find the right words.

"I'm a little nervous," he admitted, grinning as he wiped his free hand on his trousers. "I've been practicing this in my head for weeks. Then when you were looking through my sock drawer I thought everything was ruined. Of course, even if you'd found the ring this could never be ruined."

That's when his odd behavior over the past few weeks began making sense. "You had the ring in the sock drawer ... and that's why you freaked out about me looking in there. You weren't hiding anything else." I spoke more for my own benefit than his, but the realization made me smile.

"What did you think I was hiding?"

"I don't know." That was the truth. "I just knew you were acting odd and it freaked me out. You kept whispering to my mother ... and then there was the incident with my father ... and the sock drawer."

He smiled. "I asked your mother's permission. She thought it was funny and wanted to know why it took me so long. I asked your father afterward because ... well ... I thought I should. I even made sure Chief Terry knew, because I wanted to cover all of the bases."

"You've been very thorough."

His grin broadened. "I love you, Bay. I think I always have. I think from that first moment you stomped over to us at that corn maze and told us to shut our mouths I knew I was supposed to be with you.

"It's hard to explain," he continued, his voice soft. "You were ... larger than life. You made my heart race and you made my mind cloudy. I remember those first few meetings after the corn maze when I was supposed to be filling my boss in on my undercover work. All I could think about was you.

"I told myself at the time that it was because you were acting suspicious and I thought you might somehow be involved, but I knew that wasn't true," he continued. "I felt you here." He tapped the spot above his heart and the first tear slid down my cheek. "I know I broke your heart when I said I needed to think after I found out about the witch stuff.

"I think back to that time often and I'm ... angry. Not with you, with me. I didn't want to leave you that day, but I was confused. I thought I knew what my life was going to be. Then I met you and I was convinced you would become the center of my world ... and you did. The witch part just threw me.

"That day as I was walking down the hill, I could sense you behind me. You said your heart broke. Mine did too. I wanted to turn around and say it didn't matter, but I wasn't brave enough. You were already inside of me by then. I could not stay away from you because ... you're it for me. You're all I ever want.

"So, here it is." He licked his lips, his eyes never leaving my face. "This is what I want. You and me. I want to live in the guesthouse with you. Then I want to build a home with you. I want to have children with you. I want to get really excited when those children leave the house and it's just you and me again. I want to grow old together."

I fought to hold back a torrent of tears at the naked emotion in his eyes.

"I promise that I will love you forever," he said. "I promise that I'll never leave you ... or cheat on you ... or even want to look at another woman. You've crawled inside of me and made me whole. I wasn't a complete person before you.

"And I know what you're going to say," he continued, cracking a smile. "You're going to say that you don't need another person to be whole. I agree ... for other people. I need you, though. You're all I'll ever want. And while I know you can do absolutely anything you set your mind to, I think you need me."

I nodded. "I do. I ... ."

"Shh." He grinned as he lifted his finger to his lips. "This is my moment. You can gush all over me as soon as I finish. I told you I've been practicing. I'm so nervous all of this stuff is going to fly out of my head and I'm going to just repeat 'I love you' over and over again until you say yes."

"Maybe that's all you have to say," I suggested.

"Maybe," he conceded. "But I want to say more, and here it is. I don't know that I ever believed in soulmates before you. I thought it was something made up for books and movies. I was wrong. I was ... so, so wrong.

"You're the one thing in this world I absolutely cannot live without. My heart yearns for you when we're not together. You're the first thing I think of every morning, and the last thing I thank the Goddess for bringing me every night. You fill my heart with love, my mind with joy, and my life with laughter. You are ... the best thing that's ever happened to me.

"I know we've been through a lot, and there are times when I wonder how you're still on your feet because other people wouldn't be able to put up with the crushing weight that's often heaped on your shoulders. We're going to go through a lot more, but I have faith we can do it together.

"I want you to be my wife. You're already my family. You're already my heart. I want you to be joined to me forever."

The tears were back and I no longer had the urge to stop them.

"I love that crazy, wacky mind of yours," he said. "I love your crazy, wacky family. I love the way you make me feel ... and the fact that I want to be a better man for you. I love that you're crabby in the morning but still want to cuddle. I love that you're giggly at night and willing to dress up like bacon just to make me laugh. There's nothing I don't love about you. So ... ." He took a deep breath and opened the box.

The stone was bigger than I'd envisioned. It looked to be almost two carats. It was a simple setting, white gold and an emerald-cut solitaire diamond. It was my dream ring, which made me wonder if he'd had help picking it out.

"Bay Winchester, I want to give you everything you could possibly want." He dropped to one knee in front of me. "I want to be your husband. More importantly, I want to be your forever. I don't want to be without you. Not a single day for the rest of our lives. Will you marry me?"

Tears cascaded down my cheeks and I hated that I had to snort in a huge sniffle. After a few seconds of my staring at him, he cleared his throat.

"I'm starting to get a complex, Bay. You need to answer me."

That was enough to snap me out of my fugue state. "Oh." I dropped to my knees in front of him, allowing the tears to fall. "Can I speak now?"

He looked pained. "Don't you just want to say yes so we can go back to the guesthouse and celebrate?"

"Don't make this uncomfortable," a voice called from the shadows. I recognized it as belonging to my father.

That's when I realized we weren't alone. "I ... are they all out there?" Wonderment filled me as I realized the darkness beyond the butterflies was made up of silhouettes — and they all belonged to people I loved.

"I wanted you to get your moment." He brought his fingers up to brush my hair from my face. "I really need you to say yes soon, Bay. I'm going to freak out if you don't."

I nodded and held out my hand. "Yes, but you have to listen to my list of things I love about you."

"I guess I can live with that."

"You make me smile. Sometimes you're grumpy because you think I do stupid things, but I know that's because you love me. You've opened my eyes to love in a way I never thought possible, and I'm not just talking about your bacon fetish."

He laughed, the sound clear and lovely.

"You're the most loyal person I know. Even when I do things that drive you crazy you still try to bolster me. When I'm sad, you make me laugh. When I'm afraid you refuse to leave my side. And when I have to stand on my own two feet you give me the room to do it ... while standing two feet behind to make sure I don't fall."

"I never want you to fall, sweetie," he reassured me.

"I love you so much." My voice cracked, causing him to frown.

"Don't cry. I hate when you cry."

"These are happy tears."

"I think that's an oxymoron."

"Well, it's not." I moved my hands to his cheeks and grinned. "I want to be with you forever. No matter what life throws at us, I know we'll be okay because we'll have each other. I don't know much in this world, but I do know that."

"Give me your hand."

I did as he instructed, sighing as the ring slid into place. It looked natural, as if it had always belonged there.

"I meant every word I said, Bay," he whispered, his forehead connecting with mine. "You are the love of my life. You're the reason my heart keeps beating. You're my ... forever."

"I love you."

He smiled. "I love you too."

His lips met mine in a torrid kiss, and as his arms came around me, the butterflies glowed brighter, basking us in warmth and energy.

That's when the clapping began, and one by one the silhouettes emerged from the darkness.

Marcus and Thistle stood together, both grinning from ear to ear as they held hands.

Sam stood behind Clove, his arms wrapped around her and his hands resting on her stomach as they beamed.

Twila and Marnie had their heads bent together, and I had no doubt they were already talking about the food they would serve at the wedding.

Dad, Warren, and Teddy stood a bit apart, but they'd obviously been included at Landon's behest ... which meant things were coming together on that front, too.

Mom stood with Chief Terry, tears streaming down both their faces. I had to look away otherwise I would dissolve into body-shaking sobs.

When I rested my chin on Landon's shoulder, I found Viola watching from a few feet away. She looked delighted. Behind her were other ghosts. I had no idea where they'd come from or how they'd known to come.

My grandmother stood with Uncle Calvin, Aunt Tillie's husband. They both looked thrilled as they watched everyone react to the big moment.

Edith, the former ghost at The Whistler, showed her teeth when she grinned, something I was certain I would never witness.

And in the midst of them all stood Aunt Tillie. She wore her combat helmet, now adorned with a ring of flowers, and her hands glowed as she lifted them toward the sky. I had no idea what magic she was conjuring, but I knew it would be fun, not menacing for a change.

"Do you smell that?" Landon pulled his head back and looked me up and down, tentatively leaning closer. "Oh, baby, you smell like bacon."

Of course. I should've known. "You smell like doughnuts," I noted.

"That's a potent combination. Do you want to go home and see what we can come up with when we put the two together?"

"Don't make me hurt you," Chief Terry threatened, his expression darkening.

I laughed as I threw my arms around Landon's neck, my eyes finding one more ghost. It was a small one. Erika, the girl who showed Landon how to find me in a moment of great need. She'd somehow returned for this moment.

"I knew you would get here," she said, beaming.

Landon snapped his head in her direction, surprised by the voice. "You." He could clearly see her, again.

"Me," Erika agreed. "I can't stay. I just wanted to see. Remember ... keep wishing." As she pointed toward the sky and started to dissolve, a star arced and exploded, creating yet another magical moment.

I closed my eyes, determined to follow her advice, and found I had everything I ever wanted.

It was the best feeling ever.

Printed in Great Britain
by Amazon